Rachel Ryan was born and raised in Dublin, Ireland. She can usually be found writing in coffee shops, hanging around libraries, or walking the streets of Dublin, making up stories.

Her debut novel, *Hidden Lies*, was an *Irish Times* Top Ten bestseller. *Someone You Trust* is her second novel.

Also by Rachel Ryan

Hidden Lies

Someone
You
Trust

Rachel Ryan

PIATKUS

PIATKUS

First published in Great Britain in 2023 by Piatkus

1 3 5 7 9 10 8 6 4 2

Copyright © Caelainn Bradley 2023

The moral right of the author has been asserted.

A CIP catalogue record for this book
is available from the British Library.

ISBN 978-0-349-42617-4

Typeset in Bembo by M Rules
Printed and bound in Great Britain by
Clays Ltd, Elcograf S.p.A.

Papers used by Piatkus are from well-managed forests
and other responsible sources.

Piatkus
An imprint of
Little, Brown Book Group
Carmelite House
50 Victoria Embankment
London EC4Y 0DZ

An Hachette UK Company
www.hachette.co.uk

www.littlebrown.co.uk

For my mother –
for everything.

Prologue

When Amy regained consciousness, she was lying on the floor of the immaculate living room. Moonlight streamed through the floor-to-ceiling windows she had cleaned the day before, illuminating the open-plan space and stylish furniture.

She was on her side on the rug. The rug was soaked with blood.

Amy pushed herself up onto one arm, feeling a wave of the nausea that often accompanied a blow to the head. She looked at her left hand. It was covered in a liquid that appeared black in the pale light, like the hand of a child who'd been finger-painting.

Was it her blood? It couldn't be. There was too much of it. So whose . . .?

Then she saw the body on the other side of the room.

'*No.*' Amy choked out the word. She crawled on her hands

and knees across the blood-drenched rug, through shattered glass, past the broken coffee table, to the human shape lying motionless on the floor. 'No, no, no ...'

All around was silence and thin grey moonlight.

I

Three weeks earlier

Amy's phone went dead shortly before sunset.

'Oh no . . .' She slowed the car, driving with one hand and pressing the button on the side of her phone with the other. 'Don't give up on me, phone.'

But the screen remained black. The charging port in her second-hand car had broken long ago. You idiot, she berated herself. Why did you listen to music all the way down here?

The answer was simple: she hadn't realised the journey would take this long. The ad had described the location as 'peaceful and remote'. It didn't say *how* remote.

Google Maps had estimated that Amy's journey from Dublin to the furthest tip of West Cork would take five hours. She had been driving for well over six. Google didn't account for how winding and underdeveloped the roads were, for the wrong turns she would take, for the fact she couldn't drive at the speed limit the entire way.

The sun was dropping towards the horizon. Evening shadows were beginning to stretch over the land. And here she was, in a part of rural Ireland that was completely unfamiliar to her, with no map to guide her to her destination.

Great. This is just great.

She tossed her phone onto the passenger seat and continued driving down the narrow country road. It was a grey ribbon winding through green fields, running along one of the great peninsulas that formed the south-west coast of Ireland.

The landscape, wild and rugged, green and grey, felt strange to Amy, who'd lived her whole life in a city. To her right, the mountainous spine of the peninsula rose like the back of some gargantuan sea creature. To her left, the ocean shimmered under the evening sun.

On the road ahead, she saw a woman walking, a black dog trotting by her side. Thank God. Someone to ask for directions.

She pulled up beside her and lowered her window. 'Hi,' she said. 'I'm looking for a house called Sea View, outside a village called Knockcrea.'

The woman, who was fiftyish and blonde, wore walking gear and an unsmiling expression. 'Just keep driving, keep the sea on your left. You'll see it. It stands out.'

'Great,' said Amy. 'Thank you.'

'You a friend of the Carrolls?' the woman asked.

'Not exactly,' Amy replied. 'I'm going to work for them. I'm their new nanny-slash-housekeeper.'

A strange expression slid across the woman's face. 'Oh.' She nodded a couple of times. 'Well, you're nearly there. Can't miss it.'

Amy felt a stab of reticence. There was something in the woman's tone she didn't like. But she thanked her, rolled up her window and continued to drive.

A kilometre or so on, she took a bend in the road and saw the Carrolls' house for the first time. 'Wow,' she said aloud.

The woman was right: you couldn't miss it.

Futuristic and sleek, a half-cylinder wonder of modern architecture, all curved lines and gleaming floor-to-ceiling glass, Sea View looked completely out of place against the remote, rugged landscape. This far-flung corner of West Cork was sparsely populated, and the only other buildings in sight were modest farmhouses and cottages. There was something almost distasteful about the ostentatious home, its overt display of wealth.

When Amy had come across the ad last week, while scrolling through jobs websites, it had been obvious the Carrolls were using their house as an attraction. *A live-in position . . . Housekeeper/nanny/mother's helper . . . The successful candidate will have an en suite bedroom in our modern home . . . The successful candidate will be treated like a member of the family.* Multiple photos were included in the ad: the bedroom, the view, the location. Amy had seen more images of the houses when she found the mother, June Carroll, on social media. But none of it had prepared her for seeing it in real life.

She felt fresh nerves twisting her stomach. This would be her first meeting with the family. June had interviewed her on the phone and had seemed nice enough. But Amy had no idea what June's husband, Miles, was like, nor the two children. All she knew was that Tom was three and Poppy was two, that they were cute and blonde (that much was apparent from June's Instagram) and that their parents needed an extra pair of hands around the house. (No wonder, she thought, looking at the size of it. It would be no small feat to keep that place sparkling.) She also suspected, from several hints June had dropped, that they were having trouble finding someone who was willing to come all the way to this remote place.

Aside from that, Amy had no idea what she was walking into.

She pulled in the long gravel driveway and parked her shabby little Renault Clio in next to a sleek black BMW and a white Range Rover. The house loomed above her: tall, sheer, intimidating. Although the front of the building was almost entirely glass, she couldn't tell whether anyone was watching her from inside. The blaze of the sinking sun bounced off the windows, creating an opaque orange glare.

She checked her reflection in the rear-view mirror. Her long black hair needed brushing. Her green eyes had deep shadows under them. She frowned critically, took a tube of concealer from her bag and dabbed some under her eyes. She pulled a brush through her hair, put on some lip balm and began mentally preparing for the performance of meeting a new employer.

Taking a deep breath, she got out of the car. She took her bag from the boot, walked up to the door of Sea View and rang the bell.

Seconds ticked towards a minute. Nobody answered. Amy looked around, at the mountains, at the sea, then back at the door. Should she ring again?

Before she could, it was opened by a man in his early

fifties. He was an inch or two shorter than she was, and almost entirely bald. He smiled broadly at her.

'Hello, hello! Amy, I presume? Miles Carroll. Pleasure to meet you.' He grabbed her hand in his, which was slightly sweaty, and shook it. 'Welcome to Sea View.'

2

Although he was wearing comfortable house clothes, Miles Carroll gave the impression of a man who usually wore a suit. He had pale-grey eyes, a wide-lipped, almost frog-like mouth and a soft build that suggested a sedentary life.

'Apologies for keeping you waiting at the door, Amy. It's bath time here, and it's chaos. Let me take that for you.'

He picked up her suitcase. Amy noted that he had a Dublin accent, although it was moneyed and upper class, quite different from hers. While he wasn't a handsome man, Miles had an affable charisma about him that was immediately apparent.

'Thanks,' she said. 'Sorry I'm late. It took me longer to get here than I thought.'

'Most people don't realise just how remote we are.' He stepped aside. 'Come on in.'

Amy walked through the door, and for a moment, she just stared. The interior was even more impressive than it had looked in the photographs: open-plan, high-ceilinged, sleek and modern. There was a kitchen area on the left and a living area on the right.

'Your house is beautiful,' she said.

'Thanks,' said Miles. 'We like it. Come on in, make yourself at home. June's upstairs wrestling our two terrors into their pyjamas. She'll be down in a mo.' Leaving Amy's bag by the door, he led her into the kitchen area. 'Take a seat,' he said, pointing to the tall chairs by the marble island beneath hanging lights. 'Can I get you anything? Water? Tea?'

'I'm grand, thanks.' Amy sat down.

Upstairs, a child screeched, good-natured but *loud*. Miles smiled ruefully. 'They're good kids, but they lose their minds around bath time.' He took the seat across from her. 'So, you survived the drive down from Dublin?'

'It wasn't too bad,' Amy answered. 'How long have you been living out here?'

'Two years now, and we love it,' said Miles. 'Best decision we ever made. We came to West Cork on holidays, fell in love with the place, never wanted to leave. Waking up to this view every morning – the sky, the sea, the solitude – it's hard to beat. Sometimes you do miss being able to order a pizza, but the pros are worth the cons a hundred-fold. I could never go back to living in the city.'

'You can't get pizza delivered here?'

'You can't get any food delivered here.'

'Wow.'

Amy had lived her entire life in Dublin, with a variety of chippers and takeaways all within walking distance. It had never occurred to her there were places in Ireland where people couldn't get food delivered.

'Like I said, that's the only downside,' said Miles. 'Although ... I suppose the drive to work is a pain. I'm a solicitor, and I work in the nearest town. It takes me an hour to get there. But at least the car is moving and the view is spectacular. Better to be flying along past mountains and sea than sitting at a standstill alongside a thousand other saps, all twiddling our thumbs together. No,' he went on with fresh assurance, as if he'd convinced himself with this speech, 'you couldn't pay me enough to go back to the city. Just wait till you see what the stars are like out here on a clear night.'

From upstairs, Amy heard another joyful child's shriek, and the low hum of a woman's voice.

'So, Amy,' Miles asked her, 'what did you do before?'

This question struck Amy as odd. She had sent her CV along to June, who she had presumed would share it with her husband. June had said that Amy's cleaning experience was a big selling point. ('This position is as much about house-keeping as it is about minding the children, Amy. We have a large home and the upkeep is a full-time job.')

'I worked as a cleaner,' she told him. 'In a hospital.'

'Nothing wrong with being a cleaner,' Miles said heartily. 'It's good honest work.'

Amy, who hadn't suggested there was anything wrong with it, resisted the urge to point this out. 'And before that, I worked for a family in their home,' she replied neutrally. 'Babysitting mostly, but cleaning too.'

Before Miles could respond there were footsteps on the stairs. A slender blonde woman with a ballerina's perfect posture walked into the room. She smiled at Amy. 'Well, hello there! How lovely to meet you in person.'

'You too,' said Amy, slightly stunned. So June's flattering

online photos weren't just the result of good angles and editing.

'Amy and I were just getting to know each other,' said Miles. 'Where're the kids?'

'I left them watching *Dora* on the TV upstairs.' June had a genteel voice, like bells. 'We don't usually allow TV before bed, so this is a special treat.'

June had to be twenty years younger than her husband, close in age to Amy. She had perfect swinging hair, very white teeth and eyes such a deep blue they seemed almost violet. Everything about her looked freshly washed, immaculate. She was dressed head-to-toe in pastels and white – the last outfit you'd expect the mother of two small kids to wear. Amy wasn't proud of the next thought that ran through her mind: *How the hell did Miles pull this woman?*

Out loud, she said, 'I can't wait to meet the kids. Two and three – they're a lot of fun at that age!'

June had made it clear during the phone interview that they were looking for someone who could start immediately. The impression Amy had got was that the last girl had left in a hurry and the Carrolls were somewhat stuck. 'When would be the soonest you could arrive?' June had asked. When Amy said it would be a matter of days, June had basically offered her the job on the spot, on the condition that her references checked out.

'Well, you must be exhausted after the drive,' June said now. 'Take some time to settle in before I show you around. Are you hungry?'

'No, I ate on the drive down. I'm ready to be shown the ropes,' said Amy, with the automatic spirit of willingness she always showed employers, although she *was* tired.

'Have a cup of tea first, at least,' June insisted, and this time Amy relented.

'I was just telling Amy that the only downside to living around here is the lack of pizza delivery services,' said Miles as his wife put the kettle on. June touched him on the shoulder as she passed, in the unconscious manner of a couple who maintain constant physical contact.

'I *do* sometimes long for a pad thai,' she said as she busied herself with tea bags. 'I hope you won't miss takeaway too much while you're with us, Amy.'

'I'm sure I'll learn to live without. Where's the nearest shop?'

'In Knockcrea, the village,' said June. 'It's just a few minutes' drive down the road – but it's a *tiny* shop, only good for essentials like bread and milk.'

'Knockcrea isn't a village,' said Miles dismissively. 'It's a ghost of a village. There are only a couple of hundred people left living there. It was a mining town, and once the mine closed, there was nothing to keep people in the area. Now it's just a half-circle of empty houses, one shop, one pub and a closed school. The only people left are a few old fogeys and some hippy-dippy blow-in types with romantic pretensions about living in the countryside.'

He spoke with derision, apparently seeing no irony in mocking others for being blow-ins. Amy glanced at June, who was stirring tea with a completely straight face.

'If you want a proper supermarket,' Miles continued, 'you have to drive all the way to Clongrassil. It takes nearly an hour. It's a pain in the arse – but all this is worth it, Amy, you'll see. Once you get used to being out here, you won't want to go back.'

'Do you take milk? Sugar?' June asked.

'Two sugars, please. Thanks.'

June set the teas on the table, then slid onto the seat beside Miles and put a hand lightly on his. The way they sat primly side-by-side put Amy in mind of royals making a public appearance.

'So,' she asked, 'how long have you two been married?'

Miles and June gave her a short history of their relationship. They'd met at the wedding of a mutual friend. ('I had an engagement ring on her finger within the year,' said Miles. 'I know a good thing when I see it!')

They asked Amy questions about her life back in Dublin, to which she gave brief, untruthful answers. She painted a picture of a quiet, blameless life.

'And what made you want to move all the way out to Knockcrea?' June asked. 'I mean, we're delighted that you did, but I'm wondering what the appeal was for you.'

'I suppose the same thing that appealed to you,' said Amy. 'Change of scenery . . . peace, quiet . . .'

'Well, we're a married couple with kids,' said Miles. 'It's different for a young woman on her own. How're you ever going to meet someone around here?'

'*Miles*,' said June, faux-shocked. 'Who says she's trying to meet someone? Can't a woman enjoy her life solo?'

'If you say so,' said Miles. 'I'm just saying, if she wants a social life, she's come to the wrong place. I wasn't trying to suggest her biological clock is ticking or anything like that. You've got a while left on that front,' he added to Amy.

'*Miles!*' This time June's shock seemed more genuine. 'Ignore him, please, Amy.'

'What?' said Miles. 'I'm saying she's still young; she's got loads of time to have kids. That's not insulting, is it?'

June's neck and collarbone were turning pink. Maybe she'd noticed how Amy's face had stiffened. In a tense voice, she said, 'Honey, maybe just don't talk about anyone's biological clock over tea, okay?'

'All right. Christ,' Miles said comfortably. He didn't seem particularly chastened. 'Well, I for one am glad you're not too fussed about having a social life, Amy, because it's fantastic that you're here.'

June nodded, eager to move the conversation along. 'We're *so* pleased to have you.'

'And I'm pleased to be here.' Amy, too, was glad they were no longer discussing her ovaries.

'It'll make a world of difference,' said Miles. 'Having someone to rely on. Bloody nightmare, not having help. We haven't had anyone since Francisca left.'

'She had to go back to Brazil,' June said quickly. There was something pre-emptive about the way she jumped in. Amy, curiosity piqued, rather hoped Miles might blurt out something else, but he'd moved on.

'June will be able to concentrate on work again,' he said. 'I work long hours, so she's really been on her own with the kids the past few weeks.'

'What do you do, June?' Amy asked. All June had said over the phone was that she was self-employed. Amy had noticed that she had a huge number of followers online, but couldn't figure out exactly why.

'I'm a content creator,' said June. 'I use a variety of social media platforms, but Instagram is where I have the most followers, and I work with brands. A lot of my content would be about parenting, and lifestyle and wellness, that kind of thing.'

'Oh, cool,' said Amy. 'Like, sharing recipes and stuff?'

'Yes, exactly. Stuff about the kids and their routines, parenting, fashion . . .' June put her cup down delicately on the table. 'It's been difficult to keep on top of things and create consistent content since we've been without a nanny. I know people can perceive social media as not real work, but there's a huge amount going on behind the scenes: liaising with brands, for example. And you wouldn't believe how much effort goes into taking one good photo . . .'

The conversation rambled on. When they'd finished their tea and the first chunk of getting-to-know-each-other chit-chat had passed, it was time for a tour of the house.

'Honey, would you take Amy's bag to her room?' June said, touching Miles on the arm. Task delegated, she turned back to Amy. 'Let's start by introducing you to the kids.'

She led Amy up the stairs and into an enormous master bedroom, which was decorated in minimalist whites and greys. One all-glass wall faced the sea. On the king-sized bed, lying on top of a white duvet, were two tiny blonde children, their eyes focused on a huge TV.

'Hello, sweethearts,' said June, her soft voice melting to honey. She paused *Dora the Explorer* and the kids crawled over the duvet to her.

'Hiyas!' said Amy brightly, smiling her biggest smile.

The children looked at her with confused, mistrustful expressions, and clung to their mother.

'This is Tom,' said June, kissing the boy's tousled hair, 'and this is Poppy.' She put an arm around the little girl, hugging her close.

Tom was three, Amy reminded herself, and Poppy was two. 'Hi, Tom, hi, Poppy!'

Both children remained silent.

'Give them time,' June said softly. 'It's been really disruptive for them, with nannies coming and going ...' She straightened up. 'Honestly, I can't say how pleased I am to have a more mature nanny instead of one of those flighty girls just out of college who disappear at the drop of a hat. We need someone we can rely on. Someone we can trust.'

Trying not to think about all the lies she had just told June, Amy smiled at her and hoped it looked genuine.

June's attention returned to her children. 'Why don't you watch some more *Dora*, darlings? Just this once. Daddy's going to put you to bed while I show Amy around.'

Once the kids' eyes were focused on the screen again, it was easy for June to disentangle herself.

'So,' she said, returning to her normal voice as she led Amy from the room, 'the windows are obviously a big job. I get a window cleaner once a month for the outside, but the inside glass needs to be cleaned every two weeks at least. I suggest doing all the upstairs windows one week, and all the downstairs windows the following week, but of course you can do things your way if you come up with a better system.'

It was growing steadily darker outside. With the lights on indoors, and those great windows all around, Amy felt exposed. Someone could be standing outside, unseen, staring in.

'These are the controls for the blinds,' June said, 'but honestly, we leave them up more or less all the time. The nearest neighbour is a kilometre away. Who's going to be looking in?'

It was as if she'd heard Amy's thoughts.

'I'd like the floors thoroughly cleaned every second week,' she continued, now leading Amy down the stairs.

'General maintenance between deep cleans will also be your responsibility ...'

While June talked, she led Amy from room to room. The house was show-home gorgeous, the colour scheme neutral throughout – white, beige, grey. The effect was almost flawless, but here and there a plastic toy or crayon scribble interrupted the perfection.

'The kids have a playroom, and we try to keep all their junk in there,' said June. 'When they're older, we'll make it Tom's bedroom, but for the moment he and Poppy share a room.'

'Right.' Amy tried to count how many bedrooms were in this place. Four? Five?

'And this is my office,' June said, opening yet another door.

June's office was a change in tone from the rest of the house. Funky and feminine, it was done in loud, bold colours and decorated with ironically kitschy items: a zebra-print rug, a flamingo lamp, a fuchsia beanbag, an ornamental pineapple. Stylish, fun, *very* Instagrammable. 'There usually isn't too much cleaning to do in there,' she said, closing the door again. 'The kids aren't allowed in, and I keep the place neat.'

'Got it.'

Next she led Amy to a utility room off the kitchen. It was large enough that it could be turned into a small bedroom. 'All the cleaning stuff is in here. We've got the washer and dryer, obviously' – she waved at them – 'but also everything you need for housekeeping.'

'Oh, brilliant.' The shelves were fully stocked with neatly organised cleaning products. Amy felt a surge of relief. The job of maintaining this house immediately seemed more manageable.

June then launched into the children's routine. 'I handle breakfast and mornings, but on days I'm working, I usually retreat to my office around eleven or twelve, so on those days you'll do lunch. We *try* to eat about eighty per cent veggie, although that goes out the window at dinnertime! Tom won't touch corn, and Poppy turns her nose up at fish, but apart from that, they'll both eat more or less anything . . .' At this point, June seemed to register the slightly dazed look on Amy's face. 'Look, you don't need to retain all this information right now,' she said. 'And in general, if any of your duties feel like too much, tell me. I'd much rather you let me know if there's a problem, so we can resolve it. We want you to be happy here, Amy. We're looking for longevity.' Her deep blue eyes were sincere.

'Yeah,' said Amy, nodding. 'So am I.'

June smiled broadly, showing those pearly white teeth. 'I'm so happy to hear that,' she said. 'And I mean it, Amy. Don't hesitate to come to me with anything.' Then she turned and led Amy towards the back of the house, opening doors along the way. 'That's the kids' playroom . . . This is the downstairs bathroom . . .'

They were now walking down a long, narrow corridor, the darkest space in the house.

'That one,' said June, nodding at a door as they passed it, 'is Liam's room. You don't need to go in there.'

'Wait.' Amy felt like she was missing something. 'Who's Liam?'

June stopped walking and looked at her in surprise. 'We didn't mention Liam?'

'Uh . . .' Amy racked her brains. 'No, I don't think so.'

'Liam is Miles's son from a previous relationship. He's seventeen. He only stays with us for a couple of months each year, during summer. The rest of the time he lives with his mother in Leixlip.'

Amy didn't know what to say. Shouldn't they have told her this in advance?

June resumed walking. 'I'm sure I mentioned it to you,' she said. 'Anyway, it has no relevance to your role, which is probably why I didn't harp on about it. Like I said, he'll be going back to his mother's in a few weeks.'

They were almost at the end of the corridor. Amy was so busy digesting the news about the teenage son that she was caught off guard when June opened a wooden door on the left and said, 'And this is your room!'

It was huge. The floor was polished oak, the walls rich cream, the duvet cover a rose-petal pink. One wall was almost entirely glass, a window large enough to drive a car through. Amy's bag had been placed by the neatly made bed.

'It's *beautiful*,' she exclaimed.

June looked pleased by her reaction. 'There's an en suite . . .' she said, opening the door and flicking on the light. Amy glimpsed perfectly matching rose-pink soaps, towels and potpourri. 'And a walk-in wardrobe.'

'Wow. It's so beautiful,' Amy repeated. 'I don't know what to say. Thanks so much.'

It *was* beautiful – possibly the most beautiful room she'd ever stayed in in her life. But suddenly she felt exhausted. All the hours of driving, all the reasons she'd fled Dublin – it seemed to abruptly catch up with her.

June must have read the look on her face, because she said, 'I'll leave you be. Why don't you sleep in tomorrow? Take the morning to yourself?'

'That'd be great,' said Amy gratefully. 'Thank you.'

'Oh, and I just wanted to confirm.' June paused at the door. 'As we discussed on the phone, Miles and I pay cash in hand. You're all right with that?'

'Yes,' said Amy immediately. 'Yes, that's fine.'

It was better than fine. It was one of the reasons she'd taken the job. She had found over the years that people often preferred to pay their nannies and cleaners that way, and, in her current situation, it suited her perfectly. A live-in position. Money straight into her pocket. All bills and utilities in someone else's name. There was no paper trail leading to her as long as she was at this address. Legally, officially, it was like she'd dropped off the face of the earth.

'Great,' said June. 'We'll pay you weekly, on Thursdays.'

'That's perfect. Thanks for everything, June.'

'You're welcome.' June's voice became more melodic as she added, 'Goodnight.' She stepped into the corridor and shut the door gently behind her.

Amy closed the blinds over the enormous window. She put her phone on charge. Then she lay down on the rose-coloured bedspread and stared up at the ceiling.

She couldn't believe she was actually here.

Her own daring amazed her. She'd done it. She'd packed a bag, got into her car and driven away. She'd half expected an official to pull her over and say, *Amy Fagan? I'm sorry, you don't get to escape your old life that easily. Turn that car around and go back.* But nobody had stopped her as she drove out of the estate. Or as she hit a hundred on the motorway.

She sat up to turn off the bedside lamp and lay back down in the dark. It was so quiet here. She was used to the constant hum of the city, but at Sea View, the only sound was the wind whipping over the fields.

Eyes closing, she remembered that comment June had made about 'nannies coming and going'. I guess nobody stays here very long, she thought as she sank into a deep, dreamless sleep.

3

The next morning, Amy was woken by the happy shrieks of children somewhere in the house. Morning light peeked in around the blinds. She sat up, pushing her long hair back from her face.

An odd half-memory came to her. Had something woken her in the night? She recalled a drowsy feeling, a sound outside ... footsteps? A door slamming? The memory floated just out of reach, like a word on the tip of the tongue.

She sat up and stretched. It was natural to sleep lightly in a new place, she told herself. Any sound she'd heard was probably someone getting up to use the toilet.

Once up and dressed, she unpacked a few of her things. On her bedside locker, she placed a novel and a hairbrush. In the uppermost drawer, she tucked away several items with sentimental value: a photo album, an old snow globe. Then she brushed her hair, moisturised her face and checked the time: 7.48. Bracing herself, she left her room and walked down the hall into the open-plan living area.

She found June and the children sitting around the table, sunlight streaming through the huge windows behind them. Breakfast was a colourful spread: avocado toast, orange juice, a plate of sliced fruit.

'Morning, Amy,' said June, all smiles. 'I didn't expect to see you up so early!'

'Good morning.' Amy felt suddenly awkward. Would they expect her to join them?

'Sit down!' June's blonde hair looked just washed. She wore a full face of make-up – subtle, the kind that men mistook for no make-up, but a full face nonetheless – and expensive-looking grey and lilac loungewear. 'Have something to eat. Miles has already left for work.'

'Thanks, but I'm all right,' said Amy. 'I'm not really hungry yet. Morning, Tom, morning, Poppy!'

Tom and Poppy eyed her suspiciously. Tom had a chunk of avocado on his nose.

'Well, when you do get hungry, help yourself,' said June. 'You're welcome to anything in the kitchen while you're here.'

'Thanks.' Amy had a feeling that if she opened the fridge, she wouldn't find sausages and bacon. Her preferred breakfast was a fry – sizzling rashers, toast glistening with butter. Her naturally slender figure belied her eating habits. ('Skinny bitch' was how her sister, Sandra, put it, prodding Amy in the stomach. 'How can you eat all that crap and still have the same body you had at seventeen?')

'I don't really eat this early either,' said June. 'It's just coffee and orange juice for me. But these two are always starving.'

Amy looked at Tom and Poppy and the plates of green-smeared toast. 'I can't believe your kids like avocado.'

'Yes, they're brilliant eaters.' June tousled Poppy's hair and wiped the smudge of avocado off Tom's nose. 'We never let them have any sugary rubbish, and so they never ask for Coco Pops because they don't know what Coco Pops are.' She nodded at the seat beside her. 'Do sit down, Amy.'

Amy sat. 'What time do you need me to start at today?'

'Oh, why don't we say one o'clock?' said June. 'No need to rush. Does that work for you?'

'That's great, yeah. Thank you.'

June sipped her coffee. 'So. What are you going to do with your morning off?'

'I might go for a walk,' said Amy. 'Get a feel for the place.'

Suddenly Poppy spoke up. 'Lady is *new* lady,' she said, pointing a tiny finger at Amy.

'That's right!' said June. 'Amy is our new cleaner, *and* she's going to babysit you guys sometimes when Mummy is working. Won't that be fun?'

'No,' said Tom, his expression sulky.

'New *new* lady,' said Poppy, and then she fell silent again.

'I thought maybe tomorrow we could all do something nice together,' said June. 'Like go for a walk on the beach. Amy has never been to the beach here! We could show her around Knockcrea.'

Tom cheered up at this. 'Can I throw rocks?'

'You can throw rocks at the sea,' said June, smiling indulgently.

'Whoopee!' said Tom, and shoved an entire crust of avocado toast into his mouth.

Poppy continued to watch Amy mistrustfully, her blue eyes huge under wisps of blonde hair.

'Well, I'll let you guys finish your breakfast in peace,' said Amy, getting to her feet.

'Oh, nonsense, you're not intruding at all,' said June. Seeming to sense that Amy wanted to escape, she added, 'But go, enjoy your walk. The view is at its loveliest this time of the morning, I've always thought.'

Amy gave Tom and Poppy an awkward little wave good-bye. They didn't respond.

When she stepped out of the front door, the beauty of the landscape in the sunlight struck her all over again. For a full minute, she stood and stared at the rolling green fields demarcated by low stone walls, the rugged rock forma-tions on the sides of the mountains, and the vast glittering blue of the sea. In the distance, she could see the village of Knockcrea: small white houses and cottages in a rough horseshoe shape. Sea View was the only house in the imme-diate vicinity.

She walked down the driveway and onto the potholed country road, surrounded by green and a rich stillness.

Thinking back to the scene at the house, she wondered what her mornings would be like from here on out. Would she eat with the family, or make her own meals once they were finished? She wished June and Miles would hand her some sort of rulebook, or just tell her what they expected her to do. They'd done this before, whereas this was her first time living in someone else's house. She imagined herself eating alone in her room, just for some quiet and the chance to take her employee mask off. The thought made her feel suddenly, desperately lonely.

She took a packet of cigarettes and a lighter from her jacket pocket. The ad had called for a non-smoker, but surely that just meant no smoking on the job or on their property, right? It had nothing to do with Miles and June if she had a smoke on her own time, did it?

She glanced back guiltily in the direction of the house as she lit up. Cigarettes were surely on the list of things Tom and Poppy didn't know about. Did they know about baked beans and white bread and bacon? If Amy wanted a fry, would she have to cook it in secret and hide the ingredients like contraband?

She walked and smoked and thought. Birds fluttered from the thick green hedgerows that lined the road. Her phone buzzed and she took it from her pocket. It was a message from Sandra.

> **Hey, hon! Settling in okay?? I'm free for a call before work if you're up.**

This was followed by a long line of hearts, kisses and emojis.

Amy called her.

'Hi, pet!' Sandra sounded like she was rushing, which she usually was. 'How're you doing? What're the family like?'

Sandra was six years older than Amy and worked as a nurse. The two sisters were very different, but they had always been close. Growing up, Amy had been the shy one, while Sandra was loud and confident. She would charge in to stand up for her little sister when bigger kids bullied her. They looked different, too – Amy tall and black-haired, Sandra short and broad and blonde. These days, Sandra wore her fair hair shorn close to her head, a style that caused kids on the estate to occasionally – and inaccurately – shout

'Dyke!' in her direction. It was all water off a duck's back to Sandra, who was tough and thick-skinned. Amy had always admired her sister's ability to shake things off. She wished she could be more like her.

'The family seem all right,' she said, slowing to an amble. 'Bit stuck-up, maybe, but all right. They were friendly.'

'Well, that's the important thing.' Sandra sounded relieved. 'They made you feel welcome, did they?'

'They did, yeah. And the house is unbelievable.'

'Is that Amy?' A male voice in the background. Sandra's partner, Dave. 'How's she getting on?'

'Hi, Dave!' said Amy.

'Hi, Amy!'

Dave was a porter at the hospital where Sandra worked. A big man with kind eyes and a jokey demeanour, he was beloved by patients and staff alike. He and Sandra had met on her first week and had been together ever since. They had no kids, but they did have three Staffordshire bull terriers. They were the most rooted, happy couple Amy knew.

'What are the children like?' Sandra wanted to know.

'Ah, they seem sweet. Bit shy. I get the impression nannies have come and gone. It'll probably take them some time to get used to me.'

'What, they can't keep staff?' Sandra was immediately wary.

'Do they seem like good employers?' Dave asked.

'There was one weird thing,' Amy said, taking a drag of her smoke. 'There's a teenage boy living in the house too, and they didn't tell me that before.'

'What?' said Sandra and Dave together.

'Why wouldn't they tell you about him off the bat?' Sandra asked.

'They said he has nothing to do with my job,' said Amy.

'Still, it only seems fair to let you know in advance who's living in the house,' said Dave. 'What's he like?'

'I haven't met him yet.' Amy exhaled smoke. 'He was in his room when I arrived last night. All I know is his name's Liam.'

'Maybe he's one of those teenagers who never leaves their room,' said Sandra. 'Maura up the road has a son like that. Never showers. Just plays video games all day.'

'Maybe he's some kind of psychopath,' said Dave.

'Dave!' said Sandra. 'Don't say that to her!'

'Ah, I was only joking. I'm sure he's just a normal kid. Listen, Amy, I'm going to hop in the shower, but keep in touch, yeah?'

'Chat later, Dave!' Amy called.

'Don't mind him,' said Sandra as Dave left the room. 'I don't know what would happen to his ego if he realised he's not half as funny as he thinks he is.'

'I heard that!' Dave shouted from the hall.

Amy smiled, but it faded fast as she gathered the nerve to ask her sister a question.

'Sandra,' she said tentatively, 'he hasn't come to your door looking for me, has he?'

'Not yet. And when he does, I won't tell him any-thing.' Sandra's voice was steel. 'He won't get a word out of me, Amy.'

'I know.' Amy trusted her sister with all her being. 'I'm just wondering if he's realised I'm gone yet.'

'I don't know. But his head's going to explode when he does.'

There was a certain satisfaction in Sandra's tone when she

said this, but Amy just felt sick. When she hung up a few minutes later, she stood staring out at the isolated landscape, the mountain peaks and the jewel-blue sea.

Even out here, at the edge of the world, she was afraid he would find her.

4

Before

Until Amy turned fourteen, her life was ordinary. She and Sandra were raised by their mother, Louise, in a grey pebble-dash three-bedroom on a north Dublin housing estate. Cars roared past all day. Kids played football on the strip of grass across the street. A neighbour kept pigeons, and the clattering of wings as the flock rose from the rooftops sounded like home.

Louise Fagan was a nurse, a cat lover, a lifelong smoker, a devourer of romance novels and an exceptionally warm person. Her husband, Gerry, who was in construction, died in a workplace accident before Amy turned one. Louise never remarried.

Their home was warm and cosy and full of laughter. Sandra and Amy would watch *Teenage Mutant Ninja Turtles* and *Top of the Pops* together. Amy did her homework at the kitchen table and her mother would sometimes bring her a hot chocolate.

She was happy. A simple, contented kind of happiness that she was too young to appreciate. Her complaints were about small things, like her big sister being bossy, and not being allowed to dye her hair blonde. She went to and from school in a gaggle of girls, and gossiped at the bus stop, and painted her nails, and experimented with make-up, and all the uneventful days blended together into a forgettable blur.

Until one afternoon, when she was getting books from her locker and heard someone shout her name.

'Amy! Mark Keating wants to know if you'll meet him at the bus stop after school.' Samantha Rourke sauntered over to her, ponytail swinging, chewing gum like it was an accessory.

Amy felt a flutter of excitement, but didn't show it. 'He didn't really say that,' she countered, suspicious. It wouldn't be past Samantha Rourke to set you up for a laugh.

Mark Keating was sixteen. Older, cooler, notorious. The school's resident bad boy. He was also gorgeous: tall and dark-haired, with a lazy grin.

'He did. He fancies you.' There was an excited, gossipy tone to Samantha's voice that made Amy begin to believe she was telling the truth. 'He said' – and a vaguely bitter shadow crossed Samantha's features – 'that you're the best-looking girl in the whole school.'

Amy, who at fourteen looked in the mirror and saw nothing but ugliness, was stunned by this. She would have protested immediately, sure that Samantha was having her on, if not for the brief resentment she'd seen on Samantha's face, the envy that existed between fragile, hungry-to-be-loved teenage girls.

'Hmm,' she said, pretending to deliberate. She tossed back

her long ponytail of dark hair and busied herself at her locker, all to hide the fact that her stomach had flipped over. *The best-looking girl in the whole school.* MARK KEATING had said that! About HER!

'Well?' said Samantha. 'What'll I tell him?'

Amy slammed her locker shut and turned to face her. 'All right,' she said, shrugging in a pantomime of not caring much one way or the other. 'Tell him I said yeah. I'll meet him.'

When she saw Mark waiting for her at the bus stop after school, Amy's residual fear that it might all be a prank turned to elation.

Mark smiled his lazy smile. He walked her home. He put an arm around her shoulders and, later, while kissing her against a wall, a hand up her shirt.

She was his girlfriend from that day on, and for the next few months she went around starry-eyed.

5

Now

When Amy returned to Sea View after her morning walk, she tried the back entrance, eager to avoid the small-talk gauntlet. To her relief, she found the door unlocked.

In her room, she unpacked the rest of her things. It felt odd hanging up her clothes in a walk-in closet. She couldn't believe some people lived their whole lives like this, with so much space. She brushed her teeth thoroughly, making sure there was no lingering smell of smoke.

Just after she'd finished, June knocked on her door. 'I wanted to let you know I'm bringing the kids to the beach this afternoon, so you'll have the place to yourself while cleaning. It's much easier without those two underfoot!'

'Thanks,' said Amy. 'Sounds great.'

She emerged from her room, not wanting to seem rude. She made conversation with June and some efforts to bond with Tom and Poppy, who remained wary and mistrustful.

Liam did not make an appearance. On her way back to her room, Amy looked at his closed door curiously.

She passed some time by reading a few chapters of the novel she'd brought with her, *The Flatshare* by Beth O'Leary. Reading was escapism for Amy, a respite from her own life. At around 12.45, when she heard June and the kids go out, she left her room. She made buttered toast and black coffee, which she ate at the marble island, looking out at the view and listening to the quiet. Then she got to work.

Amy liked cleaning. She always had. Alone, with music playing, she could go into an almost meditative state. She liked making things neat, organised, leaving a space pristine.

She looked at the hand-written list June had left her. *Clean toilets . . . Sweep and hoover as needed . . .*

Amy threw herself into her tasks. She wiped down surfaces, scrubbed mirrors. She figured out where the fresh towels were kept and folded them in a neat pile, with one hand towel arranged decoratively on top, origami style. She loved little flourishes like that. It was the difference between nice and perfect.

She was sweeping the kitchen floor when she heard a loud bang. Amy jumped so violently she almost dropped the brush. What was that? It had come from inside the house. Miles was at work, and June and the kids were out . . .

There was another loud bang, and at the same moment, the answer hit her. Liam, she thought. It had to be. The strange noises were coming from the direction of his room. You idiot, she scolded herself. She'd totally forgotten she wasn't alone in the house.

She wanted to laugh at her own reaction. But the sudden noise had sent her heart pounding, and now unwelcome memories came flooding in.

No, she told her brain. Don't think about that . . .

But it was too late. Her body was pumping with adrenaline. Her vision became wavy. In her mind's eye she saw the flames again, dancing, crackling, as orange and vivid as if they were right in front of her . . .

No no no . . .

Amy dropped the sweeping brush, which clattered onto the floor. She made her way unsteadily to the sofa, where she sat down and concentrated on breathing deeply. It took a while for her heart to stop hammering, for her body to realise it wasn't in danger, for her brain to stop replaying the memory in high definition. She was very glad Miles and June were out.

After some time − she couldn't tell how long − she was able to look around the house and ground herself. She was here, she was safe. She got to her feet, picked up the brush and resumed sweeping.

Over the next half an hour, there were further strange noises from Liam's room. More banging, but repetitive this time. *Thud. Thud. Thud.* Amy peered down the corridor as she walked past with a bucket, but his door was still closed.

Then the noises stopped, and the huge house fell so silent that Amy could once again imagine she was the only person there.

When June, Tom and Poppy returned from the beach, June seemed delighted with the sparkling house and enthused over what a great job Amy had done.

'I'm not finished. I still have to—'

'Oh, leave it for now,' said June. 'That's *plenty* for today. The place looks *amazing*.'

Tom and Poppy were sandy and happy. When Amy tried to coax them into a silly game, Tom accepted, bursting into giggles as she made faces and pretended to grab him. Poppy hung back a little, but she was watching intently. Amy acted as if she couldn't see her. Eventually Poppy edged closer, wanting to join in. Amy took a swipe at her, and Poppy gave a huge shriek – half glee, half nervousness – and backed away again. Amy returned her attention to Tom, not wanting to overwhelm the little girl, but she was smiling inwardly. It was a start.

June, watching, smiled too. 'You're good with them,' she said.

That evening, Amy ate dinner with June, Tom and Poppy – home-made pizza with spinach, onion, cashew nuts and roasted chicken. Miles didn't join them. Neither did Liam.

'Miles has to work late this evening,' said June. 'Daddy often works late, doesn't he, my lovelies? We know he works hard to pay for the nice house we live in and the tasty food we're eating.'

The kids nodded like they'd heard this speech before.

'This *is* a tasty meal,' said Amy. 'Thanks, June.' She took a bite, chewed and swallowed before asking, 'And what about Liam? Is he going to join us?'

June, concentrating on cutting Poppy's pizza into bite-sized pieces, didn't look at Amy as she answered. 'Liam doesn't really go in for family dinners. He prefers to eat in his room.'

'Ah, I see.' Amy reached out to steady Tom's glass of water, which he'd almost knocked over. 'I suppose he's at that age, isn't he?'

'I suppose he is,' said June, still busying herself with Poppy's food.

After dinner, Amy helped June to clean up. When she said goodnight to Tom and Poppy, they said 'night night' back, and Poppy even gave her a little wave.

As she walked past Liam's closed door, she couldn't help wondering: what did he *do* in there all day? Apart from the sudden burst of thuds earlier, she hadn't heard a single sound from his room. It was unnerving.

Back in her room, she changed into the pyjama bottoms and vest she slept in. It occurred to her that while there were plenty of pictures of Tom and Poppy around the house – their blonde heads filled frame after frame – she hadn't seen a single photo of Liam. Was the poor kid terribly disfigured or something? Did he refuse to be photographed? What was going on?

Amy brushed her teeth and got into bed. She rearranged the pillows, made herself comfortable, then picked up *The Flatshare*. It was addictive, and even though she knew the couple in it would end up together, she needed to see it happen. As her eyelids began to droop, she kept turning the pages. *Just one more chapter . . . Just one more chapter . . .*

Creeaaaak.

Amy woke with a start. Her bedside lamp was still on. Her book was lying on her chest.

In the corridor, she heard soft movement. Like footsteps.

Right outside her door.

She raised her head, suddenly very awake and alert. Was that Liam skulking around out there? She stayed still, listening intently.

The footsteps moved away, creaking down the corridor. Then she heard the sound of the back door opening and closing.

Amy looked at her phone: 00.47. Where was he going at this hour? For a moment she pictured him dashing off into the night on some illegal and dangerous mission, then shook her head at her own overactive imagination. Liam was a reclusive teenager. He'd probably gone outside to smoke an illicit cigarette, just as she herself had been tempted to do earlier.

With a long exhale, she put her book on her bedside table, turned off the lamp and wriggled deeper into the bed. She lay awake for some time before falling asleep, but she didn't hear Liam come back in.

6

The next day was a Saturday. Miles was off work, and he joined Amy, June, Tom and Poppy on their trip to the beach. It was another gorgeous August afternoon. The beach was a short drive away, along potholed roads. Amy noted the number of derelict buildings they passed: several uninhabited cottages, an old grey farmhouse with boarded-up windows.

The beach was all colour: green dunes, golden sand, sapphire sea. The kids ran barefoot, squealing and giggling, while the wind whipped Amy's hair around her face.

June fell into step with her. 'After this, we'll drive up to the village and show you around.'

Miles looked up from his phone. 'Not that there's much to show. We'd offer to buy you a coffee, but Knockcrea doesn't even have a coffee shop. A packet of crisps from the pub is what passes for fine dining around here.'

'Miles,' June chided him. 'That's why we love it, right?'

June wore a pinstriped shirtdress in pastel blue and

white, and her blonde hair was loose and flowing in the wind. She looked like an advertisement for luxury beach-wear. By the sea, she had Miles take multiple pictures of her with the children. Amy stood aside and watched while June pretended to laugh, mouth wide open – revealing the bright-white ostentatious perfection of lots of expensive dental treatment. 'Come on, look at the camera, Tom! Once more for Mummy! No, Poppy – look towards Daddy!' She directed every shot. It was ages before Miles got results June was happy with, and even then she didn't seem entirely pleased. 'Hmm ... With editing, this one might be okay.'

As they walked back to the car, Amy's thoughts returned to the mysterious Liam. There had been no mention of him coming to the beach with the family. His door had remained closed as they left the house. Should she mention to Miles and June that she thought she'd heard him sneaking out at night? But she couldn't bring herself to throw the poor kid under the bus before she'd even met him. She'd started smoking in her teens. She knew what it was like to hide bad habits from your parents.

As promised, Miles drove them to Knockcrea next, where they took a walk around the village. It was a short walk. They passed painted cottages, only some of which looked lived in, a tiny church, a playground that looked like something from the 1950s, and a closed school. Now Amy understood what Miles had meant when he called the place a ghost of a village.

'Where do the kids go to school now?' she asked.

'There are hardly any kids in Knockcrea any more,' said June. 'But there's a tiny primary school in the next village over – all the kids are taught together by one teacher – and then any secondary-aged kids have to go all the way to Clongrassil.'

They reached the very small grocery shop, and Amy went in to pick up some staples. The Carrolls waited outside in the sun, Miles frowning at his iPhone, June crouched down to entertain Tom and Poppy.

Inside the shop, a wizened little woman sat behind the counter. She was grey-haired and so tiny Amy could have picked her up. 'Hello,' she greeted Amy when she walked in.

'Hiya,' Amy replied.

'You're a Dub, are you?' the woman asked as Amy took white bread and baked beans from the shelf. The shop was so small they could continue a conversation while she walked around it. 'Down here for a holiday?'

'Actually, no.' She put her items on the counter. 'I just moved down here for a job.'

The old woman glanced over at the window and saw Miles and June. Her expression changed. 'Oh!' she said. 'You're working for the Carrolls? You're the new girl?'

'Yeah, I'm working for them,' Amy confirmed.

The woman looked at her for a long moment, then turned her attention to Amy's items. She didn't scan them. She just tapped each one with a wrinkled finger, said the price aloud, then added up the total.

'Two twenty . . . Two fifty . . . That's four seventy, pet.'

Amy gave her the money in cash. While she counted out the change, the old woman said, 'I knew the last girl they had working for them. Francisca. Lovely girl. Very pretty, though not as pretty as you.'

'Eh . . . thanks.' Amy had never got used to comments like

this. She tugged at a lock of hair and tucked it behind one ear. 'Yeah, I heard she went back to Brazil.'

The woman handed her her change and glanced at the window before saying mildly, 'I'm not sure that's right. Francisca took a different job in Cork city. That's what I heard.'

Amy put her change in her pocket. The old woman's tone was casual, but her eyes were full of meaning.

'I must have gotten the details mixed up then,' said Amy. 'Maybe it was the girl before her . . .'

'Ah. Georgia.' The shopkeeper nodded as she packed Amy's purchases into a thin plastic bag. 'Lovely girl as well. She was from Brazil too, but I don't know where she went when she left. She wasn't with the Carrolls for very long either.'

The shop door swung open, the bell jangling. Tom's small head popped in. 'Hello, Peg!' he said, waving.

'Hello, Tom, sweetheart!' said the shopkeeper, and waved back until he bobbed out of sight. The door closed again. Peg handed Amy the bag.

'Well, the two little ones are lovely, anyway,' she said. 'It was nice to meet you, pet. I'll see you around, sure.'

Amy nodded. 'See you.'

Outside, Miles was still on his phone. June was all smiles. 'You met Peg? She's a darling, isn't she?' She was apparently oblivious that Peg might have some less-than-flattering things to say about her family.

As Amy followed Miles and June down the sunny street, Peg's words rang in her ears. *Francisca took a different job in Cork . . .* If Francisca had moved jobs, why had June lied about it?

Well, the two little ones are lovely, anyway.

The implication being . . . what? That the adults weren't so lovely? Or that the oldest child wasn't so lovely?

What was Peg trying to tell her?

They finished their circuit of the village and returned to the car. Again, Miles drove and June took the passenger seat. Amy was in the back with Tom and Poppy, who both nodded off the moment the car started to move.

As they left the village, Amy said, 'Thanks for showing me around. It's gorgeous here.'

June turned to smile at her. 'I'm glad you like it. Some of our previous nannies found the isolation a bit difficult to take.'

'For me, it's part of the appeal,' said Amy, watching green fields and white cottages roll past. 'It seems so peaceful. And safe.'

'Oh, it is,' said Miles. 'Very safe. People leave their doors unlocked. You rarely hear of a house being broken into or a car stolen. There's virtually no crime.'

'Well, honey,' said June, and her head tilted slightly to one side, 'that's not entirely true. There *was* all that unpleasantness—'

Miles cut her off, his voice suddenly hard as flint. 'What on earth are you bringing *that* up for? Those were minor incidents, blown entirely out of proportion by a bunch of bored housewives. Bloody morons with nothing better to do than invent ridiculous rumours. Anyone who's actually in possession of a few brain cells should know better than to repeat that nonsense.'

June went quiet. Amy took that as a cue to do the same. The back of Miles's neck had turned a flushed pink. They drove back to Sea View in tense silence.

7

Neither Miles nor June mentioned the tension in the car. Once they arrived back at Sea View, they resumed speaking in normal tones as they carried the sleeping children inside.

'You grab Poppy's bottle there, will you?' said Miles.

'Got it, honey.' June turned to Amy. 'We let them nap in the afternoons, Amy, but for no longer than half an hour, or they won't sleep at night.'

As soon as she could, Amy retreated to her room.

On the way, she passed Liam's closed door. Silence on the other side, as usual.

Amy sat down on her bed. She was embarrassed to find her heart was still hammering. During icy silences like that, she always felt, however far-fetched it was, that violence might suddenly explode.

She felt an urge for a cigarette. Having kicked her ten-a-day habit some years ago, Amy was now a sporadic smoker, resorting to nicotine only in times of extreme stress.

She'd bought the pack in her coat pocket the day before she left Dublin. You don't need a smoke, she told herself now. Just do your breathing exercises.

She lay down on the bed, closed her eyes and concentrated on breathing slowly – in for five seconds, out for seven – until her heartbeat returned to normal.

Her phone buzzed on the bedside table. She rolled over to look at the screen. It was a message from Sandra.

Hi, how're things today? Xx

She put the phone down, not ready to write back. She didn't want to tell Sandra and Dave about Miles's outburst in the car. For one thing, she didn't want to worry them. For another, it was very possible her reaction was wildly out of proportion.

Unconsciously, her hand went to the tattoo on her left shoulder.

Black ink. A name in a heart.

She sat up suddenly. Her urge for a cigarette was overwhelming. She checked the pack. Only five left. Well, after those five, she would quit for good – or at least for the duration of her post here. But she was having one *right now*.

She could hear June and Miles talking in the kitchen. She let herself out the back door.

Once on the potholed road, she began walking at a brisk pace. The day was still beautiful, the air warm and balmy. When she was safely out of sight of the house, she lit up.

She had taken this job hoping for some peace. A place where she could rest, and recuperate, and plan what to do next. A series of images flashed through her mind. Blood dripping onto an off-white carpet. Black smoke curling under a door. Orange flames dancing at the bottom of a staircase. Sandra sobbing, saying, 'You have to leave Dublin, Amy.'

She took a deep breath. *Be in the present. You're here. You're safe.*

She took out her phone and replied to Sandra's message. She decided not to mention her spiralling anxieties. She knew she was catastrophising. All she said was:

All okay. Kids seem like sweethearts. Haven't met the teenage son yet. Will update you when I do. Tell Dave I said hi! Xx

She added a heart emoji and pressed send.

After her cigarette, Amy felt calmer. For almost half an hour she walked away from the house, before deciding to turn back. In all that time, not a single car passed. Walking back up the slope towards Sea View, she was struck again by how incongruous it looked – that sleek futuristic building against the ancient mountainous backdrop.

She spent the evening watching TV shows in her room on Dave's old iPad. 'You might want the option of watching a bit of telly in your own room,' he had said when he gave it to her before she left for Sea View. While June had insisted that she was welcome to sit in the Carrolls' beautiful living area and watch movies on their widescreen TV – 'We want you to think of it as your space, too!' – Amy knew she would never be able to bring herself to march in and join June and Miles on the sofa, to interrupt their cosy married-couple evening. She could hear them watching something on RTÉ right now, hear the gentle rise and fall of their voices.

On her side in bed, with the iPad propped against a pillow, Amy tried to unwind by watching a mindless show on Netflix. But the tense, airless feeling that had filled the car kept coming back to her. She couldn't concentrate on the storyline. She couldn't relax enough to drift towards sleep.

You're completely overreacting, she tried to tell herself. Couples argue. It's normal!

Giving up on the show, Amy rolled onto her back and picked up her phone. She opened Instagram and searched for June's account.

June's Instagram feed was carefully curated: photo after photo of Tom and Poppy, of the nearby beach, and of June herself, in put-together pastel outfits, with the white-and-grey minimalist perfection of the house as a backdrop. Amy could understand why people followed this page, the aspirational draw of it; why they stared at pictures of June's blonde prettiness and her luxurious clothes and enviable house.

There was no mention that June had a full-time cleaner and nanny. Or that her husband's teenage son from a previous relationship was staying in the house too, never leaving his room. Amy wasn't sure how she felt about that. It was June's choice what she put online, and just because she shared some parts of her life didn't mean she was obligated to share everything. Amy did think it was somewhat misleading to suggest that the house looked like this without any help – but that was what advertising was, wasn't it? And it *was* advertising, she realised, as she followed the affiliate links to expensive brands of yoga pants and luxury homeware. June was selling her followers a fantasy. All the same, Amy found herself wondering how it made this Liam kid feel. To be told so clearly that the fantasy family was one without him in it.

She sat up in bed and something pricked her hand: one of her stud earrings had fallen out. She groped around the pillow, looking for the back of the earring, and then slid a hand down between the mattress and the headboard, wondering if it had fallen down there. She couldn't find it. But her fingers closed on a scrap of paper. She pulled it out.

It was a torn piece of lined A4 paper, crumpled, as if someone had balled it up in a fist. Amy smoothed it out and read the neat, cramped handwriting:

Georgia, I need to talk to you. It's urgent. Please meet me at

The rest of the words had been torn away.

She reached down the back of the bed again, hoping to find the rest of the message. She checked the bin and under the bed too. But she didn't find anything. The room had been thoroughly cleaned before her arrival. This scrap of paper had only survived because it had become jammed behind the mattress.

Who had written this? What important information had they needed to give Georgia?

Frustrated, Amy folded the scrap of paper up small and put it in the top drawer of her bedside locker. Then she sat back down on the bed. For a moment, the strangeness of her situation – living in someone else's house, so far away from everything she knew – overwhelmed her.

She opened the drawer again and took out her snow globe. Along with her photo album, it was one of the few items besides clothes and toiletries that she had packed in her hurried exit from Dublin. She shook it, watched the fake snow falling and thought about what the world would be like if people could go back in time.

8

The following day was a Sunday, and Amy was left alone in the house. Miles and June were taking Tom and Poppy to the farmers' market in Skibbereen. 'Are you sure you wouldn't like to join us, Amy?' Miles asked before they left. 'You'd enjoy it.'

'I don't want to intrude,' Amy replied. In truth, all she wanted was some time to herself.

'Oh, you wouldn't be intruding!' June said as she wrestled Tom and Poppy into their clothes.

'You guys go,' Amy insisted. 'Have a family day. I'll occupy myself here.'

When they drove away, she exhaled.

The sun was streaming down, and the sea was a royal blue that was visible through almost every window in the house. Amy opened some of those windows, letting in fresh air, and then made herself a breakfast of baked beans and buttered toast, which she ate while looking out over the spectacular view. It was peaceful to have the place to herself.

But of course, she didn't have it to herself. Every now and then she would remember, with a little jolt, that there was a teenage boy in one of the other rooms.

It was getting weird, Amy reflected, taking a bite of toast. Three days here and she hadn't even glimpsed this kid. Did he only emerge at night, like a bat?

As she was tidying up after breakfast, the strange sounds in Liam's room started again. *Thump. Thud. BANG.* What was he doing in there? She decided she would ask June about this. If Liam turned out to be a problem kid she didn't feel safe sleeping near, she could always leave. She could find another live-in job, another position that paid cash. She could disappear again.

She wiped down the table and went back to her room. She took a shower in the en suite, making sure to lock the bathroom door. As she dried herself, dressed and put on make-up, Amy noticed that the banging noises from Liam's room had stopped.

It was 10.15. She had the whole day ahead of her. She thought she might go for a drive along the peninsula. To one of the other small towns she'd seen on Google Maps, or maybe to some of the little beaches, yellow lines that looked inviting even as pixels on a screen.

She put on her hoop earrings and denim jacket, grabbed her car keys and phone and let herself out the front door. The sun was blazing, and she inhaled the fresh smell of summer air. But as she made her way to the car, she scented something else on the breeze – the pungent smell of marijuana.

She turned. There was nobody in sight. Following the smell, she walked back towards the house and around the side of the building.

She found herself face to face with a black-haired, sturdily built teenage boy. He had a fresh buzzcut and wore a crisp white T-shirt and blue jeans. He was leaning against the wall, smoking a joint and squinting into the sun.

'All right?' he said by way of greeting.

'Hi,' said Amy. 'Sorry, I just thought I smelled ...' She trailed off, glancing at the joint in his hand.

He took a drag and exhaled with deliberate carelessness. 'You're the new housekeeper, right?'

'Amy, yeah.'

'I'm Liam,' he said, looking her up and down. 'How're you getting on?'

Until now, Amy had been constructing a picture in her head of Liam as a pasty-skinned, unwashed, possibly agoraphobic kid. She was completely caught off guard by this swaggering bad boy. He was pulling on his joint and ogling her in a way that was obviously intended to be flirtatious, and it was all she could do not to burst out laughing and say, *You do realise how much older than you I am, right?*

'I'm getting on all right, thanks, Liam,' she replied. 'It's good to finally meet you. You've been a bit of a mystery.'

He shrugged. 'Have everything I need in my room. En suite, my own TV, noise-cancelling headphones ...'

Just like that, it all made sense.

'Anyway,' he continued, 'Miles and June find it easier to play happy families when I'm not around.'

'I'm sure that's not true,' Amy said automatically.

Liam said nothing, and she immediately regretted making such a trite comment. She gestured at the joint.

'Do Miles and June know you smoke?' she asked.

'Yeah,' he said, shrugging. 'What are they gonna do about it?' He took another defiant drag.

Amy suppressed a smile. He was so painfully young, his posturing paper-thin, although it undoubtedly came across as impressive to other teenagers. Liam was probably breaking hearts from here all the way back to Leixlip.

'I'll have to mention the weed to your parents, Liam,' she said.

He exhaled a plume of smoke before saying, 'June's not my parent.'

'To your dad and stepmother, then,' she amended.

'I told you, they know. They don't care.'

Amy paused as she tried to figure out how to frame her next question. She wanted to ask Liam about the strange sounds she had heard coming from his room, but she wasn't sure how.

Maybe he read her mind, because he said, 'Haven't been bothering you with the noise when I work out, have I?'

'*Oh*,' said Amy. 'That's what all the banging is?'

Liam looked amused. 'Yeah. Squat jumps, weights ... I have all my equipment in there.'

Everything clicked into place. The metallic clangs, the thumping.

'Why, what did you think I was doing?' Liam grinned.

'I had no idea,' said Amy honestly.

He laughed, and flicked the end of his joint away.

'Well, I'll see you round,' he said, pushing off the wall with a swagger so deliberate Amy wondered if he practised it in the mirror.

'You too,' she said. 'If you ever come out of your room again.'

'I leave my room,' said Liam, with a tinge of sullenness. 'I just prefer to come out when Miles and June aren't around.'

It hadn't escaped Amy's attention that Liam referred to his dad by his first name. How present had Miles been in Liam's life as he was growing up? He spoke with a far stronger accent than his father, and she wondered if it was genuine or an affectation. She found herself curious about Liam's mother and their family history.

'See you,' he said again. She echoed it back to him.

As he walked away, Amy's phone rang. Sandra.

'Hi, hon! Just checking in.'

'Well, I met the teenage son,' Amy said, walking out of earshot of the house. 'You can tell Dave that if he's a psychopath, he's hiding it extremely well.'

'What's he like?'

'Seems like an ordinary, rebellious kid.'

'Well, that's a relief,' said Sandra. 'How's everything else down there?'

'Good . . .'

Sandra talked to her about Dublin, filling her in on the gossip around the estate. As she listened to the stories of who was bitching about who, and who was having a baby, and what Mary-down-the-street's son was up to, Amy was transported back home. She could see the grey concrete, the terraced houses, the pigeons. She could hear the roar of traffic, the barking of dogs and the yells of kids playing football. All the sights and sounds that had been the backdrop to the only world she'd known, until she was forced to leave.

'You're all right for money, are you?' Sandra asked before she hung up.

'I'm grand,' said Amy. 'I appreciate you offering, but you don't need to worry about me.'

They said their goodbyes. Amy tucked her phone into her pocket, feeling a swell of love for her sister.

Over the past few years, her financial situation had been

a nightmare. Even when she was working full-time, she had struggled to buy groceries. But Sandra understood. She knew where Amy's money was going. She didn't judge, and helped when she could. The only reason Amy still had a car was because Sandra had insisted on paying her insurance, not wanting her sister to lose her last bit of independence. Amy was glad she was finally in a position where she could start paying Sandra back. A little at a time.

But that wasn't her only financial goal. She also planned to save some of the money June paid her. To hide a roll of notes in some secret place and add to it every week. It was for something important. Something she hadn't told Sandra about.

Even from her sister, Amy had some secrets.

9

Before

It was a Friday night. Sandra was in her bedroom, doing her homework. Amy was downstairs, reading on the sofa. The house was quiet.

The front door opened. 'Hello?' their mother called. 'Anybody home?' She walked into the sitting room and did a double-take at the sight of Amy in her pyjamas. 'Hi, sweetheart! What are you doing?'

'Reading,' said Amy, raising her eyebrows. 'Why, what does it look like I'm doing?'

Louise smiled. 'What I mean is, why aren't you at Kelly Cawley's party?' She sat down on the sofa beside her daughter. 'That's tonight, isn't it?'

She was right. Kelly Cawley was one of the girls Amy hung around with at school, and she had just turned fifteen. All Amy's friends would be at the party.

'Mark didn't want me going on my own,' Amy explained.

'He's in Carlingford this weekend with his cousins, so he couldn't go with me.'

'You wouldn't be on your own!' said Louise, with a little laugh. 'You'd be with all your friends.'

'He's protective of me,' Amy replied. 'If something went wrong at the party, he wouldn't be able to come and get me.'

'If anything went wrong, *I'd* come and get you. I'm your mother! And anyway,' said Louise, eyebrows raised, 'what exactly does Mark think is going to happen at this party? Kelly's parents are supervising. It's hardly going to be a wild rave.'

'You know,' said Amy with a shrug. 'There could be creepy guys or anything. He just feels better when he knows I'm safe.'

Louise considered her daughter for a moment, then said, 'So Mark is out having fun with his cousins in Carlingford, but you have to sit at home on your own, is that it?'

Amy looked up with a frown. 'What? No! That's not what it's like at all.'

Her mother's expression softened. 'Listen to me,' she said. 'It's really important that you don't stop hanging out with your friends just because you have a boyfriend. Why don't you get dressed and do your make-up, and I'll give you a lift over to Kelly's. I'll even do your hair for you.' She raised a hand to tuck Amy's long dark locks behind her ear.

But Amy pulled away. 'I can't. I told Mark I wouldn't.'

Louise was shaking her head. 'It's a bad sign if your boyfriend tries to stop you going places without him.'

'He doesn't try to stop me!' Amy jumped to her feet. 'He just worries about me, that's all!'

She couldn't believe her mother would try to spin Mark's caring nature into something negative.

'Amy, come on. Sit—'

'You should be happy that I've met someone who cares about me enough to worry. He loves me. Why are you trying to ruin this for me?'

She ran out of the room, stamped upstairs and slammed her bedroom door. God, her mother didn't understand anything. Why would Mark call her multiple times a day, why would he fret about where she went and who she spoke to if he didn't love her? The other girls in her class pined after boys who barely paid them any attention. They watched wistfully as Amy walked through the school with Mark's arm around her shoulders. She had what they all wanted. She was special, chosen. Loved.

10

Now

The weather was so beautiful that Amy decided to spend her day off walking to the village rather than going for a drive. It was too gorgeous a day to spend in her car.

She set off from Sea View, tying up her hair to let the breeze cool her neck. The winding country road was lined on both sides with lush green vegetation. There was a stillness all around. Not a true silence – bees buzzed in the flowers, birds darted past – but the stillness of being the only human in sight.

She passed the abandoned farmhouse with the boarded-up windows and followed the road that sloped down towards the village. On the horizon, the sea glittered in the sunlight, diamond-white sparkles on blue. Then she saw something up ahead that made her narrow her eyes as she drew closer. Was that . . .?

At first she thought the substance splattered over the road was blood. But then she realised it was red paint. Lots of it. The splatters of paint led to a grey metal gate into a field.

Like a trail.

She walked over to the gate. There was nothing remarkable about the field on the other side. A few sheep were grazing in the middle. In one corner stood four crumbling walls that were all that was left of an abandoned stone cottage.

Red paint splotches on the grass led in the direction of the cottage.

Amy didn't stop to think. Curiosity pulled her forward. She put a foot on the metal bars of the gate and swung herself over, landing lightly in the field. A few sheep turned their heads. The paint on the grass was fresh, as if it had been applied very recently, perhaps overnight.

She followed the trail of red towards the cottage. It put her in mind of the kind of marks that would be left if something dead was being dragged along. It's paint, not blood, she reminded herself, crouching to touch it. Paint. Dry paint.

When she reached the cottage, she stopped walking. There were words painted on the wall, in bright-red foot-high letters:

THIS IS A DEAD PLACE
NOBODY HERE IS SAFE

Above this message was a symbol: a pentagram, with an inverted cross in the middle. Both the words and the symbol had been daubed on thick, and thin rivulets of red ran down the stone.

Whoever had written this had wanted it to be found. The trail of paint proved that. But why?

Amy shuddered. How easily she had been led to this secluded location. In sudden alarm, she turned and looked around her, scanning the field, the low stone walls, the thick hedgerow. When her gaze reached the face in the bushes, it took her a moment to understand what she was seeing. Pale-blue eyes. Wild grey hair.

There was a man crouched in the hedgerow, staring at her.

She screamed. The sound sent birds fluttering up from the bushes. At the same moment the man leapt up, shouting.

Amy didn't stay to hear what he was saying. She ran. Across the field. Over the gate. Blood was thundering in her ears. Her lungs began to protest as her legs pistoned her along the concrete, but adrenaline kept her moving. She sprinted as fast as she could in the direction of the village.

When she dared to look back, the road behind her was quiet. The man wasn't following her. Still she jogged, until her breath became so ragged she had no choice but to slow to a walk.

What the hell just happened?

She could picture him clearly – a hollow face, and a shock of grey hair that stuck straight up from his head. She debated whether to call the police, but decided to take some time before making any decisions. The man had frightened her half to death, but she wasn't sure it was a 999 situation. He hadn't pursued her.

And anyway, Amy had her own reasons for preferring not to go to the police.

It was a relief to reach the village. Houses and people made her feel safe. She hurried straight to the tiny shop. She figured that if she told Peg about the strange incident, the old woman might be able to shine some light on what had happened.

But to her consternation, Peg's shop was closed. A hand-written sign in the window informed her that it didn't open on Sundays.

What was she supposed to do now?

Feeling dazed, she turned away and bumped straight into a family walking three abreast on the pavement: a curly-haired mother and two bored-looking adolescents, both glued to their phones.

'Sorry,' said Amy, stepping out of their way.

'Oh, don't say sorry!' said the woman. 'We were taking up the whole path! Hey – you're Amy, aren't you?'

'How do you know my name?' Amy responded, still on edge and adrenaline-spiky.

The woman just smiled. 'Don't worry, I'm not a stalker. Everyone knows everyone around here. You're the new girl at the Carrolls' place, right?'

'Right,' Amy replied, a little embarrassed. 'Yeah, I'm Amy.'

'Catherine.'

Catherine looked in her mid fifties. She had an enthusiastic demeanour, warm brown eyes and a mass of curly copper-coloured hair. Wide-hipped and tall, she wore flowing, bohemian clothes and a single silver pendant necklace. 'It's great to meet you,' she enthused. 'We live on the opposite side of the village. These two are Ruby and Luke.' She nudged the skinny teenagers. 'Say hello, you two.'

Ruby was a tiny, red-haired, bird-like thing, with pale freckled skin and a heart-shaped face. Luke was a couple of years younger, around twelve or thirteen, and lanky, with brown hair and massive ears. Both kids glanced up from their phones just long enough to mumble hello.

'They were small and cute once,' said Catherine with a

sigh. When Amy didn't respond, she said, 'Hey, are you okay? You look like you've seen a ghost.'

'Actually, no, I'm not,' Amy admitted. 'The weirdest thing just happened.' She looked at her hands and realised they were shaking.

Catherine's brow furrowed. 'Come over here,' she said gently, and she steered Amy out of earshot of the teenagers. 'What's going on?'

Amy told her the whole story, speaking quickly. When she got to the part where the man lunged at her, Catherine's expression changed.

'A man jumped out of the bushes at you? What did he look like?'

'Tall and skinny, maybe late sixties,' said Amy. 'With grey hair that sort of stuck straight up like a toothbrush.'

'*Oh*,' said Catherine, and to Amy's confusion, she looked disappointed. 'I know who that was.'

'You do?'

Catherine nodded, taking her phone out of her pocket. As Amy blinked at her, she made a call.

'Martin?' she said briskly. 'Bad news, I'm afraid. Our graffiti bandit has struck again.' There was a pause on the other end of the line, and then Catherine said, 'The Carrolls' new minder, would you believe … The location she described sounds like Sean Geraghty's land. Sean must have been hiding in the field in case the vandal came back, but all he succeeded in doing was giving this poor girl the fright of her life. She saw him and ran …' Another pause. Catherine looked at Amy as she spoke into the phone. 'Well, give me a text when you've talked to Sean. Thanks, Martin. Bye.' She hung up. 'Martin is the chairman of our Tidy Towns committee. He's a man of action. He'll handle this.'

'I'm sorry,' said Amy, 'but *what* is going on?'

Catherine's brown eyes narrowed. 'Miles and June didn't tell you? That there've been some . . . incidents in Knockcrea this summer?'

'No,' said Amy. 'They didn't tell me anything.'

But the way Catherine said *incidents* put Amy in mind of June's words: *all that unpleasantness* . . .

Catherine tilted her head to one side and looked at Amy like she was deciding on something. Finally she said, 'Are you free right now? Let's grab a drink.'

11

The local pub, Hartigan's, had the name above the door in red-and-gold lettering. Out front were picnic-style tables where locals sat with cigarettes and pints of Guinness, soaking up the afternoon sun.

Amy, Catherine, Ruby and Luke took the table farthest from the other patrons. As they sat down, Catherine's phone vibrated.

'It's Sean,' she said, reading the message on the screen. 'He wants to apologise to you, Amy. He didn't mean to frighten you.' She looked up. 'He said he can call and speak to you if you'd like to talk to him?'

Amy stiffened. 'Nah, there's no need … Tell him I said thanks, but I'm all right.' To her relief, Catherine didn't push it.

They got drinks. Catherine ordered a pint, Amy a 7Up. Ruby and Luke sat at the other end of the table, drinking Cokes, attention on their phones. They barely spoke to each other and seemed completely uninterested in their mother's conversation with Amy.

'It's just not right,' Catherine said as she settled down with her pint. 'Miles and June should have told you everything. If not before you came down here, then at least after you'd arrived. I mean, you're living in the same house as him!'

'As who?' said Amy. She could see where this was going, but she wanted to hear Catherine say it.

Catherine pushed some errant curls back from her face. 'Maybe I'm being unfair,' she said quickly. 'I mean, we don't *know* it was Liam. But they should have told you that a lot of people in the area think he's behind it.'

'Behind what? The graffiti?'

Catherine nodded. 'The first incident was really minor,' she said. 'Someone spray-painted swear words all over the village in red paint. Really juvenile stuff. The welcome sign outside the village was vandalised – changed from "Welcome to Knockcrea" to "Welcome to the Arsecrack of Nowhere".' She snorted. 'I shouldn't laugh. I mean, I'm on the Tidy Towns committee myself, so I was one of the eejits out there the next day with gloves and paint remover trying to scrub it off.'

She shot a glance at her oblivious kids. In a lower voice, she continued: 'That happened just two days after Liam Carroll arrived to stay for the summer. Miles told me himself that Liam didn't want to come to Knockcrea this year but his mother insisted. He's been getting into trouble in his home town. You know he lives with his mother and only stays with his father during summers?'

Amy nodded, sipping her 7Up. The sun was warm on her skin, the wooden pub bench uncomfortable beneath her.

'Well,' Catherine went on, 'Miles had a big confrontation

with Martin Doyle over it. While we were cleaning up the graffiti, Martin made some comment about how it was a disgrace that Liam wasn't helping out. Unfortunately, Miles happened to be walking through the village at the time and overheard. He and June didn't help with the clean-up either, by the way. They just carried on as if it was nothing to do with them. Plenty of people were saying exactly what Martin was saying; he just happened to say it within Miles's earshot. And ... well, Miles lost it.'

Amy could picture it. She imagined Miles, neck flushed pink, chest puffed up in outrage, storming over to confront Martin Doyle.

'They had a shouting match, and Miles insisted that Liam had nothing to do with the graffiti.' Catherine rolled her eyes. 'People get all worked up about their kids, don't they? Defend them to the hilt. But all the same ... Anyway, a week later, we woke up to find someone had graffitied the whole town again. But it wasn't as funny this time. Instead of swear words, it was satanic symbols.'

'What?'

'Yep. Goat's heads, pentagrams, great slashes of red paint ... I have to say, it was quite disturbing. People were upset. And of course, everyone assumed it was Liam.'

Amy considered this. It was hard to imagine Liam, with his crisp Nike shoes and fresh haircut, being interested in the occult. It didn't fit with his aesthetic. Perhaps that argument wouldn't hold much water in court, but in the world of teenagers, aesthetics were everything. If a seventeen-year-old had a serious interest in satanism, Amy reckoned they'd at least buy some black clothes and get a few piercings.

'There's been some petty crime, too,' Catherine said, frowning. 'Martin Doyle's tyres were slashed – just a few nights after he had that fight with Miles. And someone broke all the windows on Sean Geraghty's car. The same Sean Geraghty who gave you such a fright in the field today.' She looked at Amy pleadingly. 'He's harmless, by the way. A bit eccentric, but a lovely man. You'll meet him properly at some point, I'm sure, and then you'll see for yourself.'

Amy made a non-committal noise. She was in no rush to meet Sean Geraghty after today's events.

'He's just at his wits' end with this vandalism thing,' Catherine continued. 'Sean's a bachelor, and he lives alone on a farm a few fields over from Sea View. He's the closest thing you have to a neighbour. Now, Miles and June *swear* Liam didn't leave the house the night Sean's car windows were broken, but to be honest, random vandalism isn't very common around here. And you'd have to seek out Sean's house deliberately. It's at the end of a very isolated road.'

Amy pictured it: a lonely farmhouse, broken glass scattered in the driveway. 'The poor man,' she said. 'But I have to say, Liam doesn't strike me as the type to do something like that.'

'Of course it was Liam,' piped up red-headed Ruby. Apparently she'd been paying more attention to the conversation than she'd let on. '*Obviously.* I mean, all this started right after he got here.'

'Well, nobody can say that for sure, sweetheart,' said Catherine fairly. 'There's no proof.'

The conversation circled around those talking points for a while, then moved on. Catherine wanted to know why Amy had moved to Knockcrea. Amy told her the same lies she'd told Miles and June.

By the time they'd finished their drinks, Amy had agreed to drop over sometime to visit Catherine in her home on the other side of the village. They exchanged numbers.

As Amy stood up to leave, a final question occurred to her.

'I'm curious,' she said. 'If Miles and June insist that Liam has nothing to do with any of this, who do they think *is* responsible?'

'There's an organic farm near here,' Catherine explained, 'and they often have Woofers. You know, young people who work for free to travel on the cheap? I believe Miles blames *those bloody hippies.*'

Amy could imagine Miles saying that. She smiled. 'Listen, thanks for the drink and the conversation,' she said.

'Happy to help,' said Catherine. 'It was lovely to meet you. I'll be in touch.'

On her walk back to Sea View, Amy took a different route, avoiding the field where she'd seen the graffiti. Her head was spinning. What was she supposed to do with this information? Should she mention it to Miles and June? *Excuse me, I heard a rumour that Liam might be involved in a satanic cult?*

The more she thought about it, the more likely it seemed the whole thing was nothing more than a twisted joke. Whoever had done it was probably laughing right now, pleased with the ripples they'd caused in the village.

Then an irrational thought occurred to her: what if the graffiti was speaking directly to her? Warning her she hadn't run far enough? She pushed the idea away. She knew it was ridiculous. But she couldn't stop picturing the message.

This is a dead place.

Nobody here is safe.

With her history, was it any wonder those words sent a shiver through her?

12

Over the next few days, Amy began to settle into a routine at Sea View. She worked for several hours a day cleaning the multiple bathrooms, making the many windows sparkle. At June's request, she would spend some time looking after Tom and Poppy, so that June could retreat into her office for a little while.

Miles left at 7.45 a.m. and didn't return until late. Liam continued his habit of rarely leaving his room. In general, it felt like it was just Amy, June, Tom and Poppy in the house.

On Wednesday morning, when she woke and reached for her phone, she saw that she had been added to a WhatsApp group called 'Knockcrea Tidy Towns 2018'. It had forty-three notifications. Catherine was a member. So was Martin Doyle.

She also had a direct message from Catherine:

> **Hi, Amy! I've added you to the Tidy Towns group.**
> **This way you can keep abreast of the news around**

the village. Martin Doyle has asked me to invite you
to the next meeting. It's Friday night at 8 in Aveen
Butler's house. I'll send along the address. It won't
just be talk about the graffiti and such – it's always
a nice social event! I'll be there. Let me know xx

She returned to the Tidy Towns chat and scrolled through
the names of everyone in the group. Not surprisingly, neither
Miles nor June were members.

Sean Geraghty, however, was. He had no profile picture,
but his name was there. Amy didn't particularly feel like
socialising with the man who'd sprung out of the bushes at
her. She tapped out a reply to Catherine.

Thanks for the invite but I won't be able to make it
that night. Maybe another time!

She needed this job. She couldn't risk pissing off Miles and
June by joining a group that was pointing fingers at their
family. Before getting out of bed, she muted the notifications
on the chat.

That afternoon, Amy played monsters with Tom and Poppy.
The game consisted mostly of her chasing the children,
making silly noises, while they shrieked and ran. On this
occasion, Poppy, running while looking behind her and
laughing, went smack into the side of the table.

'Oh God, Poppy! You poor thing.' Amy went to pick her
up, but the little girl writhed away from her, screaming.

June came out of her office. 'What happened? Is she okay?'

'She gave her head a really nasty bang.' Amy felt guilty,

and wondered if June would chide her for playing such a boisterous game with the kids, but June just kissed Poppy's head and soothed her.

'There, there, darling,' she said. 'You're okay. I know it hurts, but you're okay.'

'Can we play monsters again?' Tom asked loudly, tugging at Amy's arm.

'Tom, I have an important job for you,' said June seriously. 'We need something cold for Poppy's poor head. Will you go into the kitchen with Amy and get a bag of frozen peas and a tea towel?'

Tom dashed in the direction of the kitchen before the sentence was fully out of his mother's mouth. 'Come quick, Amy! It's an important job!'

June didn't go back to her office straight away. She helped Amy put together lunch for the kids. By the time they'd eaten, Poppy had bounced back, although the bump on her forehead was impressive.

'June, I'm sorry,' said Amy, when the kids had wandered off to play and she and June were tidying up the kitchen. 'I probably shouldn't play so roughly with them.'

'Nonsense!' said June. 'The odd bump or scrape is an unavoidable side effect of childhood.'

Amy glanced over at Tom and Poppy, who were busy playing with building blocks in the living-room area.

'Actually,' she said, 'while we're here . . . there's something I've been meaning to mention to you.'

June paused in the middle of wiping down the island. 'Yes?'

'It's a bit awkward,' said Amy. 'It's about Liam.'

June put down the cloth. She took a couple of steps closer to Amy.

'What happened?' she asked in a low voice.

'It's not a huge deal or anything,' Amy said hastily. 'It's just, I saw Liam a couple of days ago, and he was, uh . . . smoking a joint. I didn't know if you and Miles knew that he . . .'

June's shoulders relaxed slightly, and Amy saw that Liam had been telling the truth. Miles and June already knew.

'We're aware it's an issue,' said June. 'Miles has talked to him about it before. Maybe it's time to discuss it again.'

'I just thought I should mention it,' said Amy, not wanting to seem like she was judging their parenting style.

'Of course. Thanks for letting us know.'

June returned to wiping the table. Amy thought she looked relieved. What was it she'd expected Amy to say?

When Miles came in the door from work, he would always scoop Tom and Poppy up into his arms. 'How are my brilliant kids? Aren't you two just the best boy and girl in the whole world?' He didn't seem to mind when Poppy wiped her snotty nose on his grey suits, or when Tom's fingers were sticky with yoghurt. It almost made Amy like him.

But she couldn't like him, not really. For one thing, she couldn't forget the way he had snapped at June in the car. She found herself on tenterhooks sometimes, afraid that he might snap again, although he'd been unfailingly warm and friendly around her since. It was as if he was aware that he had misstepped and wanted to repair his image. He would kiss June flamboyantly on the cheek as he passed, or hum a little tune to himself in the kitchen. Amy could only hope that this version of Miles would persist, and the hard-voiced man who'd made the car feel tense and airless wouldn't reappear.

There was, however, another issue.

On several occasions now, Amy had caught Miles watching her with a lascivious expression that she hoped she was imagining but knew she wasn't.

Uh oh, she thought when she felt his grey eyes follow her around the room. Please don't let anything come of this.

She did her best to pretend she didn't notice. But on Wednesday night, when she caught him looking, he didn't look away. Instead, he smiled a slow, wide-lipped smile.

Amy felt her skin crawl.

She straightened and put down the washing basket she was holding, which made a loud clatter. She walked quickly into the bathroom and shut the door behind her.

That ended that. And he did nothing more overt after. When he spoke to her, he was charming. 'Settling in okay, Amy? I hope you're not having too much trouble with these little monsters. Have you two been giving Amy trouble? Have you? Have you?'

And he'd bounce Poppy in his arms, and turn Tom upside down, until they were both shrieking with joy, and Amy would find herself almost liking him again.

She didn't mention Miles's long stares to Sandra and Dave. She didn't want to make a big deal out of nothing. Still, she couldn't help thinking about the previous housekeepers who'd arrived and left in such rapid succession.

Could the high turnover rate have something to do with Miles and his watchful eyes?

13

Before

Louise Fagan pulled her coat on over her nurse's uniform. She was on her way to the hospital for a night shift.

'Amy, I want you in bed before eleven!' she called towards the kitchen. 'No staying up late watching TV, or you know you'll be groggy in school tomorrow.'

'I *know*,' Amy called back, rolling her eyes.

'Sandra will be home at midnight, and she'll tell me if you're still up.'

Amy came into the hall. 'I don't need Sandra to babysit me,' she said lightly. 'I can put myself to bed. Stop worrying.'

Louise smiled. 'Oh, I know, sweetheart. There's some leftover dinner in the fridge if you get hungry. All right, I better run. Bye, love.'

'Bye,' Amy called after her.

When the door closed, Amy counted to three. Then she ran to the window and looked out. She could see her mother hurrying down the street. When Louise was safely out of view, she raced to the back door and opened it.

Mark was standing there, smiling his lazy smile. He'd come in from the back lane, so that the nosy neighbours who kept an eye on the road wouldn't report him to Louise.

'Coast clear?' he said.

Amy jumped into his arms.

Upstairs in her room, they lay on her bed, on top of the duvet cover, kissing until they had to come up for air, then talking in tangential circles. Amy's room was teenage-girl pink, with posters on the walls. Through the window, the city lights glittered.

As they lay on their backs, fingers threaded, the conversation moved on to their future. Things they might do, one day, when they were older.

'How many kids will we have?' Mark said idly.

'You want to have kids?'

'Yeah,' he said. 'With you. One boy, one girl.'

Amy felt as if she might burst with happiness. 'I want lots of kids,' she said. 'Like four. Or five. Maybe six.'

Mark laughed. 'Okay. We'll have six.'

'Where will we live?'

'In a house beside the sea.'

Amy turned on her side. She could see from his profile that he was smiling. 'Really? That's where you want to live?'

'Yeah,' said Mark. 'My grandparents live out in Balbriggan. Me and you could get a house somewhere like that.'

Amy was silent.

'What?' he asked. 'Did I say something wrong?'

'No,' she said. 'It's just ... Is this just joking, or do you mean it? Do you really want to live with me when we're older? And have kids and that?'

Mark turned too, so he was facing her. 'I'm serious. I know I'm not gonna find anyone better than you.'

She felt a mixture of feelings: happiness, vindication.

'Sandra laughed at me when I said that,' she admitted. 'When I told her that I hoped me and you would be together for ever.'

'When was this?' Mark demanded.

'Yesterday. Then she said that I just do whatever you say and that I have no personality of my own since we started going out. She said I'm a doormat.'

Her faced burned as she said this. Sandra's words had hurt.

'Listen to me,' said Mark. 'What would Sandra know? She doesn't have a boyfriend, does she? What would she know about being in a relationship?'

Amy nodded. She hadn't thought about it that way before.

'She's jealous,' Mark went on. 'She wishes she had what we have. And she's jealous of the way you look, too. That's the truth.'

Amy felt defensive of her sister. 'It's not that.'

'It is,' said Mark. 'You can't see yourself clearly at all. Everyone is jealous of you.'

He kissed her, and everything melted away. She was drowning in how good it felt. When they broke apart, Mark took her face in his hands and looked at her with wonder, like he couldn't quite believe how lucky he was.

It felt wonderful to be looked at like that.

'Don't listen to what anyone else says,' he whispered. 'All that matters is you and me.'

14

Now

Amy was in her room in Sea View, reading, when she heard raised voices.

'Are you kidding me?' Liam's loud, indignant voice carried from the kitchen along the corridor and through her closed door. 'You really think I'd do something like that?'

Miles said something in reply. Amy couldn't make out the words, just his tone – harsh, irritated. Unable to help herself, she got out of bed, went to her door and opened it a crack.

'We're not accusing you, Liam.' That was June speaking: fluttery, nervous. 'We're just wondering . . . I mean, we need to discuss—'

Miles cut her off. 'Look, *obviously* we need to talk about it. The whole village is talking about it. Eileen says there was three hundred euro in the jam jar behind her TV, and it was missing when she woke up this morning. She never locks her door at night—'

'Maybe she should start,' Liam said.

'You think this is funny, do you?' Miles bellowed, so loud that Amy would have had no problem hearing even through a closed door. 'Because Margaret Collins swears she saw you walking past her house at one o'clock last night! Why would she lie?'

'Honey,' said June, in a placating voice, 'the kids . . .'

'Was it you?' Miles demanded. 'Did you steal Eileen's money?'

'I can't believe this!' Liam said. 'I can't believe you're genuinely asking me if I burgled an old lady's home!'

'Well, somebody did!' his father shouted. Amy didn't need to see Miles's face to know it was red with rage.

'Bollocks!' Liam shouted back. 'Eileen's about a hundred and two! I bet she misplaced that money and then convinced herself someone stole it! She should be put in a home!'

'Oh, that's what you want me to tell her sons, is it?' Miles roared. 'Tell you what, Liam, why don't you say that to them when they come knocking at our door – they're both very eager to talk to you!'

When Liam spoke next, he sounded on the verge of tears. 'Why is everyone in this shithole village out to get me? I wasn't out last night. I didn't have anything to do with any fucking graffiti. I hate this place!'

'Oh Liam,' said June, with gentleness, 'nobody is out to get—'

But Miles bellowed over her. 'Then leave!' he shouted at his son. 'If you hate being here so much, why don't you go back to your mother's?'

There was a pause, the first in the argument. Amy wished she could see Liam's expression as he said, 'You're telling me to leave? You don't want me here?'

The hurt in his voice was obvious. Amy expected Miles to backtrack, but he blustered on.

'If you think Knockcrea is such a shithole, to use your charming expression, then I don't understand why you *want* to be here! As long as you're under our roof, I expect you to show some respect, and that means that if June and I have questions, you answer them. I notice you haven't directly answered the question about the money, by the way.'

There was another short silence.

'Well,' said Liam, 'it's only a couple of weeks till I'm back at school, so you won't have to put up with me being under your roof for much longer.'

She heard him stomping down the corridor and stepped quickly back into her room. Miles's voice rang out. 'Hey! Come back here! We're not finished.'

'I'm finished with you,' said Liam.

She heard his door slam shut and the thud of Miles's fist against it.

'Hey! Get back out here, you little shit! HEY!'

From upstairs rose a high-pitched whining. Tom and Poppy had started to cry. Amy heard June going to them, while Miles continued to bang on his eldest child's door.

Amy didn't feel much like leaving her room that evening, but eventually hunger drove her to the kitchen. The house was quiet. June sat on the sofa in the open-plan living area, dressed in grey and sky-blue loungewear. She was staring into space, slack-jawed. When Amy moved a chair, she gave a little jump. 'Amy, I didn't see you there!' She got to her feet and came over to the kitchen. 'How're you?'

It was obvious she was unsure whether to mention the

screaming match. Amy decided to be blunt. 'I couldn't help overhearing that argument earlier,' she said. 'Are you okay?'

June looked relieved and miserable at once. She glanced in the direction of Liam's room. Her words came out in an urgent whisper. 'I just don't know what we're supposed to do! He says he didn't go out last night, and I want to believe him. But Margaret Collins *swears* she saw him. Should we come down hard on him, or take his side?'

'Teenagers are hard work,' said Amy. 'It can be difficult to know which way to go.'

'Between us, I'm inclined to believe him. Margaret Collins is part of that Tidy Towns crowd, and they're a bunch of nutters,' June said fervently. 'I wouldn't put it past them to lie. But Miles has so little trust in Liam, and I understand that too.'

'It sounds like he assumes the worst of him,' said Amy cautiously.

'Well, it's not without reason,' said June. 'I mean, if you knew why Liam was expelled from his last school . . .' She trailed off.

'What happened?' asked Amy.

'Forget it,' said June, who looked horrified with herself. 'I shouldn't've . . . Look, I'm sorry you had to overhear all that earlier. None of this is fair on you. Or on Tom and Poppy. Oh God, I just can't handle this!' Her eyes were shiny with tears.

'Look, let me make you a cup of tea,' said Amy. 'You sit down. I've got it.'

June sat obediently. She dabbed under her eyes with her fingertips.

'He's a good kid, Liam,' she said, as if Amy had said otherwise. 'He's just got some issues.'

Amy gave her a tissue and made the tea. 'D'you take milk? Sugar?'

'Just black. Thanks, Amy. You're very kind.'

June accepted her mug of tea gratefully.

'Liam's going back to his mother's at the end of the month,' she said. 'You know that, right?'

Amy nodded. The subtext was clear.

Once Liam was gone, this would all be over.

But would it?

Before bed, Amy stood by the huge window and stared out at the dream-like view: mountainside and rock, sea and horizon. From this angle, just a few of the houses in Knockcrea were visible, lights in the windows beginning to glitter. The vast sky was changing colour. It was dusk.

She wondered if she would still be here in six months, a year. She felt rootless, in a way she never had before. Free-floating. Like the wind might carry her anywhere.

The one thing she knew for sure was that she couldn't go back to Dublin. She could never go back to her old life.

She brushed her teeth and changed into her pyjama bottoms and vest. She looked at herself sideways in the mirror and realised with a shock how much weight she'd lost recently. She hadn't been eating much since she got here, since eating meant imposing herself on the family's space. She'd have to get over that or she'd keep getting thinner and thinner until she disappeared.

She used one hand to sweep her hair up, looking at the tattoo on her shoulder. In the mirror, the name in the heart was backwards.

She still remembered the day she'd had it done. Mark had gone with her to Wildcat Ink in Stephen's Green. She recalled the sharp pain, the buzz of the needle. Mark had held her hand the whole time. Afterwards, as she'd stood in front of the mirror to look at the fresh jet-black lines on her skin, he had been grinning over her shoulder. 'Looks great, babe.'

He'd had a matching tattoo done on his left arm.

She had really believed that their love was for ever.

Amy let her curtain of dark hair fall back into place, covering the tattoo. She closed the blinds on that beautiful view, got into bed, and watched mindless TV shows on Sandra's Netflix account until she fell asleep with the iPad still propped against a pillow in front of her.

That night, Amy woke suddenly at 1 a.m. She lay with her eyes open in the darkness, wondering what had disturbed her.

Then she heard the distinct crunch of a footstep on gravel outside.

Just Liam smoking a joint, she told herself. But that thought didn't reassure her as much as it once had.

She got quietly out of bed. With the blinds down and shuttered, her room was utterly dark. She made her way sightlessly in the direction of the door. Her hands found the wall first, and she groped along until she touched the handle. Very slowly, she turned it and pushed the door open.

The corridor was deserted and dark. In the direction of the kitchen, she saw dim moonlight, as if filtered through thick cloud. She went the opposite way, towards the back door. She turned the handle and found it unlocked. Because

Miles and June had forgotten to lock it? Or because Liam had opened it?

As soundlessly as she could, she pulled the door open and stepped outside. Cold air touched her skin, causing goosebumps to ripple along her neck and shoulders. She looked up and saw that the sky was covered in a blanket of cloud.

Somewhere nearby, the gravel crunched again. She wanted to call Liam's name but didn't like the idea of her voice falling flat on the darkness. She made her way to the corner of the house and peered around it. Under the clouded sky, the landscape was blanketed in a blackness so complete it was hard for human eyes to make out anything.

Then, about twenty feet away, near the front of the house, she saw the orange glow of a cigarette tip.

'Liam!' she whispered.

She took a couple of steps in his direction, but he didn't seem to have heard her. He was walking away. The orange dot was bobbing down the driveway. 'Liam!' she called in a low voice. She didn't want to shout any louder in case she woke June or Miles or the kids. But Liam didn't look back. Did he have earphones in? Or was he pretending not to hear her?

He disappeared into the absolute darkness. From far off, Amy could hear the faint sound of the sea. Shivering a little from the cold, she turned and went back into the house. She closed the back door and stood looking at it, wondering whether to lock it. She decided against it. She didn't want to lock Liam out.

Then she heard a sound in the corridor behind her.

'All right?' said a familiar voice.

Amy whirled around. Her hand fumbled for the light switch.

Liam was standing there, wearing pyjama bottoms and a crumpled T-shirt and holding a glass of water. He was barefoot and sleepy-looking, squinting in the sudden light.

'*Liam?*' said Amy. 'Then who – ?' She turned to look at the unlocked door.

'What's up?' Liam asked, puzzled.

'There was someone outside the house. Just now.' Fear swelled inside her. 'I thought it was you. I tried to talk to them and they ran off.'

Liam stared at her, uncomprehending. Then he strode past her. He reached to the top of the doorframe, brought down a small silver key and locked the back door.

He made his way to the kitchen. Amy hurried after him. With all the lights still off, the great glass windows gave a panoramic view of the landscape. Liam put his glass down on the marble island. Then he went to the window and put his face right up to the glass.

'You're sure you saw someone?' he said.

'I'm certain. Whoever it was, they were smoking. I saw the cigarette.'

'Which way did they go?' Liam asked.

'Towards the village.'

He stepped back from the window.

Amy was hugging herself. 'We should wake your parents,' she said. 'I mean, your dad and June.'

Liam circled the open-plan kitchen and front room slowly, looking out of all the windows. Then he turned on the light. 'I'll wake them now.'

He went past her and up the stairs. Amy had to stop herself calling out, *Don't leave me on my own!* She stood in the middle of the open-plan space, feeling horribly exposed now the lights were on. She was acutely aware that while she couldn't see out, anyone could see in.

Miles and June came downstairs. Miles was wearing a dressing gown and an outraged expression, and talking loudly about what he'd do to any 'lowlife scum' he caught on his property. He got a torch and went out to take a look around. Liam went with him.

June, in her satin nightdress, looked pale and strained. 'Did you see the person's face?' she asked. 'Were they tall? Short?'

'I'm not sure,' said Amy. 'It was very dark.'

'What do they want?' June muttered, as if to herself.

'Maybe they were casing the place for a burglary,' said Amy.

June shook her head. There was a strange look in her eyes. 'We've lived here for two years,' she said. 'We've never had a break-in, not even an attempted one. Most of the time we forget to lock the back door. And now — at the same time as all this weird stuff is happening around the village, stuff *our* family is being blamed for — suddenly there's someone lurking outside the house?'

It was the first time she had alluded to the vandalism and cryptic messages in front of Amy.

Amy spoke gently as she asked, 'D'you have bad blood with any of the neighbours, June?'

June looked startled. 'I mean, obviously Eileen O'Reilly thinks Liam stole money from her. Her sons asked Miles to reimburse her, but Miles says that giving them money would be like confirming Liam is guilty. Which he obviously isn't going to do. So Barry and Seamus O'Reilly aren't happy.'

'Do Eileen's sons smoke?'

June nodded. 'I'm pretty sure I've seen one or both of them smoking. They're big, tough men, you know. They're the type.'

After a moment's pause, Amy said, 'I can't believe Tom and Poppy slept through all the commotion.'

'Their room is soundproofed,' said June absently. She was staring off into the distance now, deep in thought.

When the front door opened, Amy and June both jumped, but it was just Miles and Liam.

'Whoever was out there, they're gone now,' said Miles, putting the torch down. They all took seats around the kitchen island.

'Who do you think it was?' June asked Miles.

'What about that weirdo who thinks I broke his windows? Sean Geraghty?' Liam jumped in.

'Don't be ridiculous, Liam,' said Miles. 'Irritating though Sean Geraghty might be, he's not the type to harass people. In fact, the only person I can think of in Knockcrea who might act like this is ...' He trailed off.

'Who?' said June urgently.

But Miles shot a sudden glance at Amy, as if remembering she was there.

'Forget it,' he said. 'I'll tell you later.' Then, to the room at large, 'Look, let's all just get some sleep. We know calling the guards would be a waste of time. It's not like they're going to come all the way out here for this.' Amy was inclined to agree. She doubted the guards – the Irish police force – would drive all the way to Sea View over a glimpsed cigarette tip.

'You're all right, are you, Amy?' June asked before they went upstairs.

'I'm fine.'

But she wasn't. Amy drifted in and out of sleep for the rest of the night, unable to settle. She kept replaying the evening's events in her head.

Miles had said there was only one person in Knockcrea he could imagine acting like this.

Who was he talking about?

15

The house was quiet. June and the two younger children were out for the morning. Liam, presumably, was in his room. Amy was working.

She cleaned the living-room half of the open-plan space. She wiped down the coffee table, dust-rolled the pristine furniture. She carefully cleaned the television screen. The whole time, she was deep in thought.

Did Miles and June know more than they were telling her? Did Liam? Did the Carrolls have an inkling of who was watching the house?

As she fluffed up the cream and grey pillows, she remembered the glow of the cigarette tip in the dark and shivered.

It was Friday. Tonight was the Tidy Towns meeting that Catherine had invited her to. Amy decided that she would attend after all. It was a chance to get more information.

At 7.45, she slipped out the back door of Sea View, without mentioning to the Carrolls that she was going anywhere. She drove to the address Catherine had given her. It was an old house on the outskirts of the village that had been modernised, the exterior abundantly decorated with potted plants.

She parked up a little way up the street. When she rang the bell, it was Catherine who answered.

'You made it!' Catherine greeted her with a warm hug. She was dressed in layered, flowing clothes, and her voluminous curls were a halo around her face. 'Come on inside. Everyone's dying to meet you.'

Amy followed her into the hall and through a door on the right into a spacious front room lined with bookshelves and potted plants. The room had been crammed with chairs and was full of noise and people. Most were older than Amy. On a small table in the middle was an artistically laid spread of tea and biscuits.

A short, balding man in his mid forties, wearing a buttoned shirt under a beige cardigan and small square glasses, hurried in Amy's direction. 'Amy! Delighted to finally make your acquaintance. I'm Martin.'

So this was Martin Doyle, post-office worker and chairman of the Tidy Towns committee. Catherine had told her that he was kind and well-meaning, if somewhat obsessive about the village and his role.

'Lovely to meet you,' said Amy.

Martin looked like he wanted to say something else, but a red-headed woman swooped in and grabbed Amy's arm like they were old friends. 'Amy, right? I'm Aveen.'

Aveen Butler was the owner of this house. Forty-something and beautiful, with flame-coloured hair to her waist and an English accent, she was a poet and a painter. Beside Amy, she was probably the youngest person there. Born in London to Irish parents, she explained to Amy, she'd worked in advertising for over a decade before quitting the rat race and moving to West Cork. 'Best decision I ever made,' she said. 'It's like I stepped into a whole new life.'

'Aveen never came to these meetings before the vandalism started,' Catherine whispered to Amy as their hostess moved away. 'She's just here for the drama.'

As Amy made her way towards the table of biscuits, a man rose from his chair, blocking her way. She immediately recognised him by his hollow face, tall, spindly build, and distinctive grey hair that stuck up like toothbrush bristles.

'Hello,' she said to the man who had jumped out from behind the bushes at her.

Sean Geraghty flushed a deep maroon colour. 'Amy, isn't it?' He looked quickly at her face and then down at his feet. 'I owe you an apology. I never meant to scare you. I'm sorry. I tried to tell you there was nothing to be afraid of. But you ran off.'

'It's okay,' Amy told him.

'I didn't give you too much of a fright, did I?' he mumbled.

'I got a fright, yeah,' said Amy. 'But it didn't kill me.'

Something in her tone seemed to calm him. He looked up and extended his hand. Amy shook it.

'Nice to meet you properly,' she said.

He looked surprised and grateful, but still uncomfortable. Muttering something about a cup of tea, he slipped away.

Catherine appeared at Amy's shoulder. 'That was kind of you,' she said. 'He's been worrying himself sick, the poor man, imagining that you were terrified of him.'

Next Amy was introduced to Jacinta Crowley, a widow who lived alone and whose home had been vandalised.

Jacinta was a large woman, almost spilling out of her seat. She looked about seventy. She dyed her hair raven black and wore startlingly red lipstick. Clasping a cup of tea in both hands, she leaned forward to look at Amy with a frankly curious expression. 'Well, we've all been very interested to meet *you*,' she said. 'How are you getting on at Sea View?'

Something about this woman put Amy immediately on guard. 'I'm getting on grand,' she said neutrally.

'Well, tell us a bit about yourself!' said Jacinta. 'What age are you? D'you have kids of your own?'

When Amy didn't answer, Catherine said, 'You never ask a woman her age, Jacinta! And of course she doesn't have her own kids – she's live-in at Sea View, remember?'

'How are you finding living with the Carrolls?' asked Jacinta.

'Good.'

'Getting on all right with Miles?'

'Yeah, fine.'

'We're just gonna go grab some tea before the meeting starts, Jacinta,' said Catherine loudly, ignoring Jacinta's obvious frustration at Amy's monosyllabic answers. 'We'll chat to you soon!'

Amy poured herself a cup of tea and found a chair in the corner to sit on. Catherine took the seat beside her. From the other side of the room, she heard a voice she didn't recognise saying, 'Well, that June Carroll's a gold-digger, plain and simple . . .' She turned to see who was talking, but the conversation died down when she looked.

'Did you hear that?' she asked Catherine.

'Yep,' said Catherine, looking straight ahead. 'People like

to speculate about the Carrolls' marriage. What do you think? Did June marry Miles for his money?'

Amy thought of June touching Miles's shoulder as she walked past, and the warm voice she used when she called him honey. 'I don't think so. There's a lot of affection between them. I think she really loves him.'

'I agree. Incidentally, it's common knowledge that June brought more money into the marriage than Miles did. She comes from money – inherited a small fortune from a wealthy grandfather.'

'If everyone knows that, why do they go around saying she's a gold-digger?'

Catherine shrugged. 'Better story, isn't it? It's more salacious to think of the younger wife as some conniving—'

'He-hem!' Martin Doyle cleared his throat. 'All right, everyone, if we could all settle down, please.'

Amy and Catherine broke off mid-conversation and made an effort to look attentive. Martin sat in a straight-backed chair by the tea-and-biscuits table, facing the rest of the room. Jacinta Crowley had her chair pulled up beside his. Amy felt a little as if she were in school again.

'We all know what the first item on today's agenda is,' said Martin. 'The latest piece of vandalism. We were all shocked to learn that Sean's land had been targeted, for the second time.'

Everyone looked at Sean Geraghty, who stared at his boots.

'The guards have been contacted with a list of offences, and we've made them aware of our suspicions about who's responsible,' said Martin. 'Disappointingly, they've made no arrest and don't seem to be taking the situation as seriously as we'd hoped.' His expression showed his displeasure. 'But we're all well aware it's no coincidence that this antisocial behaviour began after Liam Carroll arrived in the area for the summer.'

Heads turned towards Amy, who kept her eyes on her knees.

Aveen Butler said, 'You could be a bit more diplomatic, Martin.'

'Diplomatic!' said Martin. 'Oh, come on. We all know who's behind it, and so does she.'

More heads swivelled in Amy's direction. Suddenly Martin was addressing her directly.

'Amy, could you tell us about the day you came across the vandalism?'

'Uh, not much to tell, really,' said Amy, alarmed to find herself in the spotlight. 'It was like I said to Catherine. There was a trail of paint on the ground, and I followed it. I didn't see anything beyond what you all saw – the symbol, the weird message. There was nobody around ... except Sean, obviously.' She glanced at Sean Geraghty, who looked mortified. 'I wish I could be more help, but—'

'Maybe there *is* a way you can be of more help,' said Martin. 'You live at Sea View. You could keep an eye out for us. If you see anything suspicious – or hear anything – you could let us know.'

The room had gone quiet. Amy shifted uneasily under Martin's stare. Was he asking her to spy on her employers?

'I'm sorry,' she said, playing dumb. 'I don't really know what you mean.'

Most people in the room looked uncomfortable. But Jacinta Crowley leaned forward with an eager expression, as if something juicy was being held just out of her reach.

'You could even take photos,' she suggested. 'Couldn't she, Martin?'

Martin was nodding. 'That could be helpful.'

'I'm sorry,' said Amy, 'but photos of what, exactly?'

'Well, if you see that boy do anything,' said Jacinta, like it was obvious. 'Sneak out in the middle of the night. Or come in with paint on his clothes.'

Martin cleared his throat. 'All we mean is, if you happened to see something incriminating, then why not?'

'And look, we know you're not going to want to sit awake all night looking out for him,' said Jacinta, 'so maybe one of those spy cameras could work? You can get them disguised as all kinds of things – potted plants, for example. We'd be happy to cover the cost.'

A ripple ran through the room. Amy looked at Catherine, who seemed just as shocked as she felt. Martin cringed slightly. He didn't look surprised, only embarrassed. 'Jacinta!' he said.

'What?' said Jacinta. 'We agreed we were going to ask her!'

Amy felt an unexpected flash of loyalty to the Carrolls. This bunch were like a pack of bloodhounds, and it was Liam's scent they were on. 'I'm sorry,' she said, her voice clear and firm. 'I wouldn't feel comfortable doing that.'

Most people in the room nodded at this, but Jacinta Crowley was glaring at her, and Martin Doyle didn't seem too pleased either. He shot Jacinta a furious look, as if Amy's response was all her fault.

'Look, we totally understand,' he said, adjusting his glasses. 'But if you could keep an eye out – if you could get us any evidence at all that Liam has—'

'She said no, Martin,' Catherine butted in. 'And let's say

96

she *did* get the photo you're after – June and Miles would know who'd taken it. Amy could lose her job!' She shook her head. 'I never would have brought her tonight if I'd known you were going to ambush her like this.'

'Ambush!?' said Martin, sounding greatly offended. 'We're merely *asking* – there is the issue of the greater good here.'

'It's not much, what we're asking,' said Jacinta petulantly.

'It is, actually,' Aveen Butler chimed in. 'You're asking her to spy on her employers. I don't think it's legal.'

'Painting on walls, defacing people's property – *that* isn't legal!' said Jacinta shrilly.

Suddenly everyone was arguing. Sean Geraghty was talking about privacy and respect. Aveen and Jacinta were in a heated argument. Martin Doyle was trying to shout over their heads, 'Would everybody calm down!'

Catherine stood up. 'Let's go outside for a breath of air, Amy.'

Amy jumped up to follow her.

Once they were on the street outside, Catherine said, 'I'm so sorry. I had no idea they were going to spring that on you! Normally these kinds of meetings are actually quite fun. This vandalism business is making the whole village go crazy.'

'Don't worry about it,' said Amy automatically, but she felt quite shaken.

When they went back inside a few minutes later, the room seemed rather subdued. The conversation then moved on to whether or not Knockcrea needed larger flower pots lining the main street, but it was obvious this topic was not of as much interest to people as the previous one had been. Martin Doyle had a huffy air about him; Jacinta was shooting daggers in Amy's direction. It was as if they both felt she had let them down personally. When the meeting was over, she was glad to leave.

'Lovely to meet you, Amy!' said Aveen Butler warmly. Sean Geraghty, avoiding eye contact, bade her 'Safe home, now.' But Martin Doyle's 'nice to meet you' was cold, and Jacinta Crowley barely looked at her.

Amy and Catherine walked back to their cars together. The sky above was navy blue, studded with the first stars. It was such a windless evening that the sound of the sea was carrying up over the fields.

'Honestly,' said Catherine, shaking her head, 'Martin and Jacinta really have drunk the Kool-Aid.'

'How could they think I would do that?' said Amy.

'I guess they're feeling desperate,' said Catherine with a sigh. 'This has been going on for months, and one of the first messages was written on the side of Jacinta's house. I think she was really scared. That's not an excuse for how she's acting, just an explanation.'

'What did the graffiti on her house say?' Amy asked.

Catherine took her phone out. 'I have pictures. This is what was written on Jacinta's house . . . Scroll left and you'll see what was on the school and the old mine.'

Amy took the phone and scrolled through the images. The huge red letters painted along the side of Jacinta's house read:

HE'S COMING FOR YOU ALL.

The school had been graffitied with the words:

YOU'RE NOT SAFE IN YOUR BEDS.

The message on the abandoned mine said:

RUN WHILE YOU STILL CAN.

Catherine read Amy's expression. 'You're freaked out.'

'Well, who wouldn't be?' Amy shuddered, handing the phone back.

'Whoever is doing this is trying to frighten us,' said Catherine. 'We shouldn't let them.'

'Easier said than done. And I'm on edge after that meeting, too.'

'Bloody Martin and Jacinta. I'll have words with them, I promise you.'

'Don't,' said Amy, alarmed. She already felt as if the locals disliked her, putting her in the same category as the Carrolls. 'Please just leave it, Catherine. The last thing I want is more drama. I've had enough to last me a lifetime.'

She looked up towards Sea View. It was visible even from here. All the lights were on.

She'd gone to the Tidy Towns meeting to quietly listen and had somehow ended up the centre of an argument. She'd come to West Cork looking for peace, but instead had found herself in the middle of a mystery.

Why, she thought, of all the places I could have ended up, did it have to be this creepy village? Why couldn't things have just been normal for once?

On the drive back to Sea View, Amy found herself feeling rather fragile. This wasn't due to the commotion at the meeting. It was a response to that throwaway question Jacinta Crowley had asked her earlier in the evening.

D'you have kids of your own?

Amy was relieved that Catherine had jumped in and said she didn't. She wasn't sure she would have been able to answer herself. Saying no to that question would have felt like a betrayal.

By the time she parked outside Sea View, she was crying.

She could see the Carrolls through the glass, watching TV. Amy let herself in the back door and went straight to her room. She sat on her bed, opened her wallet and took out the photograph she carried everywhere.

It had been taken on Robbie's fifth birthday. Amy was hugging him, crouched down behind him, her dark head beside his blonde one. The giant blue badge pinned to his T-shirt read: *5 today!*

She stared at the photo – at Robbie's golden-blonde hair, his dimples, his toothy smile. All she wanted was to go back in time. Have another chance to do right by her child.

She lowered a hand to her stomach, fingertips brushing the long-healed Caesarean scar. Tears ran from her eyes as she pressed the photo of her son to her lips, then to her chest.

16

Before

Amy was terrified when she told Mark about the pregnancy. After all, they were both still in school. What if he accused her of ruining his life?

But his face broke into a huge smile. 'You're pregnant?' he said. 'That's *brilliant.*'

'Really? You're not angry at me?' Her voice trembled.

'Angry? I'm happy! We're going to have a baby!'

'I thought— I thought you'd be—'

'This is good news,' said Mark firmly. He got down on his knees, pulled up her T-shirt and kissed her still-flat stomach. 'We're going to be together for ever, right? So what's the problem?'

Tears of happiness spilled down Amy's cheeks. She'd never felt more grateful to anyone. She was only fifteen and Mark was just seventeen. She'd never imagined he would react like this.

'Don't cry,' he said, with all the gentleness he could show

sometimes. 'Everything's going to be all right. I'm not going anywhere.'

'I wonder is it a boy or a girl?' Amy said, dabbing her eyes.

'A boy,' said Mark decisively. 'I know it's going to be a boy.'

He was right.

Robert Daniel Keating was born healthy, weighing eight pounds four ounces. Amy was traumatised by the birth – 'Nobody explains how much it hurts, not really,' she said to Sandra – which was difficult, and ended in an emergency Caesarean section. But when the tiny red person she'd created was placed in her arms, everything changed. That bit, it was just like everyone said: instant love.

Louise wasn't happy about her daughter becoming a teen mother. But when she held her grandchild in her arms, she was besotted. And the way Mark stood by Amy raised him in her esteem.

For the first six months of Robbie's life, Amy stayed living at home. The good parts were magic. Nothing had prepared her for seeing her child smile for the first time. Robbie was fascinated by the snow globe that sat on their mantelpiece: every time Amy shook it, he would laugh his gurgling laugh. She would sit with him for hours, playing peekaboo, counting his toes, or just shaking the snow globe and watching the joy on his face. Those months were tough, too – adjusting to parenthood wasn't easy – but her mother helped her every day.

Then Amy and Mark moved in together, into a terraced two-bedroom council house on the same housing estate.

Living with Mark was hard, harder than Amy had anticipated. The bulk of Robbie's care fell to her. Her life became nappy changes and night feeds and a feeling of constant exhaustion. Mark became increasingly snappy, frustrated with Robbie's crying.

'Why won't he stop?'

'He's a baby, Mark! Babies cry.'

'Yeah, I know he's a baby,' Mark snarled back at her. 'Jesus fucking Christ, you don't need to talk to me like I'm stupid.'

Amy was so shocked by his sudden change in tone, she didn't know what to say.

Two months after they moved in together, Mark stormed out of his job after an argument with his boss. He told Amy how glad he was to be out of there, and seemed confident that he would walk into a better job. But he didn't seem to spend much time job-hunting, although he did spend more and more time at the pub with his friends. His period of unemployment stretched from weeks to months.

The first time he broke something, it was a decorative blue bowl that Louise had bought them from IKEA. It sat on the kitchen table until Mark, in an argument over why he hadn't come home from the pub the night before, picked it up and hurled it at the wall. It shattered, causing Robbie to start screaming and Amy to cringe aside with her hands over her head.

'Oh, don't be so dramatic,' Mark sneered at her. 'It was nowhere near you.'

But she thought he looked ashamed before he walked out of the house.

Amy soothed Robbie until he stopped crying. She swept up the broken pieces with hands that shook slightly. A part of her wanted to call Sandra, but something was holding her back. Loyalty to Mark? A desire to pretend it hadn't happened?

Her phone rang, startling her. She took it from her pocket and looked at the screen.

It was Mark.

She answered. 'Hi.'

'Look, I didn't mean to do that,' he said. 'I'm sorry if I scared you. Are you all right?'

'Yeah.'

'I'm coming home now,' he said. 'And I won't go down the pub tonight either, okay? Let's stay in, watch TV and get Chinese.'

Relief flooded Amy. There was nothing to tell Sandra after all. It had just been a blip, and now things would be normal again.

'Okay,' she said. 'Chinese sounds good.'

'All right,' said Mark. 'I'll be home soon. Love you.'

'Love you too.'

Amy put her phone down. Robbie was babbling happily in his playpen, and she went over to pick him up. But before she reached him, she stopped with a wince of pain. She lifted her left leg to look at the sole of her bare foot and swore softly. A piece of blue glass she'd missed had sliced through her skin. Blood trickled from the open cut and dripped onto the floor.

17

Now

It was a sunny Saturday morning in West Cork, and Amy spent it looking after Tom and Poppy while June worked in her office. 'You don't mind working a few Saturdays just for the first month or so, do you, Amy?' June had said. 'Just while I catch up on all the work I couldn't do while we didn't have anyone.' Amy didn't mind. She needed the hours.

Tom wanted to play hide-and-seek. Poppy wanted to dress up as a princess. When all the running around and dressing up got a bit exhausting, Amy suggested reading a book. She sat down, and both kids clambered onto her lap straight away. Poppy hooked a little arm around her neck, while Tom cuddled against her shoulder.

It was enough to cause a lump to rise in Amy's throat. She swallowed it down before she began to read.

June finished work around two and took the children out for the rest of the afternoon. Amy stayed in the house to clean. She spent most of the day on the massive job of washing the enormous windows. June had told her to clock off at 5.30, so she did. She made herself a cup of tea, went back to her room and lay down. She picked up her phone, opened Instagram and sank into a state of mindless scrolling . . .

She woke up on top of the duvet, fully dressed and disoriented. Her mouth felt sticky. Her cup of undrunk tea was on the bedside locker. She checked the time on the phone beside her. Nearly seven o'clock. She heard a child shriek somewhere in the house, and realised June and the kids had come home.

She got up, brushed her hair and went to the kitchen to get a glass of water. Tom and Poppy were in the playroom. Liam was outside, smoking: Amy gave a little jump when she saw the back of his head at the window.

She was passing the foot of the stairs, on her way back to her room with her water, when she heard the voices – raised, tense – floating down from Miles and June's bedroom.

'Because you can't, Miles! You just can't do it! My God, you're not serious?'

'I am bloody serious. Why wouldn't I be serious?'

'Because . . . it's not safe!'

Miles snorted. '*It's not safe*,' he imitated her. 'Oh, fuck off, June. I've never in my life met anyone as hysterical as you.'

'Miles,' said June, low, begging, 'please . . .'

'Shut the fuck up,' Miles said coldly. 'I don't want to hear another word about it.'

Amy, at the bottom of the stairs, felt her stomach clench.

'But, Miles,' June persisted, 'you're not considering—'

'I said, I DON'T WANT TO HEAR ANOTHER WORD ABOUT IT!'

Amy's heart rate accelerated. She felt the old rush of adrenaline and fear. Quickly she slipped into her room and closed the door.

It's okay, she told herself, trying to breathe deep and slow, you're okay. Nobody's going to hurt you here.

She heard a door slam upstairs, and the heavy sound of Miles's footsteps thumping across the landing. Then a whimpering noise that might have been June crying. It didn't last long and stopped abruptly.

Amy didn't want to emerge from her room for the rest of the evening, but eventually she had to. She was hungry. When she finally made her cautious way to the kitchen, she found Miles and June at the island. Both acknowledged her in a relaxed, friendly way. As if nothing had happened. Amy ate some peanut butter on toast, loaded the dishwasher, then retreated to the safety of her room again.

That wasn't how normal couples argued, right? Amy knew her perspective on these things was skewed, and it was sometimes hard to tell if she was overreacting or underreacting. Her mind went to Sandra and Dave, the couple against whom she measured normality. Dave would *never* scream at Sandra like that, nor she at him. But perhaps this was setting the bar too high. Maybe people who weren't as bad as her and Mark but weren't as good as Sandra and Dave, couples who were somewhere in the middle, casually said stuff like *shut the fuck up* to each other all the time.

But that awful coldness in Miles's voice . . .

She pressed her fingertips against her temples and moved

them in small circles, trying to fight the gathering tension in her head. She remembered June's voice, small and pleading: *It's not safe . . .*

Maybe it was time to start looking for another job.

18

The following day was Sunday, Amy's day off. After breakfast, she shut herself away in her bedroom with a mug of
sugary tea. She settled on her bed, took out her phone and
began scrolling through jobs sites.

She used search terms like 'nanny', 'childminder', 'live-in'
and 'home help'. There was no shortage of ads.

Lively family in Galway seek energetic au pair.

*New mum seeks an extra pair of hands with four-month-old
twins. Kerry.*

Family of five needs help around the house. Sligo.

Galway, Kerry, Sligo . . . She could go anywhere.

Again, Amy felt that strange, free-floating feeling, as if
she had come untethered, like the strings that tied her to the
earth had been snipped.

The only place she couldn't go was home.

She picked up her mug of tea from the bedside table,
wrapping her hands around it for warmth and comfort. It

had been such a huge change, coming here. Such a massive, terrifying life decision. She didn't feel able to make another such change so soon. The very idea left her exhausted.

She imagined arriving at a different house and finding her bedroom was a cramped box room, full of someone else's clutter. Or that the parents were the kind of people who would pay her for less hours than she had worked, then act surprised when she asked for what she was owed. The uncertainty of it all made her want to cry.

Liam was leaving at the end of the month. Maybe all the strange happenings would stop then.

Or maybe they won't. Maybe Liam has nothing to do with any of it.

She picked up her phone again, but just looking at the ads made her feel so mentally exhausted, so bone tired, that she let it drop from her hand to the bed. She would wait. In two weeks, Liam would be gone. She could reassess then. If strange things kept happening in his absence, then she would find another job and leave Knockcrea.

She finished her tea and put the mug on her beside locker. Despite the sugar, a heavy sleepiness washed over her. She was so tired these days. She lay down on her side.

As she drifted towards sleep, she found herself thinking of the previous nannies, Francisca and Georgia. She wished there was a way she could speak to them. *Why did you leave?* she wondered. *What happened in this house? Am I safe here, or should I go?*

When she woke from her nap, she lay in bed reading for most of the afternoon. Rest seemed to be the thing her body craved most. However, when she looked out the window and realised evening was approaching, cabin fever struck. She decided to stretch her legs while there was daylight left.

Amy left the house an hour before dark. She walked in the direction of the beach, taking the longer route that kept her far away from the field where she'd found the graffiti. There were a few families on the beach: adults barbecuing food, children playing in the dunes. Quiet, but a welcome change from the total isolation around Sea View.

She looked inland. Even from here, Sea View was visible, standing tall on the slopes at the foot of the mountains. She could see the orange of the setting sun bouncing off the windows. *It almost looks as if the house is on fire.* She shivered, then shook the thought away.

If sunset was approaching, that meant she'd been out for longer than she'd thought. She checked the time on her phone and began walking briskly back the way she'd come. On the road, she passed a missing-pet poster taped to a pole. Over a low-quality photo of the ginger-furred animal, the words read: *BUBBLES. MUCH-LOVED CAT.* Underneath it said, *IF YOU HAVE ANY INFORMATION, PLEASE CALL NOLEEN HOULIHAN*, followed by a phone number.

It was a poorly made poster, clearly put together by someone with no computer skills. Amy guessed Noleen Houlihan was an older woman. Everyone knew everyone in Knockcrea, so the posters were for a very small audience: people passing through, the handful of tourists staying in the caravan park by the sea. As Amy turned away, she crossed her fingers in her pocket like a little girl, hoping Bubbles would come home soon.

Dusk settled over West Cork as she walked back. The

orange glare against Sea View disappeared as she drew nearer to the house, but there was still enough greyish light for her to see by.

Tucking her hands into her coat pockets, Amy felt the box of cigarettes. When she realised she had them, she immediately wanted one.

She turned down the potholed road to her left, the one that eventually led to Sean Geraghty's farm. The fields here were more rock than grass. She found somewhere to sit: a stretch of stone wall where she was hidden from sight of Sea View by a swell of grey rock that rose from the earth like a wave.

Crossing her legs, she lit a cigarette and exhaled with relief. The evening was still. Small birds flitted past, darting from the bushes.

Then she heard boots crunching on the road.

The large rock that concealed her from Sea View also prevented her from seeing who was approaching. For a moment, she had an urge to throw herself down behind the wall and hide rather than find out.

Then the person came into view.

'Liam!' she said.

He jumped almost out of his skin. 'Jesus!' He started laughing. 'I nearly wet myself! What are you doing hiding there?'

'Nothing,' she said guiltily.

His eyes dropped to the still-burning cigarette in her hand. 'I thought I smelled smoke,' he said, amused. 'Well, well. Miles and June wouldn't be happy about *that*.'

'Shit.' Amy dropped the cigarette and stamped it out. 'Are you going to tell them?'

He grinned. 'Don't worry. I'm not a rat. Unlike *some* people around here.'

'I'm sorry, Liam. I had to. You're—'

'Yeah, yeah,' he said. 'Underage, I know.'

Amy stood up. 'Where are you going?' she asked. She'd never seen Liam leave Sea View before.

'Just for a walk,' he said lightly. There was something about his casual tone that made Amy instantly suspect he was lying.

'Nice night for it,' she said.

'It is, yeah.' There was a bit of a grin in his voice.

Amy picked up the cigarette butt. 'I'll have to find somewhere to put this now,' she said. 'Having a secret smoking habit is more trouble than it's worth. I don't know how you do it.'

'I don't hide the fact I smoke.' Liam shrugged. 'Miles doesn't care what I do.'

'I don't know much about your family, Liam,' Amy said, 'but I think your dad does care about you.'

Liam's jaw clenched. 'You're right,' he said. 'You *don't* know much about our family.'

'I'm sorry,' she said sincerely. 'Look, I didn't mean to be patronising. You know your dad better than I do.'

'You don't know what he's like,' said Liam. 'When I was younger . . .'

He broke off. She waited. A small bird darted by.

'D'you know what, forget it.' Liam seemed to suddenly shake off whatever he'd been feeling. He put on his usual grin. 'I better get going. I won't mention the smoking to Miles and June. Your secret's safe with me.' He set off up the grey winding road.

'Liam!' Amy called after him. 'Be . . .'

She stopped herself. *Be careful*, she had been about to say, but wouldn't that sound silly? She settled for 'Be safe.'

'Yeah?' he said, making the word a kind of question, in the way of teenagers. 'I will? See you.'

He walked off and was swallowed up by the shadows. One moment Amy could see him, the next she couldn't. Where was he going? Where did this road lead, except to Sean Geraghty's farm? She knew from examining Google Maps that it looped around on the other side, eventually coming down to the village, but it was a long walk. If he was going to the village, it was an odd route to choose ... unless he didn't want to be seen.

As she walked back to Sea View, she reflected on his unfinished statement. *When I was younger* ...

When Liam was younger ... what?

19

Before

It started with slaps, shoves. Usually when drunk. Followed by apologies. The first time he punched her, Amy was stunned. She had believed that was a line he would never cross.

She applied concealer to the black eye in the bathroom mirror the next morning. She could hear the TV downstairs: Robbie was watching cartoons. The sky through the window was a cloudless blue.

The bathroom door opened. In the mirror, she met Mark's gaze. He was hung-over and miserable-looking.

'I don't know what I was doing last night,' he said. 'I was hammered. I won't drink like that again.'

Amy was quiet for a while. Then she said, 'That's your excuse?'

'If I hadn't been on the vodka, I never would have lost control like that. You know that.'

She stared at him levelly and said nothing.

He came into the bathroom and closed the door. 'Don't do

that,' he said, a note of desperation in his voice. 'Don't stare at me and not say anything. You're scaring me. You know I'd never hurt you on purpose, don't you? Tell me you know that.'

She exhaled. 'I know.'

He choked on his next words. 'Tell me you're not going to leave me.'

'I'm not going to leave you,' Amy answered reflexively. 'I'm just shocked. I never thought . . .'

He came up behind her and put his arms around her waist.

'I'm shocked at myself,' he said in a low voice. 'But I can do better. I'll stop drinking so much. I'll find a job. I'll get back on track, and we'll have the life we always wanted, me and you and Robbie. The two of you are the only thing that matters to me.'

She softened into his arms. He hadn't been this affection-ate towards her in some time. Maybe this was the tipping point and he would turn over a new leaf. She was only eighteen. She didn't want to be a single mother. She didn't want to face the world alone. The future she had dreamed of for the two of them flickered in front of her: a house in a seaside town, a quiet life.

'You'll help me, won't you, baby?' said Mark. 'You'll help me sort myself out?'

'Of course,' she said, turning towards him. 'We'll get through it together.'

They had been together for four years. They had a young son. She wanted to believe in the future he was paint-ing for her.

'Promise me you won't leave me to do this on my own,' he whispered.

'I won't.'

*

116

Why didn't you leave?

It would be years before Amy would be able to answer this question, even to herself.

It wasn't like Mark hit her on their first date. He worked up to it. He didn't hit her until they were living together, had a child together, until their lives were inextricably entangled.

Why didn't you leave?

He didn't hit her until he'd worn her self-confidence down to dust. Long before he ever raised a hand to her, Mark told her that she was annoying, that her voice was grating, that she wasn't as good-looking up close as she was from a distance. That she was stupid and incompetent, that bills and paperwork were beyond her capabilities, that she wouldn't be able to handle life without him.

Why didn't you leave?

He told her these things over and over again, and by the time the violence really took off, she had come to believe it all. That she was an annoying person with an annoying voice. That she was bad in bed and a bad girlfriend. That she was pretty from a distance, yes, which was why men whistled at her in the street, but up close and with her clothes off, she was a bit of a disappointment.

It began to seem like a miracle that anyone wanted her at all.

'But *I* love you no matter what, baby,' Mark would say. 'To me, you're the most beautiful woman in the world. You'll always have me. Always.'

Why didn't you leave?

He convinced her of the improbability of anyone else ever wanting her. He convinced her she wouldn't be able to survive on her own. He convinced her that there was nothing else for her but this.

The year Amy turned nineteen, her mother was diagnosed with terminal cancer. While her daughters were devastated, their world crumbling around them, Louise was incredibly calm. In the months between her diagnosis and her death, she spoke often of her late husband. 'I'm going to see Gerry again,' she would say, as if she'd booked train tickets to meet him for a holiday.

And then, after six months that passed like a flash, she was gone.

Looking back, Amy knew that catastrophic loss at such a young age was one of the things that kept her with Mark.

He supported her through her mother's death. He never left her side. He held her in his arms while she raged and sobbed. He caught her when she crumpled in a hospital waiting room in the face of more bad news.

After Louise's death, Amy couldn't bear any further changes. Her relationship with Mark was familiar, and at that point she clung to familiarity with everything she had.

Louise never knew that Mark had raised a hand to Amy. But Sandra figured it out. And while she never told their mother, Sandra did tell Dave, and their dislike and distrust of Mark hardened into hatred.

Leave him, they told Amy, again and again. *Leave him, leave him.*

Two days after her twentieth birthday, Amy did make an attempt to leave Mark, after a fight that got frighteningly out of control. The next day, while he was at the pub, she wrapped a scarf around her bruised neck, grabbed Robbie and fled to Sandra and Dave's. Her sister and brother-in-law lived just a short drive away, on the far side of the same sprawling housing estate.

Sandra and Dave acted like Christmas had come early. They hugged and congratulated Amy. They told her she and Robbie were welcome to stay as long as they wanted. They actually cracked open bottles of beer in celebration.

When Mark came staggering up the driveway at 1 a.m., snarling threats and profanities, Sandra and Dave roared abuse at him through the door. 'She's left you, you bastard! She's not coming back! Now fuck off!' Stuff they'd probably been fantasising about saying. The dogs leapt at the door, barking and snarling.

Mark might have been drunk, but he wasn't stupid. He knew that if he kicked that door down, he'd be torn apart. So he stood outside and called, 'Amy? Amy?'

She was in the back bedroom with Robbie, who was tucked under the duvet. With Dave's headphones over his ears and white noise playing, he slept peacefully. Downstairs, the commotion raged on.

'If you leave me, I'll die, Amy. I will. I won't have any reason to live if you and Robbie are gone.'

'Nobody gives a fuck, Mark!' Sandra shouted through the letter box.

Dave joined in. 'D'you expect us to feel sorry for you? You woman-beating piece of shit . . .'

Amy crept out to the hall to listen. Her heart was hammering in her chest.

Mark's voice carried from outside: 'If you don't come back, I'll kill myself tonight.'

Why didn't you leave?

Two of Mark's favourite threats were: 'I'll kill you, Amy' and 'I'll die without you'. Both terrified her. She saw visions of headlines: *DUBLIN WOMAN BEATEN TO DEATH BY PARTNER* or *BODY DRAGGED FROM CANAL IDENTIFIED AS LOCAL MAN MARK KEATING.*

He was the father of her child. She couldn't fathom the guilt she would feel if he killed himself because of her. In Sandra and Dave's spare room, while Robbie slept, she lay awake all night and wondered if Mark was still alive.

The next day, she went back.

Sandra and Dave were bewildered, angry at her. They felt embarrassed. They'd lost, and Mark had won. He was swaggering around the estate and Amy had a fresh black eye, and there was nothing they could do about it.

Why didn't you leave?

Amy didn't see Mark as the villain that Sandra and Dave did. She had come to believe that the abuse happened not because there was something inherently violent in Mark but because there was something inherently hittable in *her.* She really believed that if she left him and began dating someone else, they would eventually start hitting her too.

This belief was reinforced by comments she heard like: 'It takes two to tango.' Amy would walk about with bruised ribs and reflect on her role in the argument. Could she have handled his moods more delicately? She became an expert at walking on eggshells – she danced on eggshells, she pirouetted on them – and if Mark hit her, it was because she had misstepped.

'I stayed up all night waiting for you,' he said when she walked in the front door with Robbie in tow. 'I knew you'd come back. I knew you wouldn't leave me.'

'I was always going to come back,' said Amy, recognising the truth in the words as she spoke them. 'I can't imagine not being with you. I don't even know who I'd be.'

He took her face in his hands. 'You don't have to worry about that,' he said. 'I'm not going anywhere. I'll never leave you. Do you hear me? I will never, ever leave you.'

Of all the promises he made her, that one turned out to be true.

20

Now

It was a windless, beautiful evening in West Cork. The air was cool, but the saffron tint to the sky promised a spectacular sunset. On the patio outside Catherine's artisan white cottage, Amy and Catherine sat across from each other in garden chairs. Both women had blankets wrapped around their shoulders. The ocean stretching out in front of them was so still it looked like a painting.

'*I* don't believe Liam stole Eileen's money,' said Catherine.

'So who do you think it was?' Amy asked, picking up her bottle of Heineken. Seeing as 'a drink' was the social function around which this conversation was based, she had accepted a light beer, which she wouldn't finish. She rarely drank. During her years with Mark, she had developed a dislike for alcohol and an aversion to feeling out of control.

Catherine, who clearly had no such hang-ups, swirled her whiskey in the glass so that the ice clinked gently. 'Look,' she said, leaning forward with an air of confidentiality, 'the poor woman's doolally. I wouldn't be surprised if she misplaced it. There's a whiff of hysteria around Knockcrea at the moment, that's all I'm saying.'

The cottage door opened and Catherine's husband, Hugh, came out. Amy had met him for the first time when she arrived. He was six-two, with a beard, broad shoulders and a quiet solidness.

'I brought you some extra blankets,' he said. 'It's getting chilly.'

'Thanks, honey,' Catherine said. 'Have a drink with us!'

'I'm deep in work mode,' said Hugh. 'Next time. Here, Amy.' He handed her a folded blanket.

'Thanks so much.'

He gave her a funny little nod and went back inside.

'What a gent,' said Amy.

Catherine looked pleased. 'Best decision I ever made, marrying that man,' she said, putting the second blanket over her knees. 'I'd already been married once, and the first time wasn't so great. So I appreciate Hugh every day. You do when you've been with a bastard like I was with before.'

Amy's chest tightened at those words. 'How long have you been together?' she asked, trying to steer the conversation back to safe ground.

'Seventeen years,' said Catherine. 'I was thirty-four when I met Hugh, and I might as well not have had a love life before that. Nothing of note happened before I met him, d'you know what I mean? It was all just a series of mistakes.'

'I get you,' said Amy, although her love life hadn't been a series of mistakes as much as one massive extended mistake.

'Mam!' The door of the cottage opened again, and

red-haired Ruby, Catherine's daughter, appeared. She was teenage-skinny, completely hipless, in shorts and a purple vest top that clashed with her robin-orange hair. 'Are there any Oreos? Dad says there are none, but you hid some, didn't you?'

'Top of the fridge,' Catherine confirmed.

'Knew it!' Ruby said. She went back inside.

'What age is she again?' Amy asked.

'Fifteen.'

It always gave Amy a jolt to meet girls in their early teens. Their stark youth reminded her painfully of how vulnerable she herself had been at that age.

'She'll be sixteen in September,' said Catherine. 'Crazy! I can hardly believe it.' She took a sip of her drink and changed the subject. 'So, why did you choose to come all the way out here? Really.'

Amy was thrown by the swerve. 'Like I said. Peace and quiet.'

'Mm-hmm,' said Catherine with a knowing look. 'So nothing you're trying to leave behind in Dublin? Not . . . an ex-boyfriend?'

Amy flinched. She couldn't help it.

Catherine looked at her with compassion. 'My first husband was abusive,' she said quietly. 'He rarely got physical, but it was constant psychological torture, never knowing when he was going to kick off. You know?'

Amy nodded. She knew. 'My ex was . . .' she began, then stopped. 'He was . . .' She stopped again.

Suddenly she had an urge to tell Catherine everything; the whole ugly truth. But what would Catherine think of her if she knew?

'We don't have to talk about it if you don't want to,' said Catherine gently.

Tell her, said a voice in Amy's head. *Tell her what happened.* The words trembled on the tip of her tongue . . .

Then Catherine's teenage son stuck his head out the window. 'Mam!' he called. 'The Wi-Fi's cut off and I'm in the middle of a game!'

'Oh, for God's sake,' Catherine muttered to Amy. 'You can't get a moment's peace around here.' She yelled back, 'What do you expect me to do about that, Luke? Turn it off and on again!'

He slammed the window shut, and Amy and Catherine burst out laughing.

The conversation moved on then, while the sun hit the horizon and lit the heavens with shades of apricot and flamingo pink and richest gold. When the sky turned turquoise and the first stars began to glitter, Amy stood to leave.

'D'you want Hugh to give you a lift,' said Catherine, 'or are you all right to drive?'

'I only had one beer,' said Amy.

Catherine, who was on her third whiskey, seemed surprised. 'Goodness, I suppose you did!'

They said their goodbyes, and Amy walked to her car.

She drove back slowly. It was a pleasure driving through Knockcrea at this time. The lights were on in the houses and cottages she passed, and she glimpsed cosy front rooms and people watching TV. Chimneys were silhouetted against the deep green of the evening sky.

As she left the village behind and took the winding, inclined road between fields and low stone walls, her attention snagged on something in the periphery of her vision. She slowed the car and turned her head.

Something was hanging from the road sign.

She braked, pulling in to the side of the road. The sign at the crossroads was a silhouette against the evening sky, arrows pointing in either direction. From one of those arrows something had been hung by a rope. Something that was moving slightly in the breeze.

Amy turned off the engine and got out of the car. Oh no, she thought as she approached the sign. No, no, no . . .

There was no mistaking the shape. Up close, she recognised the ginger fur from the missing-pet poster. The thing hanging from the road sign was Mrs Houlihan's lost cat. The rope was tied to its tail. Its body moved back and forth as the wind picked up. It had been dead a while: she could tell by its rigidity.

As the cat swung, the rope creaked.

'Oh God.' Amy pressed a hand to her mouth. She turned and ran back to her car.

In the rear-view mirror, she caught a final glimpse of the scene: the silhouetted road sign, the teal-coloured sky, and the dead cat creaking back and forth in the breeze.

21

Amy sat on her bed in Sea View, holding her phone in front of her face. It had been less than twenty-four hours since she found the dead cat; it felt like a week. The discovery of Bubbles' corpse had sparked a fresh wave of hysteria in Knockcrea. June had personally called Mrs Houlihan to let her know her cat had been found. Miles looked rather nauseated by the story. Even Liam emerged from his room at the sound of all the excitement. Amy observed his reaction carefully: his shock and disgust seemed real.

Since last night the Carrolls had been relentlessly talking about the incident, and so, once she'd finished her work, Amy had retreated to her room to escape. Now she was on a video call to Sandra and Dave. After finding the cat, she'd resolved to tell them everything – about the graffiti, the tension between Miles and June, the drama with the neighbours – and that's what she had just finished doing.

She watched as Sandra and Dave's pixelated faces became masks of anxiety.

'That thing with the cat,' said Dave, 'that's sick. Whoever did that is really sick.'

'You need to get out of there, Amy,' said Sandra. 'This is the last thing you need. Why didn't you tell us all this was going on?'

'I'm going to leave,' Amy promised her. 'As soon as I find another live-in job.'

There was a short silence, in which the awkward, unhappy fact that Amy could not return to Dublin hung between them.

'Maybe you could stay with us for a few days,' suggested Sandra. 'Lie low. I mean, we have the spare room.'

'*No*,' said Amy. 'No way.'

In her mind's eye, she saw a nightmare vision of flames licking around the sofa in Sandra and Dave's front room, catching the curtains.

Dave said, 'If you keep your head down, and it's only for a few days . . .'

'I'm just not doing it,' said Amy. 'I'm not putting the two of you at risk. End of story.'

When the call ended, she went onto the websites that advertised nannying and housekeeping positions. Despite her exhaustion, her newly urgent desire to get out of Knockcrea blazed through the stasis and inertia she had felt before. She was now able to handle the mental effort of trawling through the ads and writing out applications, energised by that powerful motivator: fear.

She scrolled through a number of ads and dismissed each one for different reasons: four kids under ten sounded like more than she could handle; this position looked promising, but it was live-out; that one opened with a strangely aggressive tone – *We're not looking for someone who's just going to stare at their phone all day!!* – and then went on to mention hourly pay significantly below the going rate. But eventually she found an ad for a position that seemed to meet all her needs.

It was a single-parent family in Limerick. The woman smiling from the accompanying photograph had a bob of dark hair and looked around forty. Her name was Lina. She had one son, nine months old. She worked full-time and wanted a live-in childminder.

There were photos of the bedroom in question. It was far smaller than the luxurious room in which Amy currently slept, but it looked cosy, with clean white walls and a yellow bedspread. A desk by the window overlooked a street of red-brick houses.

It's perfect.

Amy felt a wave of comfort at the thought of being back in the bustle of a city.

Gathering her nerve, she typed out a professional, friendly message to Lina, expressing her interest in the job. After rereading it carefully, she pressed send. Then she put her shoes and coat on and slipped out the back door. She could hear Miles and June talking in the front room, and she didn't want to see them just now. She felt like a traitor applying for other roles, but then again, she hadn't asked for any of this. She hadn't asked for animosity with the locals, for people lurking round the house at night, for murdered household pets.

She went left, in the opposite direction to the crossroads where she'd found the cat's body. She didn't feel particularly jumpy – it was still daylight, and the landscape was so exposed that nobody could possibly sneak up on her – and what little nervousness she did feel was assuaged when she remembered she wouldn't be staying here long.

Her phone buzzed. She took it out to see that Lina had replied.

> **Hi, Amy, thanks for your message. How does tomorrow suit for a chat?**

She wrote back saying that was great. Then she messaged Sandra and Dave.

> **Got a job interview lined up already! I'll be out of here before you know it.**

It was no wonder, given the week she'd had, that Amy slept particularly badly that night. She woke at 1 a.m., and again at 2. She had nightmares in which she heard tapping at the window and opened the blinds to see Mark on the other side of the glass, grinning at her.

When, shortly before 3 a.m., there was a loud bang somewhere in the house, she sat bolt upright with her heart in her throat.

Another bang. It sounded like it was coming from the kitchen.

A thud. A male voice rumbling.

Amy jumped out of bed, completely awake. Without turning on the light, she found the handle of her door and opened it. The house was completely dark. From the kitchen, she heard the clatter of something being knocked over. Then slurred, incoherent mumbling.

She tiptoed down the corridor, feeling her way along the

wall. The kitchen came into view, full of grey moonlight that streamed in through the windows from a semi-clouded sky. In that dim light she saw Miles bumbling around the marble island like a honey-drunk bee. He was talking to himself. As she watched him, he bumped into the island, muttered something, then walked in the other direction and bumped into the fridge.

Was he drunk? High? Sleepwalking?

'Amy,' said a voice behind her.

She nearly jumped out of her skin.

'It's me,' whispered June. She flicked a switch on the wall, and Amy blinked in the sudden light. 'I didn't mean to scare you.'

'I heard noises,' Amy explained, gesturing towards Miles.

'He's had difficulty sleeping lately,' said June in a quiet voice. 'He's been taking tablets for it. If something wakes him when he's on them, he goes into this sleepwalking state.' She let out a long sigh, and rubbed her tired, raw eyes.

Miles was now facing the island, looking bewildered. In his T-shirt and pyjama bottoms, he seemed vulnerable, nothing like the self-assured lawyer he was by day.

Amy couldn't help wondering if he'd done this on purpose. She'd seen that kind of thing before. Mark used to take sleeping tablets, then deliberately stay awake just to feel high. She used to be relieved on those days. Her life was easier when Mark was on downers. They softened his hard edges, made him stupid and slow. When he was drunk, or on cocaine, or sober – that was when she had to be really afraid.

She knew that in the morning Miles would have no recollection of this. She also strongly suspected he had taken more than the recommended dose.

'Is there anything I can do?' she asked June.

'Thanks, but no.' June cringed. 'God, he'll be so embarrassed you saw him like this ...'

'Don't worry,' Amy reassured her. 'I won't mention it to him.'

'You know,' said June, 'Miles isn't the kind of person who *abuses* sleeping tablets. He's not, like, an addict or anything.'

Amy nodded, feeling awkward. 'If you're sure you don't need help, I'm gonna head back to bed.'

'We'll manage,' said June softly.

Amy mouthed goodnight and returned to her room. She lay down in her bed and listened to the sounds of June coaxing an uncooperative Miles up the stairs. It was a lengthy process.

Outside, the wind howled. The image of the dead cat hanging stiffly by its tail flashed through her mind. With a sudden movement, she got out of bed again. She took the wooden chair from the vanity table and jammed it under the door handle. Feeling a little safer, she got back into bed, and this time she slept.

22

Before

After people asked, 'Why didn't you leave?' they would sometimes follow up with: 'But what about Robbie? Didn't you want to get your son out of there?'

It was difficult for Amy to explain that Robbie was one of the main reasons she'd stayed.

Mark used their son against her like a weapon. He said that if Amy ever left him, or went to the guards about his violence, he would convince social services that she was an unfit mother and take Robbie away from her.

'I'll make sure I get full custody.' He would follow her around the house, speaking into her ear. 'They'll believe me over you, you know. You're a stupid cow who can barely string a sentence together. I'm smart. I'm persuasive. People listen to me. I'll say you hit him and starved him. Nobody likes a mother who abuses her kids. Your name will be all over the papers. Who d'you think the court is going to believe?'

He'd follow her up the stairs and into the bedroom while she tried to focus on folding clothes or making the bed.

'And if that doesn't work,' he'd continue, 'if you win in court, I'll throw Robbie in a car and drive off. When he grows up, I'll tell him his mother was an abusive, twisted bitch. I'll tell him you used to hit him until he thinks he can remember it. Believe me, Amy, if you leave me, I'll make it my life's mission to make sure you never see your son again.'

Then he would change tactics and suddenly become plaintive and earnest. 'I'm only saying this because I know we can work it out. I can change. Robbie will be happier with both his parents living in one house, won't he? And Amy' – here he would speak conversationally, gently, reaching out to stroke her hair, her collarbone – 'what if you leave and I lose the head and kill you and kill myself? What'll happen to Robbie then?'

The threat chilled her. She believed he was capable of it. Of killing her and himself and leaving Robbie an orphan. Wasn't it better for him to grow up in this dysfunctional household than with no parents at all?

Amy never reported Mark's violence. Not once. She was terrified of getting social services involved. She was terrified of losing her son. She often wondered: what would happen if they went to court? Was Mark really clever enough to manipulate the judge, to win full custody of Robbie? Did he mean it when he said he'd kidnap Robbie if things didn't go his way?

It wasn't a gamble she was willing to take.

Once Robbie started school, Amy began working as a cleaner in private homes. Mark insisted that she only work cash-in-hand, so as not to interfere with her government allowance, and that she hand all her income over to him each week. 'You've no head for numbers,' he told her. She had to ask for her own money back when she needed to buy milk or tampons, and wait while Mark hummed and hawed about whether they could afford it.

She endured it all. She kept trying to make the environment at home as calm as she possibly could. She kept playing the game of pirouetting on eggshells.

Of course, sometimes she failed. Every now and then, there'd be a crack.

And then the usual. Name-calling. Violence. On one occasion, when it was just the two of them in the house, Mark forced her into the wardrobe, locked it and then went out. Amy was trapped in the narrow dark space for over an hour, not knowing when he would come home. She had nightmares about that for a long time afterwards.

'You realise none of this is normal, right?' Sandra said, on one of the countless occasions she tried to convince Amy to leave. 'Normal people don't get locked in the wardrobe by their boyfriend. Why do you let him treat you like this?'

In Amy's beleaguered mind, 'none of this is normal' translated to 'there's something wrong with *you*'. And she already knew there was something wrong with her. Mark told her that every day. When Sandra and Dave became frustrated with her, their words echoed in her head until they became interchangeable with Mark's – a barrage of criticism.

Why do you let him treat you like this, Amy? What is wrong with you? Are you stupid? You cow, you bitch, you bad mother. You bring all this on yourself, you know that, don't you? Your fault. Your fault. Your fault.

*

Even when things were at their worst, Mark could be intermittently sweet and kind. His bursts of affection always gave Amy hope. Hope that he was about to turn a corner. Hope that things were about to change.

Hope could be deceptive.

Every good moment they shared, like a family day out at a carnival, filled her with fresh optimism. A belief that her family was worth fighting for. That if Mark could just get his problems under control, they could be like that all the time.

But when Robbie was five, something happened that changed her mind.

It was a sunny morning. Amy was at the cooker, making beans and sausages. Robbie was at the kitchen table, fidgeting, impatient for his food. Mark was upstairs, sleeping off a heavy night at the pub.

'Ma, can I have a strawberry yoghurt?' Robbie asked.

'Not until you've had your proper breakfast,' said Amy.

Robbie asked again for a strawberry yoghurt. Amy told him no, more firmly this time. And in response, Robbie called her a bitch.

'Bitch.' He said it without anger, as if he was trying the word out. 'You are a bitch, Ma.'

Amy stood still, the sausages sizzling in the pan in front of her. He could barely pronounce the word. His five-year-old teeth and tongue stumbled over the *tch*.

'What did you call me?' she asked him.

Robbie began to squirm. 'Daddy says it.'

Amy was speechless. What was she supposed to tell him? We don't use words like that in this house? A high, manic laugh suddenly escaped her.

'Ma,' said Robbie, 'can I have a yoghurt, *please?*'

She gave it to him. He spooned the pink gloop into his mouth, smearing a generous quantity on his cheeks. Amy stared at him, at his straw-blonde hair and cherub-blue eyes and innocent yoghurt-covered face.

There had to be a way she could get them both out.

23

Now

Amy's phone call with Lina, single parent of a nine-month-old boy, went extremely well. She went for a walk while she took the call, and she and Lina spoke for almost half an hour. Her potential new employer seemed particularly pleased that Amy wanted somewhere to settle down for a while. They arranged for her to visit Lina and her son, Pádraig, on Saturday. Lina told her there was no real need to come to Limerick in person – it was a long drive, she said, and they could chat over Zoom instead. But Amy, after her experiences at Sea View, preferred the idea of visiting before deciding to move there. She assured Lina the drive was no problem.

'So why are you leaving your current job?' Lina asked before she hung up.

Images raced each other through Amy's mind. Red letters scrawled on a stone wall. Miles's grey eyes following her around the room. The dead cat swinging from the rope.

'It's complicated,' she said. 'Things weren't exactly as I had been led to believe when I took the role.' (Wasn't that the truth.) 'I don't want to bad-mouth my current employers or anything, but . . . I can explain in more detail when we meet.'

'Okay,' said Lina, obviously curious. She told Amy again how lovely it had been to talk to her, then hung up.

Amy walked back to Sea View with a feeling of optimism. It was a grey, soft day, and low clouds wrapped around the mountain ridges in swirls of mist. She would miss this view. And she'd miss Tom and Poppy. They *were* pretty cute. But overall, she was delighted at the prospect of getting out of here.

Mood lifted, she put her earphones in to listen to some upbeat pop music. Humming along to Ellie Goulding, she turned the key in the front door and let herself into the house. It was only when she stepped inside that she realised she'd walked in on a blazing row.

Liam was standing in the middle of the living room, legs planted wide apart in a fighting stance. Miles stood several feet away, hands spread as if in a plea for rationality. June was in the corner, tearful, Tom and Poppy clinging to her legs. She was the only person who noticed Amy walk in.

Amy pulled her earphones out.

'. . . absolute *bollocks*!' Liam was shouting at his father. 'That's just an excuse!'

'You don't understand, because of your age!' He didn't sound as angry as his son, but even at baseline Miles was louder and more truculent than the average person. 'When you're older, you'll see that—'

'Stop fucking patronising me!' Liam roared.

Amy stood frozen on the threshold.

'Guys,' said June in a trembling voice, looking at Amy, 'can we *not* . . .'

At the same moment, Miles became aware of Amy's presence. He cleared his throat and smoothed his shirt.

'Well,' he said. 'Let's finish this discussion at another time, shall we?'

Liam shot Amy a look. Then he looked at his father. 'Why?' he said. 'D'you not want Amy to know what a bastard you are?'

June flinched. Poppy was wailing now. Amy began to make her way around the kitchen, on the far side of the island, giving the family as wide a berth as possible. 'I'll just . . . go to my room,' she mumbled.

'Amy, I apologise,' said Miles, turning to address her. She stopped walking. 'Emotions have been running high around here today, and this is just a bit of a fuss over nothing.'

'A fuss over *nothing*?' Liam's expression was incredulous. 'You *prick*!'

'Liam, that's ENOUGH!' Miles was turning an impressive purple. Amy had never known a person whose emotions triggered such vivid colour changes. 'Get yourself under control! We can continue this discussion at a—'

'Mam told me what you did!' Liam shouted. 'She told me the truth! And you haven't changed – you're the exact fucking same!'

Miles's whole body jerked, as if from a physical blow. The colour drained from his face. 'What did she tell you?' he asked, in a completely different voice.

'She told me everything! *Everything!* She's not going to lie to protect you any more!' Liam broke off, breathing heavily, eyes shining with adolescent recklessness. It was clear he had dropped the biggest bomb at his disposal, one he had perhaps been holding on to for a while.

Miles seemed paralysed. Behind him, June's expression was stricken, but not surprised. Whatever it was that Miles had done, she already knew about it.

'Liam,' said Miles. 'Liam, please.'

What he was pleading for, Amy didn't know.

His son glared at him, unmoved.

The moment stretched out like elastic. Nobody spoke. Tom and Poppy's wailing was the only sound.

There was a loud *bang bang bang bang BANG* at the front door.

Amy jumped so violently she knocked over the nearest tall chair.

Miles said 'Je-SUS! Who the hell is that?' He turned and stormed towards the door.

Amy craned her neck. Through the glass, she could see two burly men.

'Who is it?' Liam asked. He looked suddenly scared. 'Is that . . .?'

June said sharply, 'Tom, Poppy, playroom! *Now!*' Both children resisted, but June swept them into the playroom and shut the door. 'Stay in there!' she ordered them. 'Liam, come over here!'

Miles waited until Liam had backed away to the far side of the room. Then he opened the front door.

'Yes?' he said tersely to the men outside. 'What do you want?'

Amy edged closer. The two men were fiftyish, broad and burly, with the raw, reddened faces of people who spent more time in the sun than their Irish complexions could tolerate.

One was balding; the other wore a flat cap. They were so alike, it was obvious at first glance that they were brothers.

'We want to have a word with your son,' said the man with the cap.

'You can forget it,' Miles said immediately. 'I've told you both already: Liam had nothing to do with your mother's money going missing.'

Eileen's sons, Amy thought.

'Oh yeah?' said the man with the cap. 'Why don't we see what Liam has to say about it?'

The second brother unfolded his meaty arms and took a step closer.

'Liam,' said June, very quietly, '*go upstairs.*'

Liam didn't move. His eyes were fixed on his father.

'You're not getting anywhere near my son, Barry.' Miles addressed the man in the cap. 'I'm just not going to allow that.'

'Look, Miles,' said Barry conversationally, 'you're an awful prick at the best of times. But this is taking the piss, even for you. That little bollocks stole our mam's money, and he's going to answer for it.'

'My son doesn't have to answer to *you*,' said Miles. 'And if you attempt to force your way into my house, you're guaranteed I'll be pressing charges.'

'Ooh, you'll be *pressing charges*, will you?' said Barry, in an exaggerated mockery of Miles's accent. He grinned at his brother. 'Did you hear that, Seamus? We'd better be careful.'

Both men sniggered.

June was inching closer. Her expression screamed, *Goddammit, Miles, close the door!*

Miles tried to do just that. But Barry stuck a foot in the

way. 'Sorry, Miles,' he said. 'You're not getting rid of us that easily.'

And he tried to shoulder his way in.

Miles threw his weight against him. Barry stepped back, raised a massive arm and punched Miles in the face. Miles landed on the ground. Blood trickled from one nostril.

In the background, Liam looked stricken.

'Right,' said Barry, stepping forward purposefully.

A heavy wooden object slammed into his balls.

It was wielded by June. She had crept forward, picked up the wooden statue by the door and swung it with perfect timing and considerable force. Her aim was excellent.

Barry grabbed his crotch and doubled over with a roar of pain. Behind him, Seamus's jaw dropped. Miles, on the floor, gawped at his wife.

June shoved the incapacitated Barry back over the threshold, where he collided with his brother. Then she slammed the door, turned the key, and ran to Miles's side.

'Honey, are you okay?'

'Should we call the police?' asked Liam, his voice trembling.

'No need,' said Amy quickly. 'Look. They're leaving.'

'Liam,' Miles coughed. He wiped blood from his nose and looked past June, towards his son. 'Liam . . .'

Liam, who seemed on the verge of tears, hurried to his father's side. Together, he and June helped Miles to his feet.

Outside, the growl of an engine sounded as Eileen's sons drove away.

24

Early Saturday morning, when the grass was still wet with dew, Amy set off to Limerick to meet Lina. The sun hadn't yet risen high enough to shine over the mountain ridge, so Knockcrea was still in shadow, although the sky was dawn blue. She took a road between two peaks, onto the other side of the peninsula, so that she could begin her journey in the sunlight. She had told Miles and June she was going to Cork for the day, and felt guilty when June recommended some coffee shops and told her enthusiastically that she was going to love it.

As she drove, she reflected on the incident with Eileen's sons. She had been relieved when Miles didn't call the police, for her own reasons – but she had also been surprised. Miles had made a lot of noise to Barry and Seamus about reporting them. Why hadn't he followed through? Amy's best guess was that Miles didn't want to involve the guards in the situation when Liam had been accused of stealing. Maybe, despite his impassioned defence of his son, he still suspected that he was guilty.

Or maybe Miles had something else to hide.

It was a long drive to Limerick. Amy stopped in a town called Kenmare for breakfast, where she ate omelette on buttered toast and drank sugary tea in a café with plush seats and floral decor. Having eaten, used the toilet and stretched her legs, she drove on. The day was becoming increasingly sunny and warm.

She arrived in Limerick half an hour before she was due to meet Lina, and looked around curiously as she drove through the streets. She had never been to Limerick before. The truth was, in her previous life, Amy had barely left Dublin.

The address Lina had given her was quite central. A tall house on a residential street. Three doorbells signified that the building had been broken into as many apartments.

Lina opened the door with a huge smile. 'Amy, right? Come on in!'

Like June, Lina had the gleaming perfect teeth of someone who could afford the very best orthodontist work. She wore jeans and a well-cut white shirt. Her dark hair was a stylish bob. The only jewellery she wore was an understated gold necklace.

As she led Amy up the stairs to her second-floor apart-ment, she chatted away. 'How was your journey? Thanks *so* much for coming all this way. You didn't have to, but it's great to meet you in person . . .'

Amy liked her instantly.

Baby Pádraig was down for his nap, Lina explained. She gave Amy a short tour of the apartment. It was bright and cheerful and spacious.

'Can I get you a coffee?' she offered as Amy circled the bedroom that would be hers. The room was clean and cheerful, with freshly painted walls and a wooden desk by the window.

'That'd be great, thanks.'

They returned to the kitchen, where Lina made coffee, then they sat down at the table to discuss the role.

'I work Monday to Friday, nine to five,' said Lina, 'so it *is* long hours for you. But the office is only fifteen minutes from here, and I'm home at five fifteen every day on the dot. So the evenings and the weekends are yours. If I need a babysitter, I'll offer you first refusal on the hours, but if you don't want them, that's fine! And I know you're strong on housekeeping, but I'm not looking for a cleaner. This is a nannying job. Your only cleaning duties would be those relating to the baby.'

She talked a little about Pádraig, his likes and dislikes and routines. Lina's face lit up when she spoke about her son. When they'd covered the basics of the role, she said, 'You're probably wondering why it's just me and Pádraig. Most people ask me outright: "And where's his dad?"'

Amy knew too much about tangled family dynamics to ever ask why someone was a single parent. 'I understand if you don't want to tell me.'

'Oh no, I don't mind! I tell everyone,' Lina said cheerfully. 'I had him by myself. I went down the sperm donation route. I was forty and extremely single, and I just thought: fuck it. If I want a baby, maybe I'll have to go it alone. I got pregnant first try. I was very lucky. He's perfect. I couldn't be happier.'

'Wow.' Amy had never met anyone who'd had a baby by sperm donation before. 'That's very brave. Congratulations.'

'Obviously, it means I need full-time help,' said Lina,

'but that's true of loads of families where both parents work full-time, isn't it?'

In the next room, a baby's voice rose and fell on a sleepy wail. Lina's eyes lit up.

'You'll get to meet him now,' she said, getting to her feet.

Pádraig was brown-haired, blue-eyed and gorgeous. Amy held him and bounced him, and he gurgled happily. 'Oh my God, he's lovely,' she said.

'That's certainly what I think.' Lina grinned. 'But I'm biased.'

By the end of the afternoon, Amy was certain she wanted the job. She liked Lina. She liked the apartment. She was already halfway in love with baby Pádraig.

And the place seemed refreshingly, wonderfully normal.

'So,' Lina asked her, towards the end of the visit, 'why is it you want to leave your current job?'

Amy took a deep breath. 'Well,' she said. 'It's a number of things really . . .'

She had been planning to give a sanitised version, but suddenly she found herself spilling out the whole story. The drama with the neighbours. Liam. Even the dead cat. Lina was fascinated and appalled at the same time.

'I can't believe this,' she said. 'Who do you think is behind the creepy messages?'

'I don't know,' said Amy. 'But I think whoever it is wants to frighten people.'

'Well, I'm afraid you're going to find things fairly dull around here. Our neighbours are lovely. And seeing as Pádraig can't walk yet, I doubt he'll be sneaking out to terrorise the neighbourhood any time soon.'

Amy smiled. 'No secret family members?'

'None, I promise you.'

'I'll need to give June and Miles time to find a new nanny,' said Amy. 'What kind of start date were you looking at?'

'How's two weeks from Monday?' asked Lina.

'Perfect,' Amy said.

Two weeks wasn't long at all. Surely she could survive two more weeks in Knockcrea.

Back at Sea View, Miles and June were in good spirits. They greeted Amy warmly, asking how she'd enjoyed her day in Cork. Amy felt bad about lying. She knew she had to tell them she was leaving soon, but she didn't feel equal to the task just yet.

Liam was out of his room – a rare sight – and eating an oven pizza at the island, wearing grey tracksuit bottoms and no T-shirt. June seemed vaguely offended, but whether it was by Liam's bare torso or the processed food, Amy couldn't tell. Tom and Poppy, who were fascinated by their older brother and found it wildly exciting any time he emerged from his room, were watching him as if he were a creature in a zoo and firing non-stop questions at him.

'Liam, why is your hair black but my hair is blonde?' asked Tom.

'Dunno. Genetics, I s'pose.'

'What's g . . . g . . .' Tom faltered. 'What's getics?'

'Science,' said Liam.

'Can I've some that?' said Poppy, pointing at the pizza.

'No, sweetheart, that's not good food!' said June.

'Sure,' said Liam, tearing off two pieces and handing one to Poppy and one to Tom. They each grabbed their prize with both hands and began tearing into it wolfishly. Liam looked amused.

'Want some, Amy?' he asked, catching her eye.

'Nah, I'm all right, thanks,' said Amy, ruffling Tom and Poppy's fair heads.

'We had proper dinner earlier,' said June, with just the faintest emphasis on the word 'proper'. 'Home-made risotto. There's plenty in the fridge if you want some, Amy.'

'Thanks,' said Amy. She experienced another twang of guilt, like the sharp snap of an elastic band.

Miles, in the kitchen, opened a bottle of red wine. He poured a glass for himself and one for June.

'D'you want a glass, Amy?' he offered.

'Oh – no, thank you,' she said. Why did everyone keep offering her things?

'I'd like a glass, Dad,' said Liam.

'You can forget it,' said Miles immediately. 'I still haven't forgiven you for stealing my vodka and replacing it with water. What a thing to do to a man!' His voice bubbled with laughter. 'You see, Amy,' he went on, addressing the next part of the story to her, 'I had guests over, and after dinner, I went to make them cocktails. I make a mean cocktail, if I say so myself. But d'you know how these cocktails tasted? Weak. Watery. Disgusting.' He shook his head. 'Then I took a sip from the vodka bottle and I knew why.'

Liam grinned. 'I didn't think I'd watered it down enough for you to notice.'

'It was twenty per cent vodka, *max*,' said Miles, with dramatic flair. 'In ten months, you'll be able to buy your own alcohol. Until then, just stay away from mine, I beg of you.'

Even June was laughing. The attack from Eileen's sons seemed to have bonded the Carrolls. Miles's face was still bruised, but Amy had never seen them all enjoying each other's company like this. She kissed Tom and Poppy goodnight and took her portion of risotto to her room, not wanting to intrude on the family moment. As she closed her bedroom door, the sound of their laughter floated down the corridor.

25

Before

Even thinking about leaving felt dangerous. Like Mark might peer into her brain and see her treacherous thoughts. Amy tried not to think about it when he was around.

But when she was alone, the idea would return to her.

She began to consider the logistics. What to pack. When to leave. Waiting until Mark was at the pub seemed like the best option . . .

Yet the thought of actually executing these plans made her feel sick.

The first time she called Women's Aid, she hung up before anyone could answer. The second time, she called from a local park. There was nobody around to overhear, but she felt a nervy tension and a need to urinate. If Mark found out, he might kill her. She knew that. He might actually kill her. But the woman on the other end of the phone was understanding, and kind, and a chain of events was set in motion.

It was through Women's Aid that Amy was introduced to

her support worker: blonde, gentle, unshockable Karen. She would meet Karen while Mark thought she was in work, and lie about her hourly rate to explain why she was gone for so long.

In a clean, white-painted room with a fake houseplant in the corner and a box of tissues on the desk, Karen sat across from Amy and used phrases like 'trauma bonding' and 'cycles of abuse'. Clinical, dispassionate terminology that countered the myth that Amy and Mark were unique, they were *special*. From Karen's perspective, they were textbook.

It was Karen who brought up the possibility of Robbie and Amy staying in a shelter. It was Karen who first used the words 'exit plan'.

Amy put it off for many, many months. The fear was too intense. The stakes were too high. But bit by bit, the path was laid out in front of her. Karen helped her with each step.

Until finally, after almost a year of planning, the day came. It was time.

Robbie's clothes were washed and folded in the wardrobe. Amy's toiletries were lined up on the bathroom shelf, ready to be swept into a bag with one movement of her arm. She would be packed within minutes. The only sign that anything was different was that the house looked a little neater than usual.

Mark wouldn't notice that, surely?

Robbie was playing on the kitchen floor, blonde head bowed over the new Lego set Sandra and Dave had bought him. Mark was on the sofa in the front room, watching the horseracing and drinking a can of beer. The house was quiet.

Amy mentally ran through her plan for the hundredth time. At around 5 p.m., Mark would leave the house and wander down to the strip of shops with the bookies and the pub, where he would stay all night. Amy would wait for half an hour, giving him a chance to settle in. At 5.30, she would pack at super-swift speed. She would put their bags in the boot of the car, strap Robbie in the back and drive away. They'd be gone in minutes.

She hadn't told anyone what she was doing, not even Sandra and Dave. She was afraid that saying it aloud might jinx it. When Sandra had asked her yesterday why she was so pale, she'd claimed she was coming down with the flu.

Feeling a need to be in motion, she began tidying the kitchen. While washing the dishes, she looked down at the soapy suds on her hands and thought how strange this was. To wash and dry her mugs and plates, knowing that she would never use them again.

The front door slammed. Amy jumped.

Had Mark gone out? It was only three o'clock.

She ran to the window and saw him disappearing down the street. Was he going to the pub early? Or was he running some errand and planning to come back?

The swell of anxiety was so great that she could barely think. Should she take this opportunity to leave? Or wait until the time she'd originally planned?

If Mark came home when she was loading the car . . . Amy flinched at the thought. Safest to wait a couple of hours until she was sure he was settled in at the pub.

The next two hours were a kind of nightmare. She paced the house, mentally running over every step again and again: each item she would pack, the route she would drive to the shelter. She made Robbie cheese on toast and let him watch

TV, forcing herself to act natural. Every few minutes she stood up and walked to the window to check if Mark was approaching. The clock crawled.

Finally, half five arrived.

Amy looked out the window. The street was quiet.

Now.

'Robbie!' She began to move. 'Robbie, put your shoes on. We're going for a drive.'

'Where're we going?'

'Put your shoes on! No time to explain!'

Her body was pumping adrenaline as she ran first into her bedroom, then into Robbie's, tossing clothes and shoes and books into the large reusable shopping bags she had stashed for this purpose (travel bags of any kind would have attracted attention). She hurried down the stairs, a full bag in each hand. Robbie was standing in the hall, looking confused, still wearing no shoes.

'But I'm watching TV,' he said.

'Shoes on! *Now!*'

Amy hurried out to the front garden. She threw the bags in the boot, looking up and down the street as she did so. She slammed the boot shut.

It was now officially too late to turn back. If a neighbour had seen her doing this ... if word got back to Mark that his wife had been seen packing the car ... *'Amy going somewhere, Mark?'*

'Robbie, get in the car!' Amy shouted as she ran back into the house. *'Get in the car!'*

She raced back up the stairs and into the bathroom, sweeping the toiletries from their neat row into the bag. She heard a small noise behind her and turned.

Robbie was in the doorway. His blue eyes were sharp. 'Why are we going in the car?'

'Robbie, I don't have time to argue.' Amy leaned down to eye level and gripped him by the arm. 'I need you to do as you're—'

Downstairs, she heard a click that sounded a lot like a key in the front door.

She froze. Her grip on Robbie's arm tightened involuntarily.

'Ma, you're hurting—'

'*Sssh!*'

Amy stayed completely still, her senses straining. For a long moment, there was silence, and she thought she'd been mistaken.

Then she heard the sound of the front door opening.

She raised one finger to her lips, warning Robbie not to say a word. Downstairs, footsteps crossed the hall. The kitchen door opened.

A male voice called, 'Amy?'

Amy exhaled.

It was Dave.

'Come on! Quick!' Grabbing Robbie by the hand, she hurried down the stairs. Dave walked back into the hall at the sound of their footsteps.

'There yous are!' said Dave. 'How're you doing, Amy? Sandra gave me the spare keys and asked me to drop this over for you. She said you weren't feeling well.'

In Dave's arms was a basket containing painkillers, chocolate, lemon drops and a hot-water bottle. He held it out towards her. Then he noticed her hunted expression. His face dropped.

'What's wrong?' he asked, in a very different voice.

Amy caught a glimpse of her reflection in the hall mirror. She looked wild-eyed.

'We're leaving,' she said. 'Right now. Dave, help me get these things in the car.'

'Where's Mark?'

'At the pub.'

Dave understood. Moving quickly, he wedged the care package under one arm and took a bag from Amy. 'Let's go, little buddy,' he said, steering Robbie out the front door.

Amy did a last circle of the house, running through a mental inventory. Then she ran out to the front garden. Robbie was in the back of the car, strapped in. Dave was standing vigil, watching the street.

It had been less than ten minutes since she started packing. It felt like years.

'No sign of him,' said Dave. 'Amy, can you tell me where you're going?'

'I can't,' she said, jumping into the car. 'The address is supposed to be kept secret.'

'Go,' he said. 'Don't waste any time. Text me and Sandra when you're settled and safe.'

Amy nodded. Without wasting another second, she reversed out of the driveway and sped away.

As the car began to pick up speed, Robbie asked from the backseat, 'Ma, where're we going?'

As brightly as she could, Amy said, 'We're going to stay somewhere new for a few days. Just me and you!'

'Oh,' said Robbie. Then, 'What about Da?'

'He's not coming,' Amy said. She tried not to think about the things Mark used to whisper in her ear.

If you run, I'll follow you.
No matter where you go, I'll find you.
You're not getting out of this alive, Amy.
I'll never let you go.

26

Now

Amy woke early in her queen-sized bed in Sea View. Stress did this to her. She would open her eyes at sunrise, fully awake, with no chance of getting back to sleep.

'Fuck's sake,' she muttered, swinging her legs out of bed.

In her pyjama bottoms and vest, she padded down the corridor to the kitchen and living area. In the pale morning light, the sleek furniture and quiet rooms looked particularly idyllic, like a painting. On the other side of the floor-to-ceiling glass, the sky was baby pink and softly clouded.

She went to the sink and filled a glass of water. She drank it on the spot, refilled it, and had turned to carry it back to her room when she noticed the white square of paper on the mat inside the front door. It was too early for the postman to have been here, and it was a loose piece of paper rather than an envelope.

Amy put her glass of water on the island. She walked over, crouched down and read the message on the note.

if yOU knew WHAT yOuR sOn WAS reaLLY like
You WOuLdN't DeFeND him

The words had been made from letters cut from newspapers. Like something from the Enid Blyton books she used to read as a kid.

She straightened up, looking out at the driveway, the rolling fields and the distant sea. All was quiet under the shell-pink sky. The morning had that undisturbed feeling, as if no human being had interrupted nature yet.

Should she wake Miles and June? She deliberated briefly, then decided to leave the note where she'd found it. Let them come across it themselves.

She turned around and gasped aloud, hand flying to her chest. 'Jesus! You scared me!'

Liam was standing there, in grey tracksuit bottoms and a white Nike T-shirt, looking younger than his seventeen years.

'Sorry,' he yawned, rubbing his eyes with his knuckles.

'Why are you up so early?' Amy asked him.

He shrugged. 'Haven't slept. What were you looking at?'

'Nothing,' said Amy, too quickly.

Liam wasn't fooled. He walked past her and picked up the note. He read it, and his face crumpled.

'What's this? Who sent it?' He was instantly agitated. 'What do they mean, what I'm really like?'

'You don't know what they're talking about?' she asked.

'No! I haven't a clue what this is about.' To her surprise, Liam looked like he might cry. 'I'm sick of all this. What does everyone have against me? I haven't done anything.'

'I'm going to wake your dad and June,' Amy said.

*

Miles and June joined Amy and Liam in the kitchen.

'It's the bloody O'Reilly brothers,' Miles said. 'Eileen's sons. Well, if they think they can intimidate me, they have another think coming.'

He balled up the anonymous note and tossed it across the room.

June hovered to the side. She wore a satin nightdress, and her blonde hair was an unbrushed cloud. She was chewing on her lip.

'I don't know, Miles,' she said slowly. 'The O'Reilly brothers . . . aren't they more the "say it to your face" type? They probably think anonymous notes are for sissies and women.'

'Fair point,' said Miles.

Liam seemed genuinely distressed. 'You think there's someone else out there who hates me this much? Who?'

'Well, who else have you pissed off?' asked Miles. 'What else have you done, aside from stealing Mrs O'Reilly's money?'

Liam looked as though his father had hit him. 'I thought you believed me! I thought you were on my side.'

Miles took a deep breath, chest swelling up.

'Honey,' June warned, but he ignored her.

'If you're not behind all this nonsense,' he exploded at his son, 'who is? You're the only teenage boy in the village—'

'Who says it's a teenage boy?' said Liam indignantly. 'And I'm not – Luke is thirteen!'

Amy didn't really see Catherine's son, video-game-playing Luke, as the delinquent type.

'It could be Sean Geraghty,' Liam continued. 'That weirdo, living alone on his farm, can't look people in the eye . . . what about him?'

'Sean Geraghty's car windows were broken,' Miles scoffed. 'You're saying he smashed up his own car?'

'Maybe!' Liam was shouting now. 'Maybe he's crazy! Who knows? All I know is *I didn't do it.*'

In that instant, Amy believed him. She saw something in Liam's eyes – a shining sense of outrage at the injustice of the world – that convinced her he was telling the truth.

Unfortunately, his father didn't feel the same way.

'So you have no idea what this note is referring to then?' Miles said, openly incredulous.

'*No.*'

Liam held Miles's gaze steadily. The moment stretched out until the tension was palpable . . . then June broke it. She picked up the note and smoothed it out. 'We should keep it,' she said. 'If this keeps happening, we'll go to the police, and we'll need evidence.'

Miles nodded. Liam was still glaring at him.

'I'm going back to bed,' Amy said.

'Same,' said Liam, scowling. He loped off. Miles sat down. June put the kettle on. Amy picked up her glass of water and escaped to her room. Liam's indignant words echoed in her head. *I haven't done anything.*

Amy was convinced he was telling the truth.

Either that, or he was an excellent actor.

27

In a way, the anonymous note was beneficial. It made it easier for Amy to explain to Miles and June why she was leaving.

'I'm really sorry,' she told them, reciting the lines she had prepared. 'I just don't feel comfortable here under the circumstances. I have to move on.'

June looked absolutely devastated. 'Well, gosh – that's quite a shock. I mean, obviously it's your decision, but if there's anything we could do to make you feel more comfortable, say the word!'

Miles said nothing. He sat, knees far apart, hands clasped over his belly, observing Amy with a contemplative expression.

'I'm not going to change my mind,' Amy said. 'I'm sorry. I'm handing in my two weeks' notice today.'

'Well, we're sorry to lose you,' said June. 'Aren't we, honey?'

Miles looked straight at Amy as he said, 'We sure are.' There was a faintly mocking edge to his voice, as if there was a private joke only he was in on.

'Thanks for being so understanding,' Amy said to June. She did her best to ignore Miles.

'No problem,' June said.

That night, at 2 a.m., Amy was woken by the faint sound of sobbing. She swung her legs out of bed, tiptoed across her room and opened the door.

The open-plan area was deserted, lit only by the pale moon outside. She followed the sound to the door of June's office. There was a light on inside.

'Hello?' She knocked.

'Amy?' June's voice sounded thick and strange.

Amy opened the door.

The flamingo lamp filled the office with a soft pink light. June was sitting at the desk in her dressing gown.

'Did I wake you?' she whispered. 'I thought no one would hear me.'

'I'm a light sleeper,' Amy said.

'You mustn't think this is because of you,' June said quickly, dabbing under her eyes with her sleeve. 'I mean, obviously rehiring is something else to deal with, but that's not what I'm so upset about. It's just . . . everything.'

There was a box of tissues on the desk. June took one and blew her nose. She let out a long sigh, then looked at Amy with a speculative expression.

'D'you fancy a glass of wine?' she said.

'What? Now?'

June raised one shoulder in a shrug. There was a look in

her eye Amy had never seen there, a glint of mischief. 'Yeah, now,' she said. 'Why not? Fuck it.'

Amy had never heard her swear before. 'Yeah, all right,' she replied.

'Back in two minutes,' said June, and she slipped out to the kitchen.

Amy looked around the room. She had been in here before, cleaning, but it felt different being here late at night. Conspiratorial. She picked up the decorative pineapple that doubled as a jar and unscrewed the lid. Inside were a collection of pens, some hair clips and a white tube of pills. She recognised the brand name: sleeping tablets, strong ones. The label had June's name on it. So Miles wasn't the only one having trouble getting to sleep. Amy felt a wave of empathy. It seemed there were plenty of cracks in the perfect mask June presented to the world. Hearing footsteps, she screwed the lid back on the pineapple and replaced it quickly.

Soon she and June were settled with a glass of red each; June cross-legged on the office chair, Amy reclining on the beanbag.

'Look, I don't believe Liam stole money from an old woman,' said June. 'Or smashed the windows on Sean Geraghty's car.'

'I agree. It doesn't seem like his MO,' said Amy. 'So who do you think is behind it?'

'That's the thing,' said June. 'I have no idea.'

She took a large slug of wine. Amy took a small sip.

'I thought there was someone else Miles suspected?' Amy said.

'Well, for a while he suspected Martin Doyle,' said June, rolling her eyes. 'But that's ridiculous. Martin's an unpleasant, fanatical little man, but I don't think he's been running around Knockcrea smashing people's windows and slashing their tyres.'

'What about Sean Geraghty?'

June shook her head. 'Have you met Sean? He's harmless.'

Amy watched as June topped up her wine. Glass in hand, legs crossed, she looked elegant even in her dressing gown.

'Can I ask you something?' Amy said. 'If it's too intrusive, you can tell me to mind my own business.'

June looked at her curiously. 'Sure,' she said. 'Shoot.'

'What did Liam mean when he said to Miles, "Mam told me what you did"?'

There was a pause. June pressed her lips together. Amy's stomach gave an uncomfortable lurch. Had she overstepped?

'You know what,' she said, 'never mind . . .'

'No, I'll tell you,' said June. 'It's not a big secret or anything. But Miles is ashamed of it, and Liam wasn't ever supposed to find out.'

Amy leaned forward, listening intently.

'Evvie – Liam's mother – Miles barely knew her. They met in a bar. It was a brief fling. It meant nothing. When she ended up pregnant . . . well.' June faltered. 'Don't judge Miles on this. He's deeply sorry. He's spent years making up for it. But at first he wanted nothing to do with the baby. He didn't meet Liam until he was three.'

Amy's jaw dropped. 'So he dumped her when she got pregnant?'

'I know it's terrible,' said June quickly. 'But he was young, and he regrets it.'

Young? Amy thought. Miles would have been in his thirties at the time.

'Then one of Miles's friends had a baby,' June went on. 'Seeing him with his son made Miles realise . . . Anyway. He paid all the backdated child support he owed Evvie. Turned up like clockwork every second weekend. Seeing as Liam was too young to remember a time when his dad wasn't around, Evvie agreed to never mention it to him. Much better to let him believe Miles had always been there, don't you think?' Without waiting for an answer, June continued. 'I don't know why Evvie would tell him now. What's she playing at?'

'Maybe Liam asked her directly and she didn't want to lie,' Amy suggested.

'I don't want you to think badly of Miles,' June said. 'He's made up for his mistake. You've seen him with Tom and Poppy. He's a fantastic father.'

'Sure,' said Amy, although she privately thought it must be hurtful to Liam, rather than healing, to see how Miles fussed over Tom and Poppy.

'He pays for Liam's private school. Evvie could never afford it on her own. Liam was expelled from his last school, so it's hard to find a decent school that'll take him.'

'Mm-hmm,' said Amy, nodding along. Why was June so determined to convince her that Miles deserved a Dad of the Year award?

'Top-up?' June asked, pouring herself more wine.

'No, thanks.' Amy settled deeper into the beanbag. This conversation brought back something June had said before. As casually as she could, she asked, 'What did Liam do to get expelled from his last school?'

June paused with her glass halfway to her lips.

'If Miles found out I'd told you that, he'd . . .'

'I won't say a word.'

June hesitated a moment longer.

'It was a prank that went wrong,' she said. 'There was a group of kids involved. They locked a girl in the changing rooms. They knew she had claustrophobia. The sports building is out behind the school, so she was screaming and screaming, but nobody could hear her . . .'

'Jesus,' said Amy.

'It was very traumatic for her. Her parents raised hell, naturally, and the ringleaders were expelled.' June let out a long sigh, drank some wine and then changed the subject abruptly. 'So, you're really leaving us?'

Amy nodded. 'I'm really leaving. I'm sorry if that makes things difficult.'

'It is what it is,' said June, punctuating her words with a wave of her wine glass. 'I can't tell you what the past few months have been like, truthfully. With Francisca leaving so soon after Georgia . . .'

'Did they give you their reasons for handing in their notice?'

June looked at her sharply. She suddenly seemed less tipsy. 'Why? What did you hear?'

'Nothing. I was just wondering.'

'Francisca had to go back to Brazil. Her mother was sick. But Georgia . . .' June trailed off, then shrugged. 'I suppose it can't do any harm to tell you now.'

Amy waited.

June took a mouthful of wine, then continued. 'Georgia got it into her head that Sea View was haunted. She told me that she fell asleep with the blinds open one night and woke up to see a figure standing outside her window. Another time, she woke Miles and I in the middle of the night and she was absolutely hysterical. She said the ghost had gotten into her room.'

'There was someone in her room?'

'Well, that's what she thought she saw,' said June. 'A figure at the end of her bed.'

Amy shivered.

'See?' said June. 'This is why I didn't tell you! The whole thing was ridiculous. Georgia was superstitious.'

'And you're sure Miles was in bed with you at the time?' Amy spoke without thinking.

'Yes, I'm sure,' said June icily. 'Why? What are you suggesting?'

The sudden frost in the room would have turned a thermometer blue.

'I only meant ...' Amy scrambled for an inoffensive answer, 'you know, that Miles sleepwalks. I wondered if he might have wandered into her room by mistake, that's all.'

But what Amy had actually wondered hung in the air between them, turning the office wintry. The cosy, conspiratorial mood was shattered. Awkwardly Amy made her excuses and slipped away, leaving June in the office alone.

Back in her bedroom, she looked at the huge window and shivered again. Feeling glad the blinds were shut, she turned off the light and slept.

28

Before

After their escape, Amy and Robbie spent twelve weeks living in a women's refuge, and some further months in supported housing. During that time, Amy barely slept. The uncertainty of it all was exhausting. She had nightmares and panic attacks. She lived in fear of Mark finding them, and at the same time she often wondered if she'd made a mistake. She'd dragged Robbie away from the only home he'd ever known, and for what? To live out of a suitcase?

In the end, they got lucky. They were prioritised on the housing list and offered a small two-bedroom house, much like the one in which Amy had grown up, just a twenty-minute drive from Sandra and Dave's.

She kept waiting for Mark to learn her new address and turn up outside. She was ready to catch him on camera this time, so that she could prove his harassment in court. But he was eerily quiet as they readied for the court battle that would decide their custody agreement. It was like he knew exactly what she planned and wouldn't play into her hands.

'What's he up to?' she said nervously to Sandra on the phone. 'What's his game?'

'Knows better than to give you any ammunition against him ahead of the court date, I s'pose,' said Sandra grudgingly. 'Never said he was stupid.'

The house was a stable foundation on which Amy could rebuild her life. She found a full-time cleaning job in a hospital, and a new school for Robbie. He was happy there, and a local childminder collected him from school on the days Amy was working.

But the custody battle was a dark cloud over everything.

Facing Mark in court was one of the most difficult things Amy had ever done. It dragged on for months. She had stomach pains every day. The threats he had once used to control her echoed in her mind all the time.

I'll prove that you're an unfit mother.

Your name will be all over the papers.

You'll never see your son again.

None of that came to pass.

But to Amy's amazement, the judge granted Mark shared custody. He would have Robbie every second weekend.

'How can this have happened?' she asked her social worker the week after the decision. 'Don't get me wrong – I don't want to stop Mark from seeing Robbie. But I think it should be supervised visitation only.'

They were sitting in the front room of Amy's new house. She had turned it into a small fortress. There were bars on the downstairs windows and three extra locks on the front door.

'I understand your concerns,' said the soft-voiced social worker. She was mid forties and blonde, with a round face and a small mouth. 'But the court's view is that it's in the best interests of the child to promote a relationship with both parents. Some men, even if they aren't good partners, are good fathers.'

'But not Mark,' said Amy. 'Mark *isn't* a good father. My son's afraid of him. He watched him abusing me for years.'

'The thing is, Amy,' said the social worker, 'there's very little evidence of the abuse you're referring to. You never once reported it to the Gardaí, did you?'

There was something in the way she said it that made Amy think, not for the first time, that this woman didn't like her very much.

'No,' she admitted. 'I didn't report it.'

'Well, that makes it complicated, Amy. And even in cases where there are multiple convictions for violence against the mother, it's not always deemed relevant.' The social worker looked up from her notes. 'You never saw your partner physically harm Robbie, did you?'

'No. Never. But doesn't Robbie get a say?'

The social worker pursed her lips. 'Even if Robbie *were* to explicitly say "I don't want to stay with Dad", that wouldn't be the only factor in the decision-making process. Sometimes kids don't want to go stay with Dad because they've no friends on Dad's road, or because Mum has an Xbox. Those aren't reasons to sever the parental bond. The court has to consider Robbie's long-term well-being.'

When the social worker left, Amy triple-locked the front door.

She knew the house was as secure as it could be. She knew

her alarm system was state-of-the-art, and that the panic button she kept by her bed while she slept would alert the guards if she pressed it. She knew the courts believed that Mark wasn't a threat to her and Robbie any more.

But *she* didn't believe it. Not in her gut. Not in her bones.

29

Now

As Amy made her morning coffee, June approached her. She was cool and reserved, and made no mention of what had passed between them the night before. 'You don't mind working late today, do you, Amy? Till Miles gets home? I've a few bits to do.'

She wasn't being given the option to say no. June retreated to her office, and Amy busied herself with Tom and Poppy and her chores. That kept her on her feet all day.

When Miles got in from work that evening, his bad mood was palpable. He slammed the front door. He stamped up the stairs. The tension quickly permeated the whole house.

Amy retreated to her room without eating and lay on the bed. She was hungry, but not hungry enough to brave the atmosphere on the other side of the door. She tried reading a couple of pages of her book, but couldn't concentrate. Her stomach rumbled, and she thought longingly of the peanut butter and bread on her shelf out in the kitchen.

Don't be so pathetic, she told herself. Just go out there and make yourself a sandwich.

Upstairs, Miles was muttering something. A door slammed.

Amy stood up, pulled on her shoes and grabbed her car keys. She wanted to get out of here. She could drive down to Peg's shop, if it was still open, and buy crisps. And maybe Hartigan's did pub food. Maybe she could get a hearty soup and a couple of slices of soda bread. Just the thought made her mouth water. She slipped out the back door, escaped to her car and drove down to the village.

Peg's shop had closed for the day, so Amy went to Hartigan's. The woman behind the bar informed her that they didn't do food – 'You'd have to go to Clongrassil for that!' – but that there were crisps and peanuts.

'And what'll you have to drink?' the barwoman asked as Amy settled on a tall stool.

Amy hesitated. There was something unbearably tragic about the idea of sitting at a bar alone, eating crisps and peanuts with no pint.

'A pint of Guinness, please.'

She drank her pint while eating a bag of cheese and onion crisps and a bag of peanuts. Then she ordered the same again. She read articles on her phone and chatted on WhatsApp to Sandra. By the time she'd finished her second pint, she felt quite tipsy. She wouldn't be able to drive home like this.

In for a penny, in for a pound, she thought. She didn't want to go back to Sea View yet. And if she was going to keep sitting in this pub, she needed a drink to nurse.

She ordered a third and sipped it slowly.

By the time she was finished, she felt pretty drunk.

'Another, love?' offered the barwoman.

'No, thanks.' Four would have her on the floor. 'D'you have a number for a local taxi?'

'I do.' The woman handed her a card.

Amy thanked her and went outside to call the number. The cool evening air felt amazing when it hit her. God, she thought, Knockcrea really was at its most beautiful at dusk. The sun had disappeared around the globe, but the shades of gold that still coloured the horizon would linger for a long time. The sky was a vivid turquoise that darkened to deep blue over the mountains.

When she got through to the taxi service, the man she spoke to told her he was already on a job, that there was an extra fee for coming out to Knockcrea and that he wouldn't be there for forty minutes to an hour.

'An *hour*?' said Amy. 'Can't you send someone else?'

'I'm the whole company,' he said gruffly. 'You should've called in advance.'

Fuck it, she thought, tucking her phone into her pocket. She'd have to walk. It'll be grand, she told herself. It was only two kilometres to Sea View. It was still light out, more or less. The three pints had given her an optimistic courage she didn't usually have.

She set off at a confident march, munching on a bag of peanuts she'd bought before leaving the pub.

Knockcrea was lit by street lights, but once she left the confines of the village and started up the potholed country road toward Sea View, it became increasingly difficult to see. While the sky was still teal blue and gold, at ground level the light had faded to grey. Amy feared she'd twist an ankle. She walked carefully, straining her eyes to make out shapes in the gloom. Turning on a torch would have solved her problems, but even with her Dutch courage, she wasn't crazy about the idea of announcing her whereabouts by carrying a light that would be seen from kilometres around.

Neither was she crazy about walking past the fork in the road where she had found the dead cat. She decided to take the slightly longer road that looped past the abandoned farmhouse.

At that moment, she looked up and saw a falling star. She knew it was likely not a star at all, but debris from space hitting the earth's atmosphere. She'd learned that in one of the children's books she used to read to Robbie. All the same, she made a wish. She spoke it aloud, to the fields and the mountains and the sky, and hoped with every fibre of her being that it would come true. Then she resumed walking, picking her way carefully along the dark road. She could just about make out the shape of the abandoned farmhouse ahead of her.

As she drew closer, she heard a strange sound. A kind of hissing.

She stopped.

The derelict farmhouse was a pale-grey square in the gloom. That was where the noise seemed to be coming from. Amy approached it, very quietly.

Sssssssss.

Then a rattle, like a can of spray paint being shaken.

Her stomach lurched.

The vandal! It had to be.

Go back, a cautious part of her said. *This isn't safe.*

But a kind of recklessness seized her. Her feet kept moving, bringing her to the old farmhouse. If she peered around the corner, she would see the person with her own eyes.

She kept to the shadows as she crept along the side of the building. Each step was an exercise in caution.

Sssssssss. Rattle.

She took a deep breath and looked around the corner of the house.

The person was average height and wearing an Adidas hoodie, the three white stripes visible even in the gloom. The hood was pulled low over their face. Their arm moved as they shook the can: there was another rattle and hiss as they sprayed letters on the wall, using the last of the fading light to write their message. Amy held her breath as she watched.

Suddenly the person turned and looked directly at her.

Under the hood, they wore a black balaclava.

For one frozen moment, Amy and the vandal stared at each other. Then the person in the balaclava dropped the paint can and sprinted away across the field.

Amy stared after them, heart thudding. They jumped the low wall, raced up the road and disappeared into darkness. She turned on her phone light and shone it at the wall. The scrawled letters, still fresh as blood, read:

I'M TRYING TO WARN YOU

The 'U' wasn't quite finished.

With trembling hands, Amy took a photo of the message. Then she turned tail and ran towards Sea View.

30

When Amy burst in the door of Sea View shouting about the person she'd seen with the spray can, Miles and June forgot about being stand-offish with her. They swept her into the kitchen, sat her down at the island and listened open-mouthed. Miles poured wine for everyone.

'Didn't you think to run after them?' he said when she'd finished recounting the story.

'Oh for God's sake, Miles,' said June. 'Why would she do that? They could be dangerous!'

'They were more afraid of me than I was of them,' said Amy. 'I don't think I've ever seen anyone run so fast.'

'And you've no idea who it was?' said Miles.

She shook her head. 'They were wearing baggy clothes. I couldn't make out their build.'

It was frustratingly difficult to try and work out who might have been beneath that balaclava. Average height, shapeless clothes ... But one thing Amy was sure of: it wasn't Sean Geraghty. Sean was far taller.

In fact, there was no denying that the figure had looked around the same height as Liam.

'Liam doesn't have a black Adidas hoodie, does he?' she asked Miles and June. 'Like a black hoodie with three white stripes on each sleeve?'

'I don't think so,' said June. 'Have you ever seen him wear a hoodie like that, honey?'

Miles shook his head.

'Where is Liam?' Amy asked.

'He's in his room,' Miles said.

There was a brief silence.

Miles frowned and put his wine glass down. 'I'll go double-check.' He stood up and hurried off.

Amy locked eyes with June. They listened to Miles's voice echoing down the corridor. 'Liam? Are you home? ... No need to bite my head off, I'm just checking! Christ, do you have to be so bloody defensive about everything?'

He came stamping back, a bit red-faced and ruffled. 'He's been home the whole time,' he said.

'Look,' said Amy, 'please don't tell anyone that I actually saw the vandal. I'll go to the guards tomorrow and report it, but I don't want the whole village to know.' She didn't want to give Martin, Jacinta and the Tidy Towns group any reason to zone in on her again.

'If that's what you want,' said June.

That evening, Amy slept badly. She spent half the night lying awake thinking about the person in the Adidas hoodie and the balaclava. She spent the other half having dreams in which she pulled down the balaclava and saw Mark's face.

*

When Amy picked up her phone the next morning, she learned that the graffiti had been discovered. The Tidy Towns WhatsApp chat was alive with notifications as people discussed the development. Who? Why? How did they get away with it? Martin Doyle was apoplectic: he had personally purchased multiple security cameras from Woodie's and installed them in various locations in the village and around the outskirts, with the consent of the relevant homeowners. But the farmhouse that had been vandalised was on a road with no security cameras. How on earth had the culprit known to choose that spot? Was the perpetrator, perhaps, within this very WhatsApp group?

A woman named Patricia Fowler pointed out that as Martin had posted a long status on Facebook detailing his plans and the exact positions of the security cameras, and his Facebook statuses weren't private, a lot of people would have known where the cameras were.

Martin Doyle said his Facebook statuses *were* private, thank you very much, Patricia.

Patricia sent back a screenshot with his privacy settings circled to prove to him that they were set to public.

Martin Doyle told Patricia she had no right to take screen-shots of his personal Facebook page without his consent, and that by law she had to delete that picture immediately.

Aveen Butler told Martin he was being hysterical.

Catherine told everyone to pipe down and get back to the issue at hand: if anyone could have known where the recently installed security cameras were, that threw the issue wide open, didn't it?

Jacinta Crowley said that they all knew who it was, Liam Carroll, and he was the one who'd killed poor Bubbles the cat, too, so why hadn't he been arrested yet?

Catherine made a plea for calm:

> **All right, I know we're all concerned, but let's not get ahead of ourselves in blaming Liam.**

Sean Felan:

> **None of this trouble started before that gurrier arrived.**

Emily Hartigan:

> **He's a scumbag. I'm sorry, Catherine, but that's all he is.**

Noel O'Shaunghnesy:

> **If the guards won't do something about it, we should do something ourselves. I'm not afraid to say it.**

Catherine stopped responding.

Amy read all this with a growing knot in her stomach. She went out to the kitchen shortly before 9 a.m. In the living-room half of the open-plan space, Miles was on the sofa with Poppy, reading *Room on the Broom*.

'Not in work this morning?' Amy asked.

He shook his head. 'I had a dentist appointment, but it was cancelled.'

Amy made herself a coffee and sat at the marble island. On the other side of the room, Miles's phone buzzed. He picked it up, looked at the screen, then said, 'Fuck!' loudly. With a glance at Poppy, he tried rather too late to turn the word to 'fudge'. 'Fuck-uuuudge.'

Amy looked at him. 'What is it?'

'Look at this!' Miles said. 'Bloody look at this!'

She walked over and he handed her his phone. She found herself looking at screenshots from inside the Tidy Towns WhatsApp group.

'Al Thompson just sent them,' said Miles. Al Thompson was a significant landowner in Knockcrea and the only one of the locals with whom Miles was on genuinely friendly terms. 'His wife is in this bloody Tidy Towns group.'

'Jesus.' Amy had to feign surprise, but her distaste was all too real. 'That's terrible.'

'How dare they blame Liam!' Miles was going that telltale shade of peony pink that meant his blood pressure was rising to alarming levels. 'This village is full of lunatics, and they're blaming my son?' He waved the phone at her. 'How bloody dare they!'

Amy felt temporarily aligned with Miles. It was satisfying to see him outraged on Liam's behalf. She sat on the sofa and they read over the screenshots together, agreeing that the whole thing was monstrously unfair.

'Daddy,' said Poppy, 'read Room-the-Broom!'

'In a minute, petal,' said Miles distractedly. 'Daddy's busy.'

Amy turned her head when she heard June coming down the stairs. She wore a sleeveless lilac dress and her hair was loose and freshly washed. Tom was holding her hand.

'What's going on?' she asked.

'The bloody Tidy Towns lot,' said Miles, holding out his phone. 'They're blaming Liam for what happened last night. Absolute nutters.'

Amy observed that it seemed nobody was allowed to accuse Liam except Miles himself.

June took the phone. Her eyes widened as she scrolled through the messages. She looked up at Miles. 'And you're sure Liam didn't go out yesterday evening?'

'You know he was home last night,' said Miles. 'You were there when I checked!'

'Yes,' said June, with a touch of impatience, 'but was he out before that? If so, what time did he get back in? Because if he was out walking and was caught on one of Martin Doyle's cameras, this lot will have a field day.'

'I'd better ask him,' said Miles grudgingly.

Amy found herself wondering. Was it possible that Liam could have made it back from the farmhouse to Sea View before she did? Because even if she didn't believe it was him beneath that balaclava, Martin, Jacinta and the others definitely did. At this point, Amy half expected to see them coming up the drive with torches and pitchforks.

31

Before

'I don't want to go, Ma. Please don't make me.'

Robbie had shot up in the past few years. His hair had changed from the blonde of babyhood to fawn-brown. He was the tallest of all the eleven-year-old boys in his class.

'Why don't you want to go with your da, Robbie?' Amy turned from the sink to face her son, drying her hands on a tea towel. 'If he does anything to you, you won't have to go stay with him any more. We can go to court and they'll stop it. But you have to tell me. Has he hurt you?'

Robbie shook his head vehemently. 'Nothing like that. I just don't want to go to his house, that's all.'

He had made this request several times over the past few months. Sometimes he cried, sometimes he got angry. But it was only in front of his mother that he lashed out. When Mark arrived, Robbie would go with him, compliant as a lamb.

That worried Amy.

'Robbie,' she said, 'if your dad ever raises a hand to you, you can tell me, you know that, right?'

'I told you he hasn't!' Robbie shouted.

There was a knock at the front door. A frightened look flitted across Robbie's face. Then he smoothed out his features, assuming a neutral expression.

God, she used to be so good at doing that, too.

'I'll get it,' she said. She went to the door. Robbie fled up the stairs. Amy waited, allowing her son's footsteps to thump into his bedroom before answering.

She hated seeing Mark in the doorway, leering at her.

'All right, Amy?'

'How're you?' she responded.

During the first year, Mark had taken every advantage of their continued connection via Robbie to taunt, bully and intimidate her. He would prod her in the ribs. Slap her on the arse. Insist on greeting her with a kiss on the cheek. Eventually, with Karen's support, Amy had successfully obtained a court order for supervised handover. That had remained in place for two years, and while things were more casual now, the supervisor gone, some of the boundaries formed during that time had stuck.

'I'll get his stuff,' she said.

He stepped into the hall. This business of him crossing the threshold into her home was a new development, and Amy didn't like it at all.

She went upstairs. Robbie stood in the middle of his bedroom, overnight bag in one hand, not moving.

'Listen, pet,' she said quietly. 'You don't have to go with him if you don't—'

Robbie's eyes bulged. 'Shh!'

'Okay,' she whispered. 'We'll talk about it when you get . . .'

Pushing her out of the way, he hurried past her and down the stairs.

'How's it going?' she heard Mark greet him. Then the front door slammed and they were gone.

Amy rubbed her arm where her son had pushed her. She could feel the familiar sensation of a bruise forming. At eleven, Robbie was almost as tall as she was, and these aggressive outbursts worried her. But what worried her more was the look on her son's face when his father knocked at the front door. When he got home on Monday, they'd have another talk.

But when Monday rolled around, Robbie was still reticent. 'I just don't like staying in Da's, okay? I prefer staying with you.' When pressed for a reason, he just shrugged and said, 'There's no reason. But is it all right if I stop going there for weekends?'

'When will you see your da then?'

Robbie thought about it. 'We can play football on the green, or go to McDonald's.'

Amy gave the matter some consideration and decided that was reasonable. Robbie wasn't a little kid any more. He was eleven now. He could make some decisions for himself.

No more weekends where she didn't see her son for forty-eight hours at a time. No more closed doors. Robbie and Mark's time together would be supervised not by social workers, but by the general public. And it wasn't her request, it was Robbie's. She remembered arguing this very point with the patronising social worker years ago, and felt vindicated.

When Mark's next pickup day arrived, Amy told Robbie to wait upstairs while she had a word with his dad.

The doorbell rang. She went to answer it with a churning in her stomach. Things were different now, she reminded herself. She wasn't the terrified girl who would crawl to Mark with a bloody lip and apologise for making him hit her. He had no power over her any more.

At least that was what she told herself as she opened the door.

'All right, Amy,' said Mark, ogling her. 'Where's the young fella?'

'He's upstairs.' Amy kept the door half-closed as she spoke. 'Listen, Mark, there's something I need to talk to you about.'

'Oh yeah?' He put his head to one side, studying her.

'I know this isn't what we usually do,' said Amy, 'but maybe the two of you could do something different this weekend. Instead of Robbie staying in yours, maybe you could go out for the day. To Eddie Rocket's, or to play football. Or whatever – you choose, obviously; I'm not telling you what to do.'

Why was her heart thumping? Why did her stomach feel sick? She was babbling, she could hear herself.

'It's what Robbie said himself, is all,' she continued, talking faster. 'He doesn't want to sleep anywhere except here. But of course he wants to see you, you're his da!'

'I'm coming in,' said Mark, and he reached over her head and pushed the door open. Suddenly they were in the hall, and the door was closed.

'Mark . . .'

There was a tense, dangerous energy emanating from him. Amy raised her chin. She wouldn't be intimidated.

'Robbie said—' she began again.

Mark cut across her, his voice a growl. 'The fucking kid is coming with me for the weekend and that's all there is to it, Amy. Don't you fucking stand there and tell me I'm not allowed to see my own child. Who d'you think you are?'

Reality swam. Colours looked different. The world was changing around the edges.

'He's coming with me,' Mark repeated.

Amy's instincts begged her to acquiesce, grovel, fawn. To say, *Yes, Mark, three bags full, Mark.* But somehow she managed to resist the ingrained reflex. Somehow she managed to open her mouth and say, 'Not to stay over, he's not.'

Later, she would consider it a miracle that she'd got those words out. All the pep talks she gave herself when she was alone, or in the orderly rooms of the domestic violence shelter, meant nothing here. In this enclosed space with Mark, all that was revealed for the flimsy cardboard protection it was.

Mark took two steps back. He furrowed his brow, considering her. Then he punched her. One well-aimed jab.

Amy flew backwards, hit the wall and then the floor. Her nose felt broken. The pain was a white-hot shock.

Mark stood watching her with a kind of curiosity, waiting to see if that would be enough or if she needed more.

Blood splattered from Amy's nose onto the off-white carpet as she pushed herself up into a seated position. She used her T-shirt to stem the flow. It was enough. He was going to take Robbie this weekend, and the weekend after that, and nothing she could do would prevent it.

Less than five minutes alone in a room with him, and they were back to this.

'Okay,' she croaked. 'Okay.'

Mark crouched down. 'You go to the guards about this,

Amy, and I'll come back and break both your arms,' he said. 'You think I'm joking? Try it and see what happens.'

Then he straightened up. 'Robbie!' he yelled up the stairs.

Robbie appeared with the speed of a child who had been listening to everything. He looked at Amy's bloody nose in terror.

'Sweetheart, I'm okay,' she said, her first instinct to re-assure her child, but she instantly regretted it. She shouldn't be telling him any of this was okay.

'See? She's fine,' said Mark. 'Come on, let's go.'

Robbie didn't move. 'Ma? Are you sure—'

'I said *let's go!*' said Mark.

Robbie shot a frightened look at his mother, then followed his father outside. The door slammed.

They were gone.

32

Now

Miles and June encouraged Amy to leave work early, retrieve her car from the village and drive to Clongrassil Garda station – the nearest police station – to report her sighting of the vandal. The journey took almost an hour. But when she arrived, she found herself standing on the street outside the station, unable to walk in. The very first question the guards would ask would be: *What's your name?*

And what was she supposed to say?

Because Amy had something to hide. She hadn't been honest with Miles and June.

What if it got back to them that their nanny wasn't who she said she was?

Just go in, she told herself. The guards won't go digging into your past.

But she couldn't bring herself to do it. Eventually she walked away.

Amy wandered Clongrassil, killing time. She headed

down to the harbour. She did some shopping in the super-market on the main street. Fond as she was of Peg's tiny shop, it made a nice change to walk well-stocked aisles, picking up anything she needed.

The man who served her at the till was around thirty, hand-some, bearded and very interested in talking to her. 'I haven't seen you around before. You're from Dublin, are you? Yeah, the accent's a bit of a giveaway. I'm Stephen, by the way ...' He spoke with the easy confidence of a man who was used to success with women, but flirting was the last thing Amy felt like doing today. She gave polite but distant answers, then slipped away, leaving handsome Stephen looking disappointed.

On the drive back from Clongrassil, Amy was deep in thought. She took the bend that brought Knockcrea into view, revealing that picturesque horseshoe of houses nestled between the sea and the mountains. It was then that she made a decision.

Instead of going straight back to Sea View, she would drive to the village, visit Peg's corner shop and get some answers. And while she was there, she'd also get a pack of cigarettes. Fuck it, she thought. This was not the moment to be cutting nicotine out of her life.

She parked outside Hartigan's and walked to Peg's.

'Well, hello, pet,' said the old woman when Amy walked into the shop. 'What can I get for you?'

'Twenty Marlboro Red, thanks, Peg.' Amy put a bar of Dairy Milk chocolate on the counter, too. 'How're you today?'

'Not bad. Enjoying the last of the sunshine. The weather's supposed to turn tomorrow, or so I hear. How've you been getting on?'

The only other person in the shop, a middle-aged woman Amy didn't know, left, the doorbell jangling behind her.

'I haven't been great, actually,' Amy admitted when the door shut. 'Listen, Peg, can I ask you something?'

'You can.'

'What do you think about all this stuff that's going on in the village? With the graffiti and that?'

Peg looked tiny on her seat behind the counter, but her eyes were sharp.

'I'll tell you what I think,' she said. 'That graffiti business, that's the work of someone who needs help. People want to think it's some clever mastermind, but when we track down the person behind all this, we'll find some poor soul with terrible problems. What they'll need is a doctor, and some medication, and a bit of support. Nothing more than that.'

'You think?'

'I do,' said Peg. 'I had a cousin who was mentally ill – believed the devil was talking to him. He was very sick, the poor fellow. Spent some time in hospital and got a bit better, but he got sick again later. He killed himself in the end.' She said this in a calm, matter-of-fact tone.

'Jesus,' said Amy. 'I'm sorry.'

Peg nodded. 'Thank you. It was a long time ago. He was a really lovely fellow. Awful tragedy, but not uncommon. There's people up and down this country with terrible mental health problems.' She tapped each of Amy's items with a finger. 'Thirteen fifty, pet.'

Amy handed her a twenty-euro note.

'Peg,' she said, 'you knew Francisca, didn't you? The woman who worked at Sea View before me?'

Peg nodded. 'Yes. Lovely girl.'

'Did she tell you why she left?'

Peg placed the note into a drawer with her trembling hands. Then she began to count Amy's change on the counter. 'Francisca came in here a few times,' she said. 'We'd always have a chat. She said I reminded her of her grandmother back in Brazil. She told me some things about what went on at Sea View. Not long after she arrived, she started looking for a different job. You didn't hear that from me, now.'

'Was it something to do with Miles? Or with Liam?' Amy asked.

Peg pushed the change across the counter. 'What would it have to do with Liam?' she said. 'Sure he's just a kid, and he keeps to himself. Everyone knows that.'

'So it was something to do with Miles,' Amy concluded.

'I'm not saying anything,' said Peg, in the tone of someone who was most definitely saying something.

'Where did Francisca go?'

'She got a job in Cork.'

'June told me she went back to Brazil,' said Amy. 'Because her mother was sick.'

The bell on the door jangled as another customer walked in. Peg pressed her lips together, but her sharp eyes held Amy's and the word hung between them as clearly as if she'd said it aloud:

Bullshit.

33

Amy was in her room in Sea View, reading – or trying to. She lay on her back on the rose-coloured bedspread, holding her book over her face, but she couldn't concentrate. Her mind was abuzz with questions. She thought about Peg saying: *When we track down the person behind all this, we'll find some poor soul with terrible problems.* Was that the answer to the big mystery? Just someone who was mentally ill and needed medical care?

Her phone began to ring, buzzing on the bedside table. She reached over and picked it up. Lina. Why was Lina calling her? Feeling a stab of nerves, she answered.

'Hello?'

'Amy, hi. Is this a bad time?'

'No, it's fine. How're things?'

'Look, I'm not quite sure how to say this, so I'll just spit it out,' said Lina. 'I saw something about you on the internet . . . or at least, I think I did. The photo certainly looks like you, but the name is different.'

Amy couldn't speak. There was a sudden roaring in her ears.

'I feel ridiculous asking this,' said Lina, 'but is your name Amy O'Neill or Amy Fagan?'

Words wouldn't come.

'Amy? Are you there?'

Amy swallowed. 'I'm here.'

'Then can you answer my question? I'm sure you can appreciate this is cause for concern. I was all set to hire you. Your references checked out fine. But then one of my friends shared this story on Instagram. And I thought, Christ, is that the woman I've just hired as my new nanny? Amy? Do you know what I'm talking about?'

Amy closed her eyes. She knew what Lina was talking about.

'Amy? *Hello?*' Amy hung up.

A moment later, her phone vibrated. A WhatsApp message from Lina. It was a screenshot of a newspaper article. The first four words of the headline read: DUBLIN WOMAN AMY FAGAN . . . Amy didn't read any further. She knew what it said. She deleted it.

Her phone buzzed again. Lina had sent her another picture. Amy clicked on it.

There it was, filling the screen. The image she would have paid for Lina not to have seen.

She slumped back against the pillows. She could feel her future in Limerick slipping away. There was no way Lina was going to hire her after this.

Your references checked out fine . . . Of course they had. Amy's references were Sandra and Dave. While the jobs she had cited were real, she couldn't give the numbers of her previous employers. Dave had played her boss at the hospital (Dave wasn't a natural liar, but seeing as he was a porter and knew the hospital intimately, he had pulled it off) and Sandra had posed as the mother of the family Amy used to clean and babysit for.

She had used a fake surname because she'd known that if Lina googled the name Amy Fagan, she'd come across this very photo.

Amy put the phone down, rolled onto her side and lay still, her breathing shallow like a wounded animal's.

She wished she could scour the image from the internet like she scoured dirt stains from surfaces with bleach and abrasive cloths. Scrape and scrub it away until clean nothingness shone in its place and she was free to build a different life.

Maybe I don't deserve a different life.

A tear trickled onto the pillow.

Maybe she didn't deserve to escape her past. Maybe it was right that she should suffer for ever.

34

Before

When Robbie was fourteen, Mark was convicted of aggravated assault after attacking a neighbour who confronted him over a parking issue. He was sentenced to five years in prison, two suspended. Amy's relief was enormous. For now, at least, Mark was gone.

Sandra and Dave came around with champagne.

Amy laughed when she opened the door, shaking her head. 'Don't let Robbie see you with that.' She led them into the kitchen. Dave filled three glasses and insisted on a toast.

'Good riddance,' said Sandra, raising hers.

Dave joined her. 'With a bit of luck, the bastard will fuck up in there and get more time. Cheers!'

'Don't get my hopes up,' said Amy, clinking her glass against his.

Sandra downed her champagne in one and put the empty glass on the table. 'I hope he dies in there,' she said.

'Sandra!' said Amy, genuinely shocked. 'Don't you ever say that in front of Robbie.'

'Robbie's probably relieved. He's afraid of Mark. He'll be better off if he never sees him again. I mean it. I hope he dies inside.'

There was an uncomfortable silence. The frivolous, irreverent mood had fizzled out. Dave cleared his throat.

'Look, emotions are running high,' he said. 'Let's take it down a notch. We're glad you're safe, Amy, that's all.'

He went over and put an arm around Sandra. Something unspoken passed between them. Sandra sniffed, nodded, then turned to Amy.

'I won't say that again,' she said. 'Let's just enjoy this glorious day.'

'Cheers to that,' said Amy, raising her glass.

'More champagne!' said Dave.

When Sandra and Dave left, around 3 p.m., Amy set about tidying away the signs of merriment before Robbie got home from school. He didn't need to know they'd been celebrating his father's imprisonment. Dave had even brought party hats and streamers.

She hid the evidence at the bottom of the bin, returning the mood of the house to appropriate solemnity, but she couldn't help thinking that Sandra was probably right. Yes, Robbie was going to be upset, but ultimately, wasn't everything going to be better now? Mark was gone. It was over.

When she heard Robbie's key in the front door, she hurried down the hall. 'Hi, sweetheart. How was . . .'

But he ran past her and up the stairs. She heard his bedroom door slam.

Amy stood staring after him, a new unease rising inside her.

*

Over the months that followed, Robbie went off the rails at a speed Amy couldn't believe.

At the time, she didn't understand it at all. Her well-behaved boy, who had only ever lashed out during rows about going to his father's house, was suddenly staying out all night. Coming home drunk and stoned. Being brought back in Garda cars by serious-faced officers in blue uniforms who would inform her that he had been caught fighting. Shoplifting. Riding as a passenger in a stolen car.

Shortly after he turned fifteen, he was caught with three hundred euro worth of weed in his pocket. 'What is wrong with you, Robbie?' Amy said, dazed, after driving him home from the station. 'You're only fifteen years old. What do you think you're doing?'

He had his phone out and was texting, ignoring her.

'That's not your normal phone.' Alarm bells clanged in her brain. 'Robbie, where did you get that phone? Is that a burner?'

'Fuck off, Ma, would you?' He didn't even look at her, just tried to walk out the front door.

She barred his way. 'Where do you think you're going?'

'Out.'

'No, you're not.'

He glared at her.

'I'm not stupid, Robbie,' Amy went on. 'Who gave you that phone? Who gave you the grass the guards seized?'

'Fuck OFF, Ma.' He grabbed her by the arm and tried to haul her out of the way.

There was a scuffle. Amy held her ground, but found herself thrown sideways and into the shoe rack. She hadn't realised how strong he'd grown.

For a moment, she thought he was going to apologise. But then he slammed the door and was gone.

Amy tried scolding, threatening, shouting. She tried begging, pleading, guilt-tripping. None of it worked. She knew that gangs in the area got young kids to do their dirty work. The articles she read online called it 'grooming'. Amy had always known it happened; she'd just never thought it would happen to her child.

She tried to create a sense of normality at home. She needed to show Robbie an alternative to the dangerous glamour of running the streets with older friends who had money and cars and drugs. She began obsessively cooking meals from scratch, as if this problem could be solved with roast dinners. She tried to be warmer, gentler, regretting every time she had ever raised her voice to him. She bought him an expensive speaker and a brand-new bike.

But none of it was enough.

Six months after Robbie turned fifteen, there was a knock at Amy's door.

She went to answer it with no idea that her world was about to be turned upside down.

35

Now

The next day, Amy went about her tasks as if in a dream. She cleaned windows, scrubbed surfaces, changed bed sheets. The whole time, the photo kept flashing in her mind's eye. She felt sick to her stomach at the thought that Lina had seen it. What must she think of Amy now?

When Sandra had first told her the picture had gone viral on social media, along with screenshots of the article, Amy had prayed it would die down in a day or two. But it kept attracting more and more shares.

She knew she should send some explanation to Lina, but every time she tried to imagine what she might say, she experienced a wave of debilitating exhaustion. She couldn't summon the energy or the courage. Her mind was buzzing with anxiety.

That picture is all over the internet now. It'll follow you for ever. Wherever you go, for the rest of your life, people will ask you to explain it.

Amy couldn't face that thought. So instead she concentrated on the tasks in front of her.

She put fresh soap in the bathrooms. She arranged fruit in the glass bowl on the table. She washed the sheets with fabric softener that smelled like lavender.

After work, she went for a long drive. She wanted to keep busy, keep moving. Catherine texted her, inviting her over for dinner on Sunday. Sandra messaged her on WhatsApp, asking if she'd like to do a video call with her and Dave later. Amy ignored them both.

She didn't want to tell Sandra that Lina had seen the picture. She didn't want to see her sister's disappointed expression or hear her say, 'It might still be okay, Amy – maybe if you call her and explain, she'll understand?'

She drove the length of the peninsula and back again, staring in a kind of stupor at the grey and green landscape that rolled past. By the time she returned to Knockcrea, it was getting dark. When she parked in the driveway, she sat in silence for a while before checking her phone.

The first notification on her screen was a message from Lina.

> **Hi, Amy. I've decided to give the job to another candidate. I'm sure you can understand why I've made this decision.**

So. That was that.

She put the phone back in her pocket and got out of the car. A cold sea breeze lifted her hair from the back of her neck. Through the huge windows, she could see Miles and June drinking red wine on the L-shaped sofa in front of the television, while Tom and Poppy played with an upended box of toys on the floor.

Amy let herself in the back door. She went to her room and changed into her pyjama bottoms and vest even though it was just past eight. She felt bone-tired, so bloody exhausted that the only thing that held any appeal was sleep. She climbed under the duvet and passed straight out.

Amy slept fitfully. She dreamed of smoke, of orange flames. She saw Mark's face floating in front of her – hollow-cheeked, pale – saying, 'I'm going to find you, Amy. I'll never let you go.' Then Mark disappeared, and she found herself locked in the wardrobe, with someone knocking at the other side of the wood . . .

Rap-rap-rap-rap-rap.

She sat up in bed, disoriented.

She was in her room in Sea View. She had fallen asleep with the lamp on. Her phone screen read 1.02 a.m. And somebody was knocking on her bedroom door.

Rap-rap-rap-rap-rap.

'Amy?' a low voice called. 'Amy?'

Miles.

Amy got out of bed. She was suddenly conscious that she was wearing no bra. She glanced around, wanting to pull on an oversized sweater, something that would swamp her form, but she had nothing to hand.

'Amy? I can see that your light's on.'

There was a thick, slurred edge to his voice. Amy remembered the red wine he and June had been drinking earlier. She stood still and stayed silent. Maybe he'd go away.

Then the handle turned and the door opened. Miles was

standing on the threshold. He wore pyjama bottoms and a dressing gown.

'Is everything okay?' he said in a stage whisper. 'I heard shouting.'

Amy folded her arms across her chest. 'I was asleep, Miles. You woke me up. I didn't hear any shouting.'

He frowned. 'No, it was you who was doing the shouting. I thought you were calling for help.'

She had a sinking feeling in her stomach. 'You heard me calling for help?' She glanced at her bed. Her duvet and blankets were a mess, like she'd been kicking in her sleep.

He nodded. 'I came to see if you were all right.'

'I'm sorry,' she said. 'I sometimes have bad dreams. I hope I didn't wake you.'

Miles hiccupped. 'I thought maybe someone was lurking around the house, frightening you ...'

No one but you, Amy thought.

'It was nothing like that,' she said out loud. 'I appreciate you checking on me. But I'm fine.'

He didn't move from the doorway. 'If you're sure.'

'I'm sure,' she said, with a new note of firmness.

Still he didn't move. He was peering at her curiously, and she thought she saw a meanness in his alcohol-bleary eyes.

'Who's Robbie?' he said suddenly.

Amy gave a little jolt, as if an electric shock had run through her. 'What?'

Miles was watching her closely. 'That's the name I heard you shouting,' he said. '*Robbie, Robbie* ... Who is he? An old boyfriend?'

She swallowed hard.

'I'm going back to bed now,' she said after a moment. She

walked forward and took hold of the door in a way that made it clear she was about to close it. 'Goodnight, Miles.'

He looked a little shamefaced. Maybe there was something in her expression that made it obvious he'd pushed hard on an old wound.

'Goodnight, then,' he said, stepping back.

Amy shut the door on him with a little bang. She kept a grip on the handle to steady herself as a flood of dizzying memories washed over her.

In her mind's eye, she saw Robbie at five. Robbie at twelve. Robbie at fifteen, which was how she thought of him most often. One of the photos she kept in her bedside locker was of the two of them on his fifteenth birthday. He was already taller than her, his arm around her shoulders.

It was that photo she took out and looked at most.

Amy staggered over to the bed and sat down, then leaned forward until her forehead touched her knees. She hated that Miles had heard her shouting for Robbie in her sleep. It was like he'd peered into her most private thoughts, a place he had no right to look.

As long as she'd lived here, she'd feared that Miles and June would find out what had happened to Robbie. The thought filled her with a burning shame. Why should anyone trust her to look after their children when she hadn't been able to protect her own son?

36

Before

In her small house in Dublin, Amy was washing dishes. The doorbell rang. She dried her hands and went to answer it, humming to herself. Maybe it was Sandra and Dave; they'd said they'd try to pop over today.

When she saw the young man standing on her doorstep, her welcoming smile faded.

He was in his early twenties, and had vivid carrot-orange hair. He wore a designer tracksuit and an expensive watch. He had a boxer's build and swagger, and a sharp-featured, vulpine face. She had never spoken to him, but she knew his name. Craig Keane. He was a well-known drug dealer from the area.

'All right, Amy?' he said, like they were old friends. 'How's things?'

'What do you want?' she asked, trying not to let her fear show.

'Just a chat,' said Keane easily. 'Do you know who I am, Amy?'

She said nothing.

He walked into her house like he owned it. Amy followed him down the hall, heart pounding. He took a seat at her kitchen table and looked at her appraisingly. She stayed standing, arms folded.

'What do you want?' she repeated.

'We need to talk,' said Keane, leaning back in his seat. 'About Robbie.'

'What about him?'

'Robbie's run up a bit of debt with myself and my colleagues,' he replied. 'Four grand's worth of debt, or just about. If he can't pay it, that debt falls to you.'

'Four grand?' said Amy. 'He's just a kid. You know he doesn't have that kind of money!'

Keane's eyes were a staring pale pebble grey. 'And *you* know what'll happen if that debt's not paid. Not just to you, not just to this house, but to Robbie. Now, you don't want anything bad to happen to Robbie, do you?'

The juxtaposition between his conversational tone and the things he was saying was terrifying.

'I don't have four grand,' said Amy, with the defiance of the uninitiated. 'And even if I did, I wouldn't give it to you! Now get out of my house.'

Keane calmly stood and walked to the front door. Before he left, he looked back. 'People get shot for a lot less than four grand. D'you want to be sitting at your son's funeral, thinking your credit union savings were more important?'

Amy couldn't speak. She felt dizzy.

'You have a think about it,' said Keane. 'I'll be back.'

When he was gone, she double-locked the door with shaking hands. Then she went to the bathroom and threw up.

She called Robbie, who sounded drunk. Music blared in the background. 'What is it, Ma?'

'Robbie, where are you? I need to talk to you.'

'Ah, leave me alone, would you? I'm out with my friends. I'll be home in a few days.'

'Robbie, wait! Don't hang . . .'

He hung up. When she called back, his phone was off.

Amy sat on the stairs with her head in her hands. She couldn't call the police and report Keane. She knew what happened to 'rats'. She felt completely trapped.

The next day, an envelope arrived through her letter box with a bullet in.

The day after that, her windows were smashed in.

On the third day after Keane's visit, Amy was woken at 4 a.m. by a phone call. The caller ID was withheld. 'Hello? Who is this?' She could hear commotion on the other end of the phone – thumping, shouting – then she recognised her son's voice, sobbing in pain.

'Robbie?' She sat bolt upright in the dark. Defiance was a distant memory. Her son was sobbing and she couldn't reach him. '*Robbie!*'

Men in the background were laughing while Robbie cried out.

The line went dead.

Minutes later, Amy received a photo via WhatsApp of her son's bloody, battered face. The text underneath read:

Pay up or next time we keep kicking till he's dead.

The following day, Amy went to the credit union and took out all her savings. It wasn't enough to cover the entire debt, but she also applied for a small loan. Sandra helped her to make up the difference while she was waiting.

She had bought her child's safety, but only for a time.

Within a matter of months, Robbie had run up an even bigger tab. Again Amy opened her door to find orange-haired Keane standing there. He informed her, in his friendly, conversational way, that she had a debt to pay.

If she didn't, he calmly told her, he'd burn her house to the ground.

Her life had become a nightmare. No matter how much she paid, the dealers demanded more, constantly adding money onto the debt she was trying to pay. Her teenage son was taking hard drugs, staying out for two, three nights at a time. She would lie awake in the small hours with no idea where he was. Her greatest fear was that Robbie would OD in some crack den, with nobody around him who cared enough to notice as his breathing slowed and then ceased.

Her only relief was that Mark was in prison. But time was passing, month after month flying by. Word reached Amy that there had been an appeal, and that his sentence was being reviewed by the parole board. She tried not to think about it. Then one day Sandra came by to let her know it was no longer a possibility, but reality. In a far-off institution, some faceless official had stamped a form approving the prisoner Mark Keating for release.

Mark would be out soon.

37

Now

It was a sunny morning in West Cork, the gorgeous weather totally incongruent with Amy's mood. She wanted nothing more than to lie in bed all day, but she had to work. She got dressed and brushed her teeth on autopilot.

In the kitchen, she found Miles, June, Tom and Poppy at the island. Miles was wearing a suit, ready for work, and drinking coffee. June, who looked pale, her make-up not quite hiding the dark circles under her eyes, was sipping a green juice. She was speaking to Miles in a low, urgent voice. Tom and Poppy were sitting across from them, eating avocado on toast.

'Morning, Amy!' said Miles when she walked in. 'Fancy a cup of coffee? There's plenty made.'

'I'd love a cup,' said Amy. 'Thanks, Miles.'

'Good morning, Amy,' said June distractedly.

Miles gave no sign that he remembered his drunken intrusion into Amy's room. She wondered if he'd forgotten, or if he was embarrassed by his behaviour. She studied his face closely as he poured her coffee: Miles's skin, as always, gave him away. There was a faintly pink tinge to his cheeks.

'Thanks,' she said, accepting the cup. She ruffled Tom and Poppy's hair. 'Morning, you two.'

June turned away from her, and Amy felt a sudden lurch in her stomach: did June know Miles had gone to her bedroom last night? Did she think something had happened? But as the conversation picked up again, she realised that June's tense mood had nothing to do with her. Busying herself with the sugar, she tried to look like she wasn't listening in.

'I'm telling you, Miles,' June was saying in a hushed voice, 'I know what I saw. There were three people. They did a circle of the house. I couldn't see their faces, but from the way they moved, I thought it was two men and a woman.'

'You're sure?'

'*Yes*, I'm sure!' There was a serrated edge to June's voice. 'If you hadn't been stocious drunk last night, you would've seen them too! I couldn't wake you. It was terrifying.'

'Daddy!' said Poppy. 'Want orange juice!'

'I'll pour her some,' said Amy, and did so.

'D'you think it was the O'Reilly brothers?' Miles asked June.

'Definitely not.' June sounded certain. 'They didn't have that stocky build. One of them was very tall. They just circled the place and left.'

Amy, putting the pieces together, went cold. Three people had been hanging around the house last night?

'Can you work from home today?' June was asking Miles.

'I'm sorry, honey, but not today. It's just not possible.' He pulled his wife closer and kissed her cheek. 'But all of this is going to be okay. You'll see.'

June was stiff, resisting his hug. He kept an arm around her, kept talking.

'I'll call an electrician and ask about installing a state-of-the-art new alarm system,' he said. 'I'll get security cameras in every window. I'll get a locksmith down to put double locks on all the doors. I won't stop until you feel totally safe – okay?'

'I'll call the Garda station at Clongrassil later and make a report,' said June.

Miles nodded. 'We'll find out who's behind this juvenile campaign of intimidation,' he said. 'And when we do, they're going to be very sorry. Okay?'

June relaxed against him then, and allowed him to kiss her on the lips. 'Okay.'

Miles went to ruffle Tom and Poppy's hair. 'All right, you two, Daddy's got to go to work. I love you millions and billions.'

'Byee!'

'Bye, Daddy!'

'See you later, Amy,' he said, friendly and casual, and off he went.

Tom and Poppy finished their avocado toast and disappeared to the playroom. June made eye contact with Amy. Together the two women began to clear the table.

'They did a full circle around the house before they left,' said June, gathering the plates. 'Miles wouldn't wake up, he was so drunk. I was shaking him and shaking him. I was so scared, but then they got back in their car and drove away.'

Amy wiped crumbs from the island top. 'You said one of them was very tall?' she said, thinking of Sean Geraghty.

'Tall and bulky,' said June, eliminating Sean instantly.

'Did you see what kind of car it was?'

'It was too dark. I just saw the lights and heard the engine.'

'And you didn't see their faces?'

June shook her head. 'They were all wearing masks.'

'What?'

'You know, like Halloween masks,' said June. 'The hard white one with holes for eyes.'

Amy shivered. She could picture it. Three masked figures creeping past her window while she slept.

Was the house being cased for a burglary? Or was it something darker?

Could it be something to do with her?

The tattoo on her shoulder seemed to tingle. Just as it had on the day she'd had it done in Wildcat Ink, with Mark squeezing her hand . . .

She pulled herself out of the past. Concentrate. Three people outside the house? That didn't fit. They weren't here for her. This was something to do with the Carrolls, she told herself, and whatever strange business they were mixed up in.

'June,' she said, 'maybe it's time to get Tom and Poppy out of here. Just until you know what's going on.'

'And bring them where?' June held her head high. 'Miles thinks the people behind this are trying to intimidate us. Well, they won't succeed.'

'But if things escalate ... I know first-hand how out-of-control situations like this can get.' Amy swallowed. 'I've seen it with my own eyes, back in Dublin.'

It was the most personal thing she'd ever said in front of June. But June seemed too distracted to notice. She was loading the dishwasher, brisk and purposeful, as if mundane household tasks could put a barrier between herself and all this menace.

'Let's say someone *is* trying to intimidate you,' said Amy slowly. 'Have you any idea who? Or why?'

'No. But whoever it is, I won't be frightened out of my own home,' said June, with a naïve courage that Amy couldn't help but admire a little.

As she collected her cleaning things from the utility room, Amy wondered if she should ask the Carrolls if she could stay a little longer, just until she found something else and they found someone else. But then she thought of the dead cat, and the strangers in masks circling the house, and wondered how she could even consider sleeping in this house a night longer than she had to.

Just get out of here, said a sensible voice inside her. *Whatever is going on, you want to be as far away from it as possible.*

A more easily panicked part of her brain responded: *But where am I supposed to go? What am I supposed to do? What if I end up homeless?*

As she got stuck into her work, she began to think more clearly. The activity of making a place clean and orderly always made her feel calmer. While she mopped the kitchen floor, she gave herself a pep talk.

You'll find something else. Get on the internet, start searching. It doesn't have to be perfect. You just need a bit of money and a roof over your head.

She plunged the mop head into the bucket and squeezed out the excess water.

You'll manage, she told herself. *You've survived so much. You'll survive this.*

That evening, after she'd finished cleaning the kitchen and all of the downstairs windows, she applied for a new job. (*Family of four, Waterford, mother, father, two boys; live-in housekeeper/childminder needed.*) Sitting up in bed eating a bag of Doritos, she carefully wrote the parents a message from the iPad Dave had given her. She gave her name as Amy O'Neill and sent the application from the matching email account she'd created – amyoneill012@gmail.com. She had a slightly sick feeling in her stomach as she pressed send, but what else could she do?

A fake name was her best option. Firstly, it made her harder to find online. She didn't want even a nannying profile with the name Amy Fagan to exist. That was too much of a digital footprint.

Secondly, it prevented employers from coming across the photograph she didn't want them to find.

Amy O'Neill was the name she'd used to apply for the job at Sea View. It had been easy. The new email address was all it took. She had had several cash-in-hand cleaning jobs over the years, and she'd guessed that Miles and June wouldn't ask for ID. They hadn't. Hopefully this family wouldn't either.

She put the iPad down and took another Dorito from the bag. As it crunched in her mouth, her phone buzzed.

It was a message from Catherine.

Amy, I saw this being shared on social media! What's going on? Are you all right?

The next message she sent was a link to a social media post. Oh God. Catherine had seen it too.

Amy's stomach began to churn. She clicked into the post

and stared at the photo. Trying to see it through Catherine's eyes. Through Lina's.

It was a photo of a poster. At the top, in large black letters, was the word *MISSING*, above a black-and-white image of Amy's face. Her expression was slightly lost, slightly sad. It was an eye-catching photo, chosen to turn heads.

She read the words at the bottom, even though she'd read them many times before.

Amy Fagan, of Barrymeade, was last seen on the 28th of July, wearing blue jeans and a red coat. She is 5ft 9 in, with long black hair. She may be erratic or confused. If you see Amy, please call this number or contact Barrymeade Garda station.

The phone number was in huge print underneath. She had hoped the poster would fade away. But it had gained traction on social media, Amy's symmetrical face and sad eyes generating thousands of clicks and shares.

She swiped to the next image in the post. A screen-shot of a newspaper article. DUBLIN WOMAN AMY FAGAN MISSING SINCE JULY, the headline read. Underneath it said, *The family of Amy Fagan are desperate for news . . .*

Her phone began buzzing suddenly in her hand. Catherine was calling her.

She answered it.

'Amy, are you all right? The poster said you were . . . well, that you might be feeling a bit confused.'

'I'm not confused at all. Look, Catherine, I know this seems crazy, but there's an explanation. I'll tell you everything when I see you. Just . . . please don't call that number. Please don't tell anyone where I am. And don't mention the poster to anyone else in the village. Please.'

There was a short silence.

'Amy,' said Catherine, 'if you're in some kind of trouble . . .'

'I've got things under control. But don't call that number. I'm begging you.'

Catherine cleared her throat. 'I won't. I'm guessing you had good reason to leave Dublin. I know you haven't done anything wrong.'

'I don't know about that,' Amy murmured.

'What?'

'Nothing . . . Listen, if we can meet up, I'll explain everything. I'll tell you the whole story. Has anyone else in town seen the poster?'

'Not as far as I know,' Catherine said.

'Okay.' Amy exhaled. 'Are you free for a drink tonight?'

'I'm in Bantry tonight visiting family.'

'How about tomorrow?'

'I'm free tomorrow evening,' said Catherine immediately. 'You could come over to mine?'

They decided on a time and hung up. Amy slumped down on the bed, exhausted. She could feel the walls of her old life closing in on her. How much would she tell Catherine? Would she be brave enough to tell the full truth?

In a dream-like state, she opened the top drawer of the bedside table and took out her photo album. On the duvet cover, she spread out her favourite photos of Robbie. The one that had been taken on his fifth birthday, back when he was so small she had to crouch to hug him. The one taken on his fifteenth birthday, when he was taller than her.

217

Her hand shook slightly as she held that photo up to the light.

Robbie, baby, I'm so sorry. I tried to protect you. Everything just —

Everything just got out of control.

Amy lay down on top of the duvet, fully clothed, Robbie's photos loose around her. Tears trickled down her temple. She stayed like that for a long time, staring unseeingly at the wall.

She slept badly that night.

She dreamed about the fire.

In the dream, she was in her old house in Dublin. She was asleep in bed when a loud bang downstairs woke her. She got out of bed and turned on the light. Black smoke was pouring under her door. Covering her mouth and nose, she stumbled out onto the landing and looked down.

Orange flames danced at the bottom of the stairs, blocking her way to the front door.

Usually this was the point in the nightmare when she woke up. But tonight, her subconscious kept her in the memory a little longer. Forced her to relive the part where she stumbled to the bedroom door next to hers — and found it locked.

She pulled uselessly at the handle. She hammered at the wood. 'Robbie! *Robbie!*'

The flames crackled and blazed below.

'Wake up! There's a fire! WAKE UP!'

She was coughing and choking. The smoke was getting thicker. She slammed her foot against her son's door, trying to kick it down.

'ROBBIE!'

Then she woke in West Cork, gasping for air, with tears on her cheeks and Robbie's name on her lips.

38

The next day, Amy raised the blinds to find the morning overcast and grey. Low clouds had blown in and wrapped around the mountains, enveloping the peaks in opaque white. She dressed and ate breakfast in the kitchen, then got to work on the enormous job of keeping the house in immaculate condition. For now, she still worked at Sea View.

But next week, her notice would be up.

After that, who knew where she'd go?

When she'd completed her cleaning duties, she spent two hours playing with Tom and Poppy so June could get some work done. They read *Room on the Broom* multiple times, and played a vigorous game of hide-and-seek.

When she'd finished up for the day and eaten some micro-waved lasagne for lunch, Amy put on her warmest coat and went for a walk. She called Sandra, who answered immediately. 'Hi, hon! Is everything okay?'

As she walked, she told Sandra how Lina had come across

the MISSING poster. How it had sent her into a despair spiral. How she'd pulled herself out of it and applied for a new job.

'And the new job just emailed me back,' she explained. 'They seem very keen and we have an interview set up for tomorrow, so things are looking up. *And* they want someone to start asap, so I could still be out of here by Monday after next!'

'Amy, that's great,' Sandra said hesitantly. 'But couldn't you explain the poster to this Lina woman? If she understood the circumstances, maybe she'd—'

'I can't,' said Amy immediately. 'I just can't, Sandra. I can't go into all that with a stranger. I'd have to tell her about . . . about Robbie, and the fire, and . . .'

She broke off.

'Okay,' said Sandra. 'I won't push it. So what's been going on in that crazy house you're staying in? Any more drama?'

'Yes, actually . . .'

Amy told her about the people in masks who had been spotted outside the house. Sandra's amusement turned to horror.

'Jesus,' she said. 'Amy . . . you don't think Keane could be behind this, do you?'

Amy shook her head as if Sandra could see her. She wasn't worried about Keane. The dealers had preyed on her out of convenience: she was local and vulnerable. Once it became clear she couldn't be easily located, they'd move on to some other unfortunate parents in the area.

'Keane wouldn't bother tracking me down,' she said. 'I don't have enough money to make that worth his while. He's a businessman.'

'You're right,' said Sandra. '*Keane* wouldn't.'

There was a short, uneasy silence in which her implication hung in the air.

'I'm telling you, Sandra, whoever it was was after Miles and June,' said Amy. 'The Carrolls are involved in something.'

'Amy, you need to get out of there.'

'That's exactly what I'm trying to do.'

'Oh shit, my manager's just come back in.' Sandra dropped her voice to hushed employee-on-the-phone levels. 'Gotta go! Chat to you soon!'

She hung up.

Back at the house, June asked Amy if she wouldn't mind working a couple of extra hours that evening.

'I'm meeting Miles after work, and I don't want to drag Tom and Poppy all the way to Clongrassil and back.'

'Yeah, course.'

'Thanks a million. We might grab a bite to eat, and if we do, I'm not sure how long we'll be. If we're back late, could you put the kids to bed?'

'Okay.' Amy hoped they wouldn't be too late. A couple of hours was fine, but she was supposed to be meeting Catherine for a drink at nine. She sent Catherine a quick message letting her know she might be delayed. Then she settled the kids on the sofa, underneath a blanket, with a lamp on in the corner and *Peppa Pig* on the big screen. Through the great windows, she watched June drive away in the white Range Rover. When the sound of the engine faded, she went around making sure all the doors and windows were locked.

When she was confident the house was secure, she made

herself a cup of sugary tea and two slices of buttered toast. She sat down at the island and stared out at the grey sky and storm-coloured sea, chewing. When her phone rang, Amy gave a startled little jump. She picked it up and looked at the screen. It was Catherine. 'Hello?' Amy assumed she was calling about their plans to meet. But Catherine sounded tense and anxious.

'Amy, hi. Ruby's not there with you, is she?'

'What?' For a moment, Amy thought she'd misheard. Ruby? Catherine's red-haired daughter? 'No. Why would Ruby be at Sea View?'

'Jacinta Crowley saw her walking out of the village with Liam about half an hour ago. Now she's not answering her phone.'

Amy pushed away her half-eaten plate of toast and sat up straight.

'Ruby and Liam?' she said. 'Are you sure? I didn't know they knew each other.'

'Neither did I.' She could picture Catherine shaking her head, bouncy curls moving from side to side. 'But Jacinta insists she saw them together. Are you sure she's not there?'

Amy turned her head to look around the huge, high-ceilinged house. She had assumed Liam was in his bedroom, silent as usual. Had he slipped out without her noticing?

'I'll go and check,' she said, standing up.

'Thanks,' said Catherine. 'Call me back after?'

'I will.'

Tom and Poppy were curled quietly on the sofa, glazed eyes fixed on the screen. Peppa Pig and George were jumping in muddy puddles. The house was that kind of early-evening shadowy, when the daylight was no longer bright enough to fill the rooms but nobody had got around to turning all the lights on yet.

Amy walked down the corridor to Liam's room. She rapped lightly on the door.

'Liam?' she called.

She waited. The big house was very quiet. The only sound was the TV.

Amy leaned closer to the door. Actually, she could hear something on the other side. A faint, persistent, tinny sound.

She knocked again. 'Liam?'

No answer. But that faint noise continued. Was there someone in there?

'I'm coming in,' she said loudly, and opened the door.

The room appeared to be empty. After a moment's hesitation, Amy walked in.

Liam kept his space surprisingly tidy. The bed was made. The floor was clear. On his desk was a wide-screen computer monitor, and an array of headsets and hand-held controllers for various video games. There were posters on the walls, mostly for bands Amy had never heard of, although she recognised Wu-Tang Clan. Against one wall were a variety of weights and dumb-bells, and a rolled-up exercise mat. The blinds were down, but the window was open. The room felt airy.

The faint, tinny sound seemed to be coming from the computer.

'Liam?' Amy called.

She checked the en suite. She even looked under the bed. No Liam. No Ruby.

She walked over to the desk. Picking up the headphones

emitting the quiet, muffled sound, she put them over her ears. Liam had left music playing, some kind of autotuned clanging hip hop. She took the headphones off and moved the computer mouse. The screen lit up. The computer was unlocked.

In the corner of the screen was a chat box with Ruby.

Amy hesitated. She moved the mouse over Ruby's name. The temptation to click was enormous. Beside her name was a profile photo of her, red-haired and smiling.

Amy clicked into the chat.

Scrolling back, reading fast, she skimmed through the reams of messages Liam and Ruby had been sending each other. They went on and on. The two teenagers had been in almost constant contact for weeks. Did Miles and June know about this?

She returned to the most recent conversation.

Liam:

come on. it'll be fun I promise

this is our last chance you know. my dad is making me go back to Leixlip

he's a prick

Ruby:

I'm just nervous my mam is going to catch me. she'd kill me

I really want to though

I'm just scared

Liam:

don't be scared. we won't get caught

I've done it loads of times before

Amy frowned. What was it Liam was trying to convince Ruby to do?

She scrolled further back into their messages. When she saw some photos, she stopped, allowing them to load.

The first image was of Ruby in her underwear, posing in her bathroom mirror. Everything from the exaggerated arch of her back to the way she pursed her lips screamed teenage insecurity.

In response to the photo, Liam had written:

sexy. now let's see one with you bent over.

Amy yelped. She closed the chat and jumped back from the desk as if the mouse had burned her hand.

Shit.

So Ruby and Liam had a secret relationship. Amy wasn't looking forward to explaining this to Catherine. Reeling at the development, she was turning to leave the room when she noticed something odd. The poster on the far wall was for some rap group called Fastman. Amy had never heard of them. The colours were garish yellows and reds, but what had caught her eye was the symbol in the centre of the design – a huge pentagram, with an inverted cross in the middle.

Just like the symbol that had been painted on the abandoned cottage.

She stared at the poster for a long moment. Then she went to the door and looked out into the corridor. Tom and Poppy were still watching *Peppa Pig*.

She stepped back into Liam's room. She had to move fast. Any compunction she'd had about intruding on his privacy had disappeared.

She opened the wardrobe. His clothes were hanging neatly or folded on a top shelf, but at the bottom she saw a black gym bag. She crouched and unzipped it.

It was full of tins of red spray paint.

Amy picked one up. Thin lines of paint ran down the cylinder like dried blood. She stared at it, stunned. Then she reached into the sports bag again. This time, her fingers found soft material. She pulled out a hoodie.

A black Adidas hoodie, with three white stripes down each sleeve.

'Oh God,' she said aloud, her voice cracking. She didn't want to believe that charming, funny Liam had done this. But the evidence was in her hands.

And Ruby was alone with him.

39

After cramming the items back into the gym bag and returning it to the bottom of the wardrobe, Amy returned to the
lamplit front room. 'After this episode it's bedtime, okay?'
she said to Tom and Poppy.

Her head was spinning. Who should she contact first?
Catherine? Or Miles?

Catherine made the decision for her by calling back. 'Is
Ruby there?' she asked urgently.

'She's not here. Neither is Liam.' Amy drummed her fingertips on the island surface. Did Catherine have a right to
know about the items she'd found in Liam's room? It felt like
something she should discuss with Miles before mentioning
it to anyone else. But what if Ruby was in danger?

'She's not answering her phone. I don't know what to do.'
Catherine sounded close to tears. 'How worried should I
be, Amy? I know there are a lot of rumours about Liam, but
none of it's true, is it?'

'Look, I'll try and get in touch with Liam now,' said Amy. 'I'll call you back if I find out anything, okay?'

'Thank you, Amy.'

Once Catherine hung up, Amy called Miles. He didn't answer. She sent him a message.

Hi, Miles. Could you text me Liam's phone number, please? It's important.

A minute later, her phone pinged with the number. Standing by the window at the front of the house, staring out at the quiet country road, she called Liam's phone.

No answer.

A dark shape fluttered by the glass – a bird, or a bat – and Amy nearly jumped out of her skin.

Calm down, she told herself. Liam's got issues, sure, but he's just a troubled kid. There's no need to panic. Ruby's not in danger.

An unwelcome memory flashed through her mind: the anecdote about the claustrophobic girl Liam had locked in the changing rooms at school.

She remembered his message to Ruby: *Come on. It'll be fun.*

She tried calling Miles. Again he didn't answer. Again she texted him.

Miles, please give me a ring when you see this. It's urgent.

She rang Liam's number again. This time, he answered.

'Hello? Who's this?' There was wind in the background. He was outside.

'It's Amy. Where are you? Is Ruby with you?'

Silence.

'Liam. Come on.'

'Yeah, she is,' he said. 'So what?'

'I need the two of you to come back to Sea View.'

'Why? We're just having a picnic on the beach over at Salt Point.'

Amy was surprised that he'd offered their location so easily. Was he telling the truth, or was this a ruse?

'Jacinta Crowley saw the two of you together, and Ruby's mam is going mad,' she said. 'I'm sorry to ruin your picnic, but I need you to—'

'This is so unfair!' Liam exploded. 'What did I ever do that Ruby's mam doesn't like me? No, hang on, Ruby, let me finish.'

Amy could hear the girl trying to interrupt. She felt a wave of relief: Ruby sounded fine.

'I know what it is,' Liam continued. 'The reason Ruby's mam is going mad is because she thinks I'm not good enough for her. She thinks I'm some kind of scumbag. For no reason!'

'Nobody's calling you a scumbag, Liam,' said Amy. 'Ruby's mam is worried because her daughter sneaked out without telling her where she was going.'

'What does she think is gonna happen?' Liam said belligerently. 'Everything's grand. We have a fire here and we're watching the sunset. We'll cycle back later.'

Amy could see the picture he painted – a small fire on the beach under the dying light; a shared blanket. Was that really all they were doing?

'Can I speak to Ruby?' she asked.

There was a scuffle as the phone was passed over.

'Hi, Amy,' said Ruby in a small, shy voice. 'Could you please tell my mam I'm okay, and that me and Liam will be back later?'

'Ruby, I'm not going to pass along messages to your mam for you,' said Amy firmly. 'Tell her yourself. Answer her calls.'

Liam took the phone back. 'This is why Ruby didn't tell her mam she was seeing me. She knew she'd act like this! It's not fair. I haven't DONE anything.'

'You haven't done *anything*, have you not?' said Amy, reaching breaking point. 'You didn't spray-paint *anything* in the village?'

'No! Well . . . okay, I did the first one.'

'What?' Again, Amy found herself caught off guard by his honesty.

'Yeah,' said Liam. There was a shrug in his voice. 'I did the first load of graffiti. I changed the "Welcome to Knockcrea" sign to say "Welcome to the Arsecrack of Nowhere". And I drew some dicks and swear words around the place. I was pissed off about being stuck in Knockcrea for the whole summer. But then me and Ruby got talking, and I was glad I was stuck here. If you've heard me sneaking out at night, it's because I've been going to see her. But all the creepy messages and that other shit, none of that was me. None of it.'

He sounded so convincing. Amy was torn.

'Look, we can talk about it when you're back,' she said.

'We're not going back,' said Liam. 'Why should we? This is our last night together. I'm being sent home to my mam's tomorrow. My dad won't let me stay in Knockcrea, even though I begged him.'

'You begged him to let you live here?'

'Yeah,' said Liam bitterly, 'and he told me he'd think about it. But then a few days later he said no. That was the fight you walked in on.'

Amy decided to put her cards on the table.

'I found the stuff in your room,' she said.

'You were in my room?' said Liam, and then, 'What stuff?'

'You know. The stuff you were hiding in your wardrobe.'

'What are you talking about?' He sounded utterly baffled. 'There's nothing hidden in my wardrobe. Have you gone mad?'

Amy didn't know what to believe. 'Please just bring Ruby back to Sea View,' she said. 'The two of you could hang out here.'

'No,' said Liam. 'We're staying where we are.'

He hung up.

Amy tried to call back. It went straight to voicemail.

Shit.

She looked out the window in the direction of Salt Point, where Liam had said he and Ruby were having their picnic. Evening blanketed the landscape. The windows of distant farmhouses were squares of light in the gathering dark.

What should she do now?

Turning away from the window, she registered Tom and Poppy, still tucked under a blanket in front of *Peppa Pig*, small heads drooping onto shoulders. Walking over, she plastered a fake smile on her face. 'All right, you two!' she said, picking up the remote. 'Time for bed!'

Once Tom and Poppy were sleeping soundly, Amy went back downstairs. She turned on the main lights.

No sign of Miles and June. No sign of Liam and Ruby, either.

Sunset was over, and the evening outside was turning

into night. She checked her phone. Two missed calls from Catherine. She'd given Ruby ample time to call her mother herself. Now to find out if she'd done it.

As she unlocked her phone, there was a sudden clattering sound outside, like something had been knocked over.

Amy went still, like a spooked animal.

'Hello?' she called, and then wished she hadn't.

She walked over and put her face close to the window. The dark wasn't so complete yet that she couldn't make out the cars, the trees, the low stone walls that demarcated the fields. There was no sign of movement out there.

She waited a minute. Then two.

Then she made a decision and slipped on her shoes. She typed 999 into her phone. Thumb hovering over the green button, ready to dial at a moment's notice, she unlocked the front door.

'Hello?' she called as she stepped outside. 'Is somebody there?'

A slight wind rustled her hair. She began to make her way around the side of the house, her footsteps crunching softly on the gravel.

At the back of the house, she saw that the yard brush with the long wooden handle was lying on the ground. So that was the sound she'd heard. She picked it up and propped it against the wall again. She circled the rest of the house, seeing nothing suspicious. It must've fallen over by itself.

Tucking her phone into her pocket, she lingered by the front door, looking in the direction of the beach again. The clouds were thinning and the moon was rising. Amy saw the glint of far-off headlights and wondered if it was Catherine, driving around looking for Ruby.

She walked back inside. The lights were off, and the interior of the high-ceilinged open-plan area was dim and shadowy. It took a moment for her to realise what was wrong with this picture.

I left the lights on, she thought, hand halfway to the switch. I definitely, one hundred per cent left the lights on.

Who turned them off?

She lowered her hand. She didn't want to draw any attention to herself. She moved cautiously forward, her eyes darting from left to right.

Then she heard a small sound behind her.

Bracing herself, Amy turned around.

40

A tall, black-haired man was standing inside the house, blocking Amy's way to the front door. He looked thinner than the last time she'd seen him, his face gaunt and yellowish. His eyes were locked on hers.

Instead of terror, Amy felt a kind of resigned calm. Of course this was happening. Of course he had found her.

'Who told you where I was?' she heard herself say.

He shook his head slowly from side to side. As if to say, Does it matter?

She supposed it didn't. She felt it couldn't have ended any other way than this.

'You left me.' His voice cracked. 'I looked for you, and I couldn't find you. You abandoned me.'

Amy's heart broke – and at the same time, fear spiked through her. 'I'm sorry!' she cried out. 'I didn't have a choice . . .'

He stepped forward. She saw violence in his eyes.

She ran for the back door.

It was hopeless, of course. He was six foot one, with long legs and huge strides. He caught up with her in a couple of steps. She felt his hand close on her hair, right at the top of her head, then he was dragging her back along the floor.

'You don't get to fucking run away from me!'

Amy tried to stay quiet, cognisant of Tom and Poppy asleep upstairs. If they heard her scream . . . If they woke up to this . . .

He dragged her along the floor, kicked her, pummelled her. Arms over her head, body folded up as small as she could make it, she endured it all.

'Bitch,' he called her, and she didn't disagree. 'You *abandoned* me,' he said again, and she sobbed, not from pain, but from guilt.

He was right. She had.

He was standing over her, breathing heavily, when the front door opened behind him. Attention entirely focused on Amy, he didn't notice.

But Amy saw the door swing open. She saw Catherine walk in. Looking for her daughter.

She pictured the nightmare scene through Catherine's eyes. Amy in the foetal position on the kitchen floor with a bloody lip. Black tendrils on the tiles where her hair had been ripped out. A man standing over her, his back to the door, his fists clenched.

Catherine's eyes widened. But she didn't make a sound. She looked Amy in the eye and raised a finger to her lips. *Shh.*

Then she bent down, picked up the same wooden statue that June had used in the fight with the O'Reilly brothers and began to creep forward.

Amy was struck by her courage. But she couldn't allow her to do what she was about to do. As Catherine drew nearer, raising the statue above her head, Amy cried out, 'No!'

She lunged forward and grabbed Catherine around the knees. Both women crashed onto the ground. The statue flew from Catherine's hands, bouncing harmlessly across the floor.

There was a male roar of rage. 'What the *fuck* . . .'

A size-eleven shoe collided with Catherine's abdomen, leaving her gasping. A large hand grabbed a fistful of her thick curls. Her bag was wrested from her arm, her phone from her pocket. Her eyes, shocked and betrayed, stinging with tears, met Amy's.

I'm sorry, Catherine, Amy thought desperately. I couldn't let you . . .

Amy's loyalty had not earned her any kindness. She too was kicked in the stomach, then grabbed by the hair and dragged across the tiled floor. Her phone was taken from her. She was shoved into the utility room with the washing machine and dryer. A moment later, Catherine was thrown in after her.

The door slammed. The lock clicked.

Catherine propped herself up against the wall, one hand on her stomach, still struggling for breath. 'What did you do that for?' she gasped. 'How could you be so stupid?'

'I'm sorry,' said Amy. 'I had to. Something that heavy, straight to the head – you could've killed him.'

'Look what he's done to you! Christ, Amy. I've been in an abusive relationship myself – I know it's not as simple as just hating your partner – but *Jesus* . . .'

'He's not my partner.'

'Your ex, then!' Catherine snapped. 'Whatever you want to call him!'

'He's not my ex, either,' said Amy.

Confusion furrowed Catherine's face.

'Then who is he?'

Amy closed her eyes.

'That was Robbie,' she said. 'My son.'

41

Before

Shortly before his eighteenth birthday, Robbie was arrested for possession of heroin: a small amount, for personal use. Amy couldn't wrap her head around it. He was her baby. She'd tucked him into bed at night. This couldn't be happening.

She knew he was expecting her to shout at him when she collected him from the police station. Over the past years, Amy had done plenty of shouting. Plenty of crying and pleading. But today she stayed silent. She watched Robbie from the corner of her eye as he got into the car. He was over six foot tall now. His hair had darkened from brown to black, like his father's. He looked gaunt, older than his age.

They didn't speak on the drive home, or as they parked outside and walked into the house. She could see him watching her covertly, waiting for her to explode.

She closed the front door behind her.

'Are you hungry?' she asked.

He looked at her suspiciously. 'What?'

'Are you hungry?' she repeated. 'I think I'll stick on a pizza. You want one?'

After a pause, he nodded.

Robbie went into the front room and began texting furiously. Amy resisted the urge to demand to know who he was talking to, or try to grab his phone. Instead, she put on two cheap oven pizzas and some garlic bread. When the house was full of the warm smell of food, she went into the front room and sat down on the sofa beside Robbie. He tucked his phone into his pocket.

'Robbie, I have to ask you something.'

He groaned. 'Ah, Ma, don't start.'

'I'm not going to go on about the drugs,' she said. 'I know there's no magic word I can say to make you stop.'

He blinked at her. 'What, then?'

Amy took a deep breath. 'You know how I told you once that I went to school with a girl who'd been sexually abused?'

Frowning, Robbie nodded.

Her heart was thumping so hard she felt like it should be visible through her chest. This was the hardest thing she'd ever had to say out loud. 'Robbie, I need to ask you if your dad ever did anything like that to you.'

'What?' He leapt to his feet, hangover forgotten. 'No! Fucking hell. Jesus. *No.* Why are you asking me that?'

'I had to ask!' Amy jumped up too. 'I'm glad the answer's no, but I had to ask!'

Robbie looked utterly disgusted. 'That's sick. He never did anything like that, *ever.*' He ran a hand over his shorn hair, and paced the room as if he was trying to shake the question away.

Amy persisted. 'Did he ever abuse you in other ways? Like

hit you? Get physically violent with you?'

Robbie stopped pacing. He stood facing her, breathing heavily. He was four inches taller than she was.

Eventually he said, with aggression, 'Well, what the fuck do you think?'

Amy felt suddenly unsteady, like the ground had tilted. 'He used to hit you?' she whispered.

And then, out of nowhere, he was roaring at her. Screaming as if he'd been waiting to say this for years. 'YOU KNEW WHAT HE WAS LIKE! DON'T ACT SURPRISED! YOU FUCKING KNEW!'

He whirled around and swept the ornaments and photos off the nearest shelf. He picked up a hand-held speaker and threw it at the wall with such force that it made a dent.

'Robbie,' said Amy, 'no! I didn't – I didn't know ...'

'You knew what he was like! And you made me stay with him anyway!'

The world was swimming around her.

'I didn't know he was hitting you! I would've—'

'You would've *what*?' Robbie spat at her. 'You never kept me safe. You never did what a ma is supposed to do. You made me live with him when I was little, and even when *you* got away from him, you let him take me every second weekend. Why didn't you protect me?' He was crying now, choking out ugly sobs. 'Fuck you,' he said through his tears. 'I *hate* you.'

Amy felt as if she was going to break in half. 'Why didn't you tell me?'

'He said that if I told you, he'd beat you into a coma and make me watch.' Robbie wiped his nose with the back of his hand.

'But . . .' Amy's head spun. 'I never saw any bruises.'

'He only hit me where my clothes covered. And it wasn't all hitting. He used to lock me in the wardrobe for hours.'

Amy started to sob. 'Oh God.'

Robbie looked at her with open disgust. 'Ma, stop acting like this is a big shock. How could you not have known?'

'I asked you!' Her voice shook. 'I asked you if he hurt you! I said you could tell me!'

He let out a roar of frustrated, wordless rage that she flinched away from.

'DON'T YOU BLAME ME!'

'I'm not blaming—'

'When he hit you, and people asked about it, you used to lie, didn't you?' Robbie was crying like he did as a baby, snot and tears running down his face. 'So why did you expect the truth from me when I was just a kid?'

Those words slammed into her with as much force as Mark's fists ever had.

'I didn't want you to spend weekends with him!' she said desperately. 'I went to court for supervised visits. I tried – I fought for it!'

'You didn't fight hard enough!'

He grabbed the TV and hurled it across the room. It smashed against the wall. Amy yelped, dodging away from the broken grass.

'I would've stopped him . . . Robbie, I swear, if you'd told me . . .'

'STOP FUCKING BLAMING ME!'

He rushed at her. It wasn't like Mark's attacks: careful, well-aimed jabs. It was like he was flailing in frustration and rage and his mother happened to be in the way. His swinging arms still landed some painful blows – one to her head, one to her midriff. She fell back onto the sofa. He stood over her, his face shiny with tears.

'I'm sorry!' she cried. 'I just meant that I wish I'd known! That's all I meant!'

Her arms had been raised in self-defence. She lowered them slowly to her sides. She no longer cared if he hit her. Right then, she felt she deserved it.

But Robbie was backing away. His face was tear-stained and wounded and ashamed. The anguish Amy felt in that moment would follow her for the rest of her life.

'I'm sorry, Robbie,' she sobbed. 'I'm so sorry.'

He kicked the door. He stamped on the already broken TV. He punched a hole in the wall.

Then he stormed from the house, leaving Amy shell-shocked, her whole body humming with pain.

The disintegration of what was left of their relationship destroyed Amy. It felt like clutching at sand.

Robbie came and went. Staying in the house some nights. Other nights staying God knows where. Despite his increasing violence towards her, Amy couldn't throw him out. The thought of her son sleeping in a doorway was too much for her. Every time she thought about the awful things he'd screamed at her during that life-changing fight, she went numb.

Keane kept knocking at their door. Amy kept paying him. She knew his threat to have her son shot wasn't an idle one. What else could she do?

She handed over everything she had. It was never enough.

*

The stress took its toll. Amy lost her job at the hospital after too many missed days. Now on welfare, she collected her dole from the local post office every Tuesday.

This Tuesday, as on every other, she handed her social security card to the dour-faced woman behind the till. The woman gave her a docket to sign and counted out her money unsmilingly.

Then Amy left the post office and crossed to the other side of the road, where Keane was leaning against the wall, waiting for her. His hair looked crayon-orange in the sun. He was wearing a brand-new Balenciaga tracksuit.

'All right, Amy?' His tone was light and friendly, with just a hint of cordial flirtation. 'How're you?'

Wordlessly Amy counted out the notes and handed them over. Keane took the money and counted it again, nodding to himself.

It wasn't all Amy's dole for the week, but it was most of it.

'Keane?' she said tentatively. 'Can I keep an extra twenty this week? Please? I need a filling, and my medical card won't cover another, so I'm trying to save ...'

'Yeah, course you can!' said Keane, in a surprised tone, as if to say, God, I'm not a *monster*!

He handed her back a twenty. She felt relief swell.

'I'll just take it out of next week's,' said Keane.

Her relief vanished as quickly as it had come. The thought of having even less to live on next week left her feeling winded.

He folded up the notes she'd given him, tucked them into his pocket and winked at her.

'See you next week,' he said. Amy watched him striding off in his expensive tracksuit, with that macho lilt to his walk.

She felt so tired she thought she might collapse to the concrete and melt into the earth.

Amy sometimes went hungry rather than ask Sandra for money. Sandra and Dave had limited finances. They worked hard and deserved the small, nice things they earned: subscriptions to their favourite streaming sites, their yearly fortnight in Lanzarote.

There was a soup kitchen in town that handed out food packages. Amy never sat down to eat there, but she did go in a handful of times to collect a hamper. On one occasion, as she left with a parcel in her arms, she passed two women in the street who looked like mother and daughter. The older woman glanced at Amy and sniffed.

'Nobody in our society actually goes hungry,' she said to her daughter in a carrying voice. 'They all get their dole, don't they? The types who'd go into a soup kitchen in this day and age are just chancers. After anything they can get for free.'

'Mu-um!' said the younger woman, looking embarrassed. 'Shh!'

Blood rushed to Amy's cheeks. She swallowed the lump that rose in her throat and controlled her emotions the whole way home.

It was only with the front door closed that she finally allowed herself to cry.

Shortly before Robbie's twentieth birthday, he came home late one night drunk and high. Amy was woken by the sound of him crashing up the stairs. She jumped out of bed. 'Robbie? Is that you?'

He stumbled into her room. In a slurred voice, he told her that he'd done something stupid. He'd been holding a parcel for the dealers, as a way of working off some of the money he owed them, and had lost it. The debt had now gone up by another ten grand.

Something inside Amy snapped.

'Ten grand?' she said. 'Robbie, I had to get a tooth pulled last week because I couldn't afford to have a filling done. Where do you expect me to get *ten grand*?'

'You know how it works,' he mumbled. 'You pay it off bit by bit.'

'No,' she said, shaking her head. 'Not this time. I'm not doing it.'

'If you don't pay them, they'll kill me.' His voice was getting louder. 'It's your fault my whole life has turned out shit, and now you're gonna let me get shot?'

'We have options. You could leave Dublin, start over.'

'Wherever I go, they'll find me!' he shouted at her. 'You'll find the money somewhere. You could go to loan sharks.'

'I'm not going to loan sharks!' Amy shouted back. 'I already live off scraps! I'm not making things worse for myself – I won't do it!'

He lunged at her, and suddenly she was on the ground. There was a roaring in her ears, so she couldn't quite make out what Robbie was shouting, but she heard something about Mark and his childhood. He pulled a knife from his pocket. She really believed, in that moment, that he was going to kill her. A trickle of urine ran into her underwear.

Then he stuck the knife into the mattress and stormed out.

The next week, Amy went back to the DV centre to see

Karen. Blonde, soft-spoken Karen, who had helped her leave Mark all those years ago.

'I'm experiencing domestic violence again,' she told her, sitting across from her in that same clean white room. 'But this time, it's at the hands of my son.'

She held firm to her decision. She told both Robbie and Keane that she wouldn't be taking responsibility for Robbie's latest debt.

Three weeks later, she was asleep in bed when she was woken by a loud noise downstairs. It sounded like glass breaking. She lay very still, eyes wide open in the dark. Was someone trying to break in? She'd had bars fitted on the windows when she'd first moved in. It wouldn't be easy to break into this house. She strained her ears, listening for another sound . . .

Then she smelled the smoke.

She sat up in bed, sniffing the air.

Burning.

Fire.

The moments that followed were stand-out terrifying. Afterwards, Amy would be able to remember every second. She leapt out of bed, switched on the light and saw black smoke pouring through the crack under the door.

Pulling her pyjama top over her face, she opened the door. She stumbled to the top of the stairs, looked down and saw the image that would haunt her for the rest of her life.

Orange flames danced below, blocking her way to the front door.

She turned, coughing, and made for the closed bedroom door on her left.

'Robbie!'

She grabbed the handle. The door was locked. 'Robbie? *Robbie!*' She hammered on the wood, screaming his name. He often came home drunk. What if he was passed out in there?

The smoke was getting thicker. She could barely breathe. She took a step back and dealt the door an almighty kick. Then another.

'ROBBIE!'

Smoke billowed. Heat rose from the flames below. Amy gave one more great kick.

This time, the door swung open.

Robbie's bed was empty.

He wasn't home.

Amy experienced one second of blinding relief before she staggered into her own room, eyes streaming, lungs struggling. She slammed the door shut and stumbled to the window, survival instinct propelling her. She opened it and leaned out, gulping in the cold, clean air. Then she climbed out onto the window ledge. From there, she swung herself onto the roof of her next-door neighbours' single-storey extension, with an athleticism she could never have achieved under other circumstances. The roof was slanted, and she slid over the tiles. She glimpsed her neighbour's startled face through his bedroom window as she sailed past.

She landed in the garden next door with a thump, but no broken bones. It was, as Sandra said later, a fucking miracle.

Amy staggered to the back door and banged on it. Her neighbours, a middle-aged couple, came rushing out.

'Are you all right?' the woman asked, her eyes enormous.

'Call the fire brigade,' said Amy, and then she did

something she'd never done before: she fainted, crumpling to the ground.

The petrol bomb that had started the fire was found by the firefighters in her living room – a twisted piece of blackened glass and metal.

Keane approached her in the street the next day. 'Sorry to hear about your house, Amy,' he said. 'But maybe pay us what you owe us next time, yeah?'

At Sandra and Dave's, Amy sat on the sofa in quiet shock, drinking cup of tea after cup of tea.

'You could've been killed,' said Sandra, tears in her eyes. 'I think you need to leave Dublin, Amy. At least for a while.'

'But what about Robbie?'

'Amy,' said Dave, leaning forward, 'Robbie is one of the reasons you need to leave. We're worried he might do serious harm to you.'

Amy shook her head, wanting to deny it. Then she burst into tears.

'But what if Keane and the others come after *you*?' she said.

'They won't,' said Sandra. 'They pick their targets.'

It hurt Amy to hear this, but she knew it was the truth. Sandra and Dave had each other, and three large dogs. They didn't have a child in the throes of addiction. It was Robbie who made Amy vulnerable, and yet it was Robbie who tied her to the city. She agonised over her decision. What would happen to him if she left?

But even before she'd been burned out of her home, she'd lived in fear of his increasingly erratic behaviour.

She wasn't sure who she was more afraid of any more – Keane or her own son.

When she came across the ad online, it seemed like the perfect escape route. *Live-in position looking after two fantastic kids, aged 2 and 3 . . . Competitive pay . . . A remote, beautiful location in West Cork . . .*

She spoke to June and was offered the job. She packed her bags. She changed her phone number.

Then she left to start over at Sea View.

42

Now

'How can you have an adult son?' said Catherine. 'You're not old enough!'

'I'm thirty-five,' Amy told her. 'Robbie's twenty. He's my son.'

They sat across from each other in the utility room, pale-faced and shaken. Catherine's curls stuck up where they had been torn almost out of her head.

'You're thirty-five?' Catherine sounded disbelieving. 'So you had him when you were *fifteen*?'

Amy didn't know what to say.

'You told me you'd come to Knockcrea to get away from an abusive ex!' Catherine said.

'I let you believe that,' said Amy. 'I didn't know how to tell you the truth. Robbie's dad *was* abusive towards me. But he's been in prison for years. When I came to Cork, it was my son I was running from.'

She put a hand to the tattoo on her left shoulder. Mark had

held her hand while she was getting it done. But it wasn't his name that was inked on her skin. The lettering in the heart read: *Robbie.*

Mark had never been released from prison. A week before his date, he got into a scuffle with another prisoner. He stabbed the man. The man died. Mark wouldn't be getting out for a long time. For the past five years, it had just been Amy and Robbie.

'Do you know where Ruby is?' Catherine demanded.

'She's at the beach with Liam,' Amy said in a quiet voice. 'I got through to them on the phone before Robbie appeared. She's safe.'

'You're sure? You spoke to her?'

'I did. She's fine.'

Outside, they could hear Robbie clumping around the house. Amy cringed at a particularly loud bang.

'Tom and Poppy are in bed,' she whispered. 'God, I hope he just takes it all and leaves without waking them.'

'Takes what?' Catherine asked.

'Well, he's going to burgle the house,' Amy said matter-of-factly.

Catherine was staring at her like she'd never seen her before. 'I could've stopped him. I was trying to *help* you!'

'I couldn't let you hurt him. You know I couldn't. You're a mother.'

Catherine's expression softened. 'I can't believe your own child did that to you,' she said, eyes on Amy's injured face.

'He didn't have an easy childhood,' said Amy, wiping blood from her chin. 'He blames me. He says I didn't do a good enough job of protecting him from his father. Maybe he's right. If I could go back in time and do it all differently,

I would ... But it's too late now. And he's so *angry* with me.'

Robbie's anger scared and awed her. His rage was like red-hot lava, blistering anything it touched.

'How did he find you?' Catherine asked.

'Remember that MISSING poster of me you saw on Facebook?' asked Amy. 'Well, Robbie made it. Put my face on it and his phone number. Got it circulating online. He also used a fake news generator to write an article. With a poster and a screenshot from what *looked* like a real news site, I can see why the post got so many shares on social media. It looked legitimate.' Amy spoke without emotion. 'Somebody around here must've recognised me and called the number. I'm sure they thought they were doing a good thing.'

Catherine's face was a mask of shock. 'Jesus,' she said.

They could hear the thuds and clunks of Robbie carrying something downstairs and outside. Amy guessed he had a car parked somewhere nearby.

'We need to think,' said Catherine. 'We need to get out of here.' She looked around the room. The only window was a narrow rectangle too small for anyone to squeeze through.

'I don't think there is a way out,' said Amy.

'Well, we can't just sit here,' said Catherine in frustration. 'Do you have a hairpin?'

Amy bit her lip to stop herself saying that picking a lock was harder than it looked on TV. Without a word, she took a bobby pin from her hair and handed it over.

While Catherine fiddled with the lock, Amy wondered what Robbie was thinking. His erratic, violent behaviour terrified her, and yet it was easy for her to see the hurt little boy he was inside, to imagine how abandoned he must have felt when he discovered she'd fled Dublin. She wished more than anything that he was small again, so she could comfort him without fear. So she could protect him this time.

'What was that?' said Catherine in a sudden whisper.

Amy started. 'What?'

'I heard voices!'

Amy crawled over and pressed her ear against the locked door. She heard the rumbling of a male voice.

Then footsteps. Two pairs.

She drew a deep breath, and called softly through the door: 'Who's there?'

43

Amy and Catherine were silent in the utility room, listening.

'Who's there?' Amy called again.

'Amy?' It was Liam's voice on the other side of the door. 'Where are you?'

'Keep your voice down!' she hissed. 'We're locked in the utility room. Let us out, quick!'

The key turned. The door swung open.

Liam stood there, baffled. Ruby was a few feet behind him. She had Liam's hoodie around her shoulders. Her mouth fell open when she saw her mother.

'Ruby!' Catherine jumped to her feet and grabbed her startled daughter by the hand. 'We have to go, now.'

'Why?' Ruby asked. 'What's going on?'

There was a loud thud upstairs, followed by the sound of Robbie swearing. Both teenagers jumped. 'Who's that?' said Liam sharply.

'Just get out of here,' said Amy, steering them in the direction of the door. 'All three of you.'

'What about you?' asked Liam. He was staring in frank alarm at Amy's bloody lip.

'Tom and Poppy are upstairs,' she said. 'I can't leave them. But you three need to go, now, before—'

'Nobody's going anywhere,' said a new voice.

All four of them whirled around to see the young man who'd appeared at the bottom of the stairs. He had vivid orange hair and a sharp vulpine face, and he was wearing a flashy designer tracksuit.

'No,' said Amy helplessly.

'All right, Amy?' said Keane, approaching her. 'How's things? When Robbie said he'd found you, I said I'd drive down with him. Thought it might be interesting.' He glanced around at the huge house. 'I was right, wasn't I?'

Catherine, Ruby and Liam stood stock still. The sense of danger emanating from Keane had fixed them in place.

'You've been here the whole time?' Amy asked, horrified.

Keane nodded, grinning. 'Thought I'd have a look around while you and Robbie had your little reunion.'

Behind him, Robbie came stumbling down the stairs with a TV in his arms. He looked gangly and pitiful in contrast with Keane's tense, composed presence. Amy gave him a pleading look. She couldn't believe he'd brought Keane here. Shamefaced, Robbie looked away.

'So,' said Keane, his pale eyes flicking from person to person. 'Who owns this house?'

'The homeowners are out, but they'll be back any minute,' Amy answered. It was a lie. She doubted Miles and June would get back from Clongrassil any time soon.

Keane's gaze settled on Ruby and Liam, who looked terrified. 'And where did you two come from?' Ruby shrank back, and he smiled at her. 'No need to be shy, love. Do you live in this house?'

Liam put an arm in front of her and moved her back while he took two steps forward. 'She doesn't live here,' he said. 'I do.'

Ignoring Liam, Keane turned to Catherine. 'This your daughter, yeah?'

Catherine took a deep breath, as if considering denying it, then nodded.

'Where do you go to school, sweetheart?' Keane asked in his easy manner.

'John of God's?' Ruby answered on a question mark, glancing at her mother.

'And what's your name?'

'Ruby.'

'Very good,' said Keane.

Then he turned to Catherine.

'Listen,' he said. 'If you cooperate, yous can all go home safe tonight. You, your daughter, her boyfriend. But if you don't, well . . . there'll be trouble.' He shrugged, in an apologetic, it-just-can't-be-helped way. 'See, I know Ruby's name now. I know her face. I know where she goes to school.'

Catherine blanched.

'If you care about your daughter,' he continued, 'you won't go running to the cops tomorrow. Just do what you're asked tonight and keep your mouth shut afterwards, and you'll never hear from us again.'

As he spoke, he pulled a knife from his pocket. The blade gleamed silver in the moonlight that streamed through the windows.

'What do you want?' Catherine asked hoarsely.

'First, phones,' said Keane. 'You two' – he nodded at Ruby and Liam – 'hand them over.' They did. 'Robbie, you have the two other phones, right?'

'Yeah.'

'All right,' said Keane, 'here's what we're gonna do. You three' – he waved the knife at Amy, Liam and Ruby – 'are going to stay here with Robbie. You and me,' he addressed Catherine, 'are going to go for a little drive. How many credit cards do you have?'

'Three.'

'Each with a daily withdrawal of five hundred or so, is that right?'

'Yes.'

'So a grand and a half.' Keane nodded. 'That's a start.'

'No fucking way!' Liam said, suddenly and loudly. 'Don't go anywhere with him, Catherine! Don't give him any money!'

In a flash, Keane turned the blade in Liam's direction. 'Enough of that,' he said in a quiet voice that was more threatening than any shout. 'If you don't keep your mouth shut, I'll have to put this knife through you.'

Liam fell silent.

'Keane,' said Robbie, 'there's enough stuff in the house to—'

'Shut the fuck up, Robbie, and go keep an eye on the door,' said Keane. 'The owners could be back any minute.'

Robbie complied.

Keane turned his focused gaze back to Catherine. Her face was milk white. She said quietly, 'Just do as he says, Liam, Ruby, *please*. It's not worth anyone getting hurt.'

'Very good,' said Keane. 'Very smart. Your daughter's safety – that's more important than a few quid, isn't it?'

Eyes on the blade, Catherine nodded.

'All right,' said Keane, gesturing. 'Let's go.'

Catherine moved reluctantly towards the door.

Ruby gave a small, terrified shake of her head. 'Mam, please don't leave me.'

'Shut up,' said Keane, the sharp tip of his blade swinging around so that it pointed towards her stomach. Ruby made a whimpering sound and drew back.

Then Liam stepped in front of her.

'Don't point that at her,' he said stupidly.

No, thought Amy. No, no . . .

Keane began to laugh. Robbie moved away from his post at the window and began drifting casually towards Liam's other side. Between these two men, Liam looked exactly like what he was: a schoolboy. Young. Scared.

But he kept standing between Ruby and the knife.

Catherine was frozen, unable to tear her eyes from her daughter.

'Listen, pal,' said Keane to Liam. 'Get inside that room.' He nodded towards the utility room. 'The three of you. In there, now.'

Robbie said, 'Come on, let's go,' almost soothingly, and reached out and grabbed Ruby by the arm.

'Don't touch her!' Liam shouted.

Then everything happened very fast.

Liam knocked Robbie's arm away. Then Liam and Robbie were grappling. Keane leapt in. Amy dragged Ruby back.

'Go, get out of here!' she yelled.

'*Liam!*' Ruby screamed.

Liam was being pummelled, tossed from side to side like

a rag doll. Ruby tried to run to him. Amy pulled her away and pushed her towards the front door. '*Run*, Ruby!'

Then Catherine had Ruby by the arm. In the chaos, she managed to escape with her daughter into the night.

Amy turned back to the melee. She jumped onto Keane's back, trying to drag him off Liam. He shook her off like a dog shaking off water, and she fell back onto the kitchen floor. He turned around. While Robbie and Liam continued to grapple, he advanced on her, his face a mask of icy rage.

Then a heavy object shattered over his head.

Amy blinked. It took her a second to realise what had happened. After getting her daughter outside, Catherine had come back in. She'd grabbed the ceramic fruit bowl from the kitchen table and smashed it over Keane's head.

Keane didn't collapse like people did in the movies. He blinked a couple of times, ceramic and dust on his shoulders, then turned to Catherine. She backed away rapidly, but he caught up with her in two strides and punched her with a boxer's trained precision.

She hit the floor and didn't move again.

'Catherine!' Amy cried out.

Keane turned to Robbie and Liam, who were still tussling. Liam seemed to be holding his own, more or less, until Keane waded in. He was animalistic – grappling, writhing like an eel in his thrashing movements.

Amy looked around for a weapon. She saw the poker by the fireplace and ran to grab it. When she turned back around, the fight had moved to the living room. Keane caught Liam with a blow that knocked him off his feet and sent him crashing through the glass coffee table.

'*Liam!*' Amy screamed.

She swung the poker at Keane. It hit him in the ribs. He wrenched it from her grasp and then aimed a punch at her. Unlike Catherine, Amy was used to deflecting blows. She dodged, avoiding the worst of the impact.

Then Robbie grabbed her.

Amy couldn't fight her son with the same spark and rage she could use to fight Keane. Fatigue overcame her. She let Robbie push her back towards the kitchen. When she tried to dodge past him, his fist connected with her temple, harder perhaps than he meant it to.

She hit the ground.

The world swam. She raised her head. On the other side of the room, Liam had struggled to his feet. Both Keane and Robbie were on him in seconds. She saw them scuffling, and saw Liam knocked to the ground. She couldn't see what was happening then, but she heard him cry out in pain—

'Come on!' Keane said to Robbie. 'Fuck this. It's not worth it. We need to get out of here.'

'Fuck,' said Robbie. 'What've you done?'

'Just move, would you?'

The door slammed.

They were gone.

Amy tried to stand, but she was too dizzy. 'Liam?' She tried to crawl to him, but her consciousness was ebbing, the world darkening. Before she could reach him, she sank down onto the bloody, glass-scattered rug and passed out.

44

When Amy regained consciousness, she was lying on the floor of the immaculate living room. Moonlight streamed through the floor-to-ceiling windows she had cleaned the day before, illuminating the open-plan space and stylish furniture.

She was on her side on the rug. The rug was soaked with blood.

Amy pushed herself up onto one arm, feeling a wave of the nausea that often accompanied a blow to the head. She looked at her left hand. It was covered in a liquid that appeared black in the pale light, like the hand of a child who'd been finger-painting.

Was it her blood? It couldn't be. There was too much of it. So whose . . .?

Then she saw the body on the other side of the room.

'No.' Amy choked out the word. She crawled on her hands and knees across the blood-drenched rug, through shattered glass, past the broken coffee table, to the human shape lying motionless on the floor. 'No, no, no ...'

All around was silence and thin grey moonlight.

'Liam, please wake up,' she sobbed.

Memories of the fight flooded back to her in vivid detail. Robbie saying to Keane: *What've you done?* Now she understood why they'd fled the scene.

Amy didn't know CPR. She had never learned how to pump and breathe a body back to life. She felt for a pulse, but couldn't find one. Was he breathing? She put her ear to his mouth. To her immense relief, she felt air moving in and out of his lungs. 'Oh, thank God, thank God ...'

Ambulance. She needed an ambulance.

She felt in her pockets for her phone. Then she remembered that Robbie had taken it. The Carrolls didn't have a landline.

'No,' she whispered. Then she screamed it. '*No!*'

At that moment, the front door opened and Catherine came rushing in, Ruby behind her. Catherine turned on the main light. Ruby saw Liam and let out a strangled cry.

'We need to call an ambulance!' Amy shouted.

'There's one on the way,' said Catherine. 'I called it before I went to find Ruby.'

Ruby ran to Liam's side. Catherine walked over and crouched down. She had the beginnings of two black eyes.

'How did you call an ambulance?' Amy asked. 'They took our phones.'

'I found this one on the ground,' said Catherine.

'That's my phone,' said Amy in confusion. Was this an accident, or had Robbie dropped it intentionally? She filed the thought away for later and put the phone into her pocket. All that mattered now was that an ambulance was on the way.

Ruby knelt in Liam's blood and pulled his head onto her lap. 'Liam, please wake up,' she sobbed.

His head lolled.

'Please God, let that ambulance get here soon,' whispered Catherine.

'He's going to be okay, isn't he?' Ruby asked. 'Tell me he's going to be okay!'

'He's breathing,' said Amy, which was all she could say. She didn't know which of Liam's organs the knife had penetrated. He was losing a lot of blood.

Ruby was stroking his hair, sobbing. Catherine and Amy made eye contact, expressions fearful. Then something outside caught their attention.

Over the mountain ridge, flashing blue lights appeared, and the wail of an ambulance echoed across Knockcrea.

When the paramedics came rushing in, Amy hung back. She didn't mention her own injuries. She didn't want to distract them from Liam.

'Can I go with him in the ambulance, Mam?' Ruby asked. Her face was streaked with mascara-stained tears.

Catherine nodded. 'We'll both go.' She looked at Amy.

'I need to stay here,' Amy said hollowly. 'I can't leave Tom and Poppy.'

Catherine looked a bit startled at the reminder of Tom and Poppy's existence. Thanks to the soundproofed walls, the two younger Carroll children had slept through everything. 'I'll use one of the paramedics' phones to call Aveen Butler,' she said. 'I'll ask her to babysit. As soon as she gets here, follow us to the hospital, okay?'

Then she hurried after Ruby to the ambulance.

Amy stood at the window and watched the blue lights disappear over the ridge of the mountain again. She had never been particularly religious, but in that moment, she prayed.

Aveen Butler arrived within twenty minutes. She was full of questions, but Amy barely acknowledged her. She raced outside, leapt into her car, and put the name of the hospital into Google Maps.

That long, agonising drive was one of the worst experiences of her life. She would never forget it. When she arrived at the hospital, the woman behind the desk tried to send her to the emergency department. Amy brushed aside her concern. 'I'm fine! I don't need help. I'm looking for someone. Liam Carroll.'

They sent her to a waiting room on the third floor. On her way there, people stared, reminding her how bad she looked. When she opened the swinging doors, she found Catherine and Ruby sitting in plastic seats. Catherine's face was badly swollen. Ruby was still wearing Liam's hoodie, and her clothes were covered in his blood.

'Is he okay?' said Amy.

'We don't know,' said Catherine. 'We haven't heard anything yet.'

Amy sank down into a nearby seat and closed her eyes.

Please let him be okay. Please God, let Liam be okay.

If he wasn't, it was her fault.

They sat for a while in silence. It was interrupted when the waiting-room door slammed open and Miles and June walked in. Miles was still wearing his grey work suit. His face was pale.

'How's he doing?' he asked. 'Is he awake?'

June, behind him, was sobbing. Her hair was a mess and her cheeks were tear-streaked.

'We don't know anything yet,' said Catherine quietly. 'We're waiting for the doctor.'

'Oh God,' said June. 'Oh God.' She clutched at Miles.

Amy couldn't speak. She couldn't look at Miles or June directly. Catherine was the one who had called them. Amy hadn't been able to face it. Out of the corner of her eye, she watched them sit down.

'Tell us what happened,' said Miles.

Catherine summarised the events briefly, avoiding un-necessary detail. Miles didn't seem to care about much beyond the very basics: there had been a burglary and Liam had been stabbed. That Amy had known the men, that it was her presence that had caused this disaster – none of that seemed to register with him, not at that moment. His focus was entirely on his son.

When Catherine finished, June's eyes were on Amy. 'You have an adult son?' she said quietly. 'You never told us that.'

Amy didn't know what to say.

Miles buried his face in his hands. 'Dear God,' he said in a muffled voice, 'please let Liam be all right. Dear God.' He raised his head, caught Amy watching him and spoke directly to her. 'There are things I regret. The first three years of his life . . . If I could change . . .'

The door swung open and a doctor walked in. He was a tall man with a kindly face. Everyone stood up.

'My son?' said Miles.

The hope and fear contained in those two words were unlike anything Amy had ever heard.

'You're the family of Liam Carroll?' asked the doctor.

Miles nodded.

The doctor raised a hand in a reassuring gesture. 'He's going to be fine,' he said.

Miles sat down again, with a shaky noise somewhere between a laugh and a sob. June collapsed into the seat beside him and threw her arms around him. Ruby burst into tears, and Catherine hugged her.

'His vitals are all good,' the doctor continued. 'He's lost a lot of blood, but no internal organs were punctured. He's recovering well.'

Amy felt dizzy with relief.

Oh, thank God. Thank God.

The relief lasted only seconds. Then fresh guilt struck. Liam had been *stabbed*. Because of her.

She clapped a hand to her mouth, jumped to her feet and ran for the bathroom. She made it to a toilet just in time, leaning over the bowl to vomit until she was bringing up bile. Afterwards, she stood at the sink and stared at herself in the mirror. Her hair was tangled and her lip split. She was covered in blood, some of it Liam's, some her own. She looked like what she was: trouble. Everywhere she went, violence and chaos followed.

Without saying a word to anyone, she walked out of the hospital and into the clear-skied, indifferent night. In the back of her car, on the side of the road, she pulled a coat over herself and fell into a fitful sleep.

45

One week later

Two men have been arrested in connection with the stabbing
of a juvenile in Cork. Craig Keane, 25, of Barrymeade, Dublin,
who has 19 previous convictions, has been remanded without
bail. The second man involved in the incident, Robert Daniel
Keating, also of Barrymeade, has been charged with burglary
and aggravated assault . . .

Amy looked up from the newspaper. Raindrops dotted the
windscreen of her car. She had read the article many times
since she bought the paper that morning.

For the past week, she had been sleeping in her car in
Cork city, a two-hour drive from Knockcrea. Unable to face
returning to Sea View to collect her things, she'd bought
cheap clothes from Penneys and toiletries from a chemist.
She used the bathrooms at the public pool to shower. She
saw women staring at her bruised body and knew what a
shocking sight she made.

At the Garda station in Clongrassil, she had given a state-ment. She'd tried to say as little as possible, claiming the blow to her head had affected her memory. She knew Catherine was giving a detailed statement, and so her own lack of cooperation would make little difference. Still, she couldn't bear the thought that her own words might be used against Robbie in court.

She looked down at his photograph in the newspaper, then closed it over. Her phone began to ring. She picked it up. Catherine.

'Hi, Catherine.'

'How're you?' said Catherine. 'Did you see the news?'

'Yeah, I saw.'

'D'you want to talk about it?'

'Not really,' said Amy, pushing the newspaper aside.

Catherine had been calling her every day and filling her in on all that was happening in Knockcrea. The village was buzzing with excitement. Burglary! A stabbing! And the housekeeper's *son* was involved! Rumours were flying around that Amy had been colluding with Robbie and Keane, and that she'd taken the job at Sea View in order to case the house and steal from her employers.

'I was calling to discuss Liam, actually,' said Catherine.

'What about him?' Amy said in sudden panic. 'Is he okay?'

Liam was still in hospital. Amy lived in fear of hearing he'd taken a turn for the worse.

'He's fine,' Catherine reassured her. 'I brought Ruby to visit him yesterday, and he's doing well. Actually, I was thinking that you should visit him.'

'What?' said Amy. 'Catherine, if Miles and June caught me there, they'd kill me.'

'Miles and June won't be at the hospital tomorrow,' said Catherine briskly. 'The only other person who'll be there at visiting hour is Ruby. You should go and see her and Liam.'

'Why?'

'They've both been asking for you,' said Catherine. 'They went through this deeply traumatic experience with you. You can't just disappear without ever speaking to them again.'

'I really think it'd be better for everyone if I stayed away,' said Amy weakly.

'You're wrong,' said Catherine firmly. 'The kids need to see you. It'll help them heal.'

Guilt gnawed at Amy. 'You really think so?'

'I do,' said Catherine without hesitation.

When the call ended, Amy slumped in her car. She was experiencing a sensation like seasickness. She dreaded facing Liam when it was her fault he had almost died.

But Catherine had been persuasive. The next day, Amy found herself outside the doors of the hospital at 2 p.m. Following the instructions Catherine had texted her, she got the lift to the third floor, walked down the corridor on the left and went through the last set of swinging doors.

In the bed by the window, Liam was propped up on pillows. Ruby was sitting in a chair beside him, the sun shining through the glass behind her. There was an open Domino's pizza box on Liam's lap. On his bedside table was a second pizza, a two-litre bottle of Coke and two boxes of cookies. Ruby and Liam, deep in laughter, turned their heads as Amy walked in.

'Hi,' she said hesitantly.

They waved her over. She took the uncomfortable chair on the other side of the bed.

'Your poor face, Amy,' was the first thing Ruby said. 'Does it hurt?'

'It's not that bad, honestly. I'm just glad Liam's all right.'

'I'm fine,' said Liam through a mouthful of pizza. 'They say I can go home in a couple of days.' Unscrewing the lid of the Coke, he added, 'I'm going to have a bad-ass scar, too.'

Amy suppressed a shudder as she remembered the dark pool of blood on the living-room floor.

'We really wanted to talk to you, Amy,' said Ruby shyly. 'We wanted to make sure you were okay.'

'I'm fine,' said Amy, as convincingly as she could. 'You don't have to worry about me.'

Liam offered her the box of pizza. She shook her head.

'There was some stuff we wanted to tell you, too,' he said, putting the box back down on his lap.

'Like what?' Amy asked.

He and Ruby exchanged a furtive look.

'Remember the night you saw somebody smoking outside the house?' he said. 'That was Ruby.'

'That was *you*?' Amy couldn't believe it.

Ruby made an apologetic face, but there was a grin in her eyes. 'Yeah,' she said, reaching for a cookie. 'Sorry about that.'

'I felt bad when I saw how scared you were,' Liam said to Amy. 'But I had to really commit to pretending there was an intruder. If Miles and June had figured it out, they would've told Ruby's mother.'

'My mam would've hit the roof,' said Ruby.

'And the night Eileen misplaced her money?' Liam continued. 'Well, I *was* out that night. Margaret Collins did see me. I went to meet Ruby. But I couldn't admit that in front of my parents.'

'Your mam knows now, right?' Amy said to Ruby.

Ruby nodded. 'And she searched my room and found cigarettes, so I'm grounded for, like, a month. But I'm allowed to visit Liam. Mam loves Liam now.'

Liam grinned. 'Turns out getting stabbed for your girlfriend is a pretty effective way of impressing her parents.'

As the conversation meandered on, Amy came to understand the messages Liam had sent Ruby (*I've done it loads of times . . . We won't get caught*). He'd been trying to convince her to climb down the rocks onto Salt Point, where they'd watched the sunset. That beach was private land, and Ruby had been worried that they'd get in trouble with Al Thompson, the notoriously grumpy landowner.

'There was something I wanted to ask you,' Amy said to Liam when he'd finished describing their trip to the beach. 'You know that Fastman poster you have on your wall? It has a pentagram on it, with an inverted cross, just like the symbol I saw painted on the cottage.'

'Does it?' Liam looked honestly puzzled. 'To tell you the truth, I never noticed. Lots of bands go for that kind of imagery.'

Amy pictured the person in the balaclava. 'And neither of you know who was behind the graffiti? Or who planted the stuff in Liam's room?'

'Wasn't it your son who was doing all that stuff?' said Ruby.

'Of course not,' said Amy gently. 'The graffiti started before I arrived in Knockcrea, remember?'

'My room's on the ground floor,' said Liam. 'Anyone could've climbed in.'

There was a pause. Amy cleared her throat. 'You know, I came here to apologise,' she said. 'For what happened.'

'I don't blame you,' Liam said. 'It wasn't your fault.'

Tears sprang to Amy's eyes. The hospital room blurred. 'I *am* to blame, though,' she said thickly. 'And I'm so sorry.'

'You didn't stab Liam,' Ruby said firmly. 'Keane did.'

'Well.' Amy wiped her eyes. 'Thank you both for saying that.'

She said goodbye a short while later, leaving Ruby and Liam to their pizza. She stepped out of the hospital feeling lighter. Catherine had been right. She had needed to see Liam, happy and whole.

The visit had been a tonic.

Back in her car, she found the courage to make a phone call she had been putting off. She had a pit in her stomach as she pressed the phone to her ear. When a woman said 'Hello?' in a warm Limerick accent, she almost hung up.

But she steeled herself. 'Lina, it's me. Amy.'

'I got your text,' said Lina warily. 'You said you had something important to tell me?'

'I'm not asking for the job back,' said Amy. 'I understand you've given it to someone else. But I wanted to explain. See, I have a son, and he has addiction issues . . .' Speaking calmly and precisely, she told Lina the truth behind the MISSING poster and how it was a ruse to find her. 'I know this isn't going to make you want to hire me,' she said when she was finished, 'but I wanted you to know the truth.'

There was silence on the other end of the phone.

Then Lina burst into tears.

'Lina?'

'Oh God,' Lina said. 'Oh God.'

In a rush of words, Lina admitted that she was the one who had called the number on the poster and reported Amy's location. She had believed that Amy really was erratic and confused, and that her family was worried. She had believed she was doing the right thing. Amy felt strangely calm as she listened.

'They're going to find you!' said Lina through her tears. 'You need to get out of there!'

'They already found me,' said Amy. 'But it's not your fault – please don't blame yourself.'

Before she knew it, she was telling Lina all about what had happened in Knockcrea. The fight. Liam's stabbing. By the end of the phone call, both women were in tears.

'You have no idea how sorry I am,' Lina kept saying.

'It's not your fault,' Amy said over and over. 'How were you to know?'

When she finally put the phone down, she sat in her car for a while, just thinking. A little more of the terrible weight she had been carrying seemed to have eased.

She pulled her seat belt across her chest. She suddenly felt she had the energy to return to Sea View and collect her things. It would be foolish not to. Although she still felt nervous at the thought of facing Miles and June, she was too low on money to replace all the items she'd left behind.

Something occurred to her. Ruby had been the person smoking outside the house, and Liam was the one who'd been sneaking out at night. Which meant that nobody had been watching Sea View, except for the three strangers in their Halloween masks.

Unless . . .

Several memories flashed in her mind's eye – a pineapple-shaped jar; a figure in a balaclava – and a theory began to form.

No, she told herself. That's crazy. There's no way . . .

But it would explain everything.

Frowning, she turned the key in the ignition. She would have plenty of time to think on the drive to Knockcrea.

46

Amy arrived at Sea View in the late afternoon. The sun was low but bright in the sky as she pulled into the driveway. Although she had her keys, she rang the doorbell.

June answered. She looked put together as always, in the sleeveless lilac dress she often wore around the house, but her expression was stony.

'Hi, June,' said Amy.

June didn't return the greeting.

'Your things are there,' she said, nodding towards a packed suitcase.

Amy nodded. So they didn't want her in their house for a single second.

'Did you pack my iPhone charger?' she said. 'I think it was under the bed.'

Irritated, June stepped aside. 'Go on, then,' she said. 'You can look for it.'

Amy walked into the house. It had almost been returned

to its previous immaculate state. Almost. The coffee table hadn't been replaced yet. Neither had the rug Liam had bled on. The middle of the room looked bare.

Miles was sitting on the L-shaped sofa in front of the empty space where the coffee table had been. He looked dishevelled, with dark shadows under his eyes.

'Ah, Amy,' he said, looking up from his phone. 'I'm surprised you have the nerve to show your face around here. You know, I never did thank you for getting my son stabbed and almost killed. Really, I'm delighted we hired you.'

'Just two minutes and I'll be gone, Miles.'

Amy walked quickly to the beautiful bedroom where she had briefly lived and would never sleep again. She could hear Miles and June talking in the front room, their voices a low hum. She didn't look under the bed for the iPhone charger. After all, it was in her car. She just waited, peering around the door, until June sat down on the sofa with Miles.

Once they were distracted, she tiptoed out, light as she could, past Liam's bedroom and towards June's office. The door was open. She darted inside and made straight for the desk. Unscrewing the ornamental pineapple jar, she took out the tube of sleeping tablets with the name *June Carroll* on the label. She tucked it into her pocket, then walked back to the living room.

Miles and June were still on the sofa, talking in low voices. Amy went over and sat on the smaller sofa across from them.

They both stared.

'Is there a reason you're still here?' said Miles.

'I have something to tell you.' Amy's heart was racing. What if the theory she had been thinking over on the long drive down here was wrong? She looked from Miles to June and back again.

'Spit it out,' said Miles. 'Then you can be on your way.'

Amy swallowed. 'Firstly, I'm sorry. You have no idea how sorry I am. Liam was hurt because of me. I'll carry that with me the rest of my life.'

'Sorry can't undo the damage you've done to our family,' said June. '*Sorry?* Is that all you have to say for yourself?'

'No,' said Amy. 'There's more.' She looked directly at Miles. 'I know who's been vandalising the village. And I know why they wanted to frame Liam.'

Miles sat up a little straighter, tucking his phone into his pocket. 'You do, do you?' He sounded sceptical. 'Who was it, then?'

'Your wife,' she told him.

He stared at her like he was sure he'd misheard.

June laughed, a high-pitched, fluttery sound. 'That's absolutely ludicrous.'

'She's the one who planted the items in Liam's room,' Amy said, still speaking to Miles. 'She sent the anonymous note. Remember those masked figures who were supposedly lurking outside the house? That was all bullshit. Nobody saw them but June. She invented them.'

'Is this your idea of a joke?' Miles said loudly.

'She's been behind the graffiti the whole time. She got the idea when Liam vandalised the "Welcome to Knockcrea" sign – he did do that, that *was* him. But June found the spray-paint cans he'd thrown out, and decided to frame him for something worse. She broke Sean Geraghty's car windows. She slashed Martin Doyle's tyres. She stole Eileen's money. She wrote cryptic messages in red paint around the village. She wanted everyone – but especially you, Miles – to believe that Liam was this dangerous kid. That it wasn't safe to have him around. She copied the pentagram from a poster in his room – another way to link everything to him.'

'This is insanity,' said June. She was clutching her husband's arm like it was a prize she'd won. 'She's lying, honey. I mean, *why* would I—'

'You've got this wrong,' said Miles. 'June wouldn't do that.'

'I think she did,' Amy told him. 'And I think she drugged you with sleeping tablets so you wouldn't notice her sneaking out at night.'

'Sleeping tablets?' he scoffed. 'I've never taken a sleeping tablet in my life.'

'June, do *you* take sleeping tablets?' Amy asked.

June said nothing. Her lips were a thin line.

'Neither of us do,' Miles answered for her.

Amy took the tube of pills from her pocket and handed it to Miles. 'Then why does she have these in her office?'

'What's this?' said Miles, his face screwed up in confusion as he peered at the label. 'June? How long have you been taking these?'

June swallowed. 'I've been having trouble sleeping recently. I didn't want to worry you.'

'She used them to drug you,' Amy said to Miles. 'Get a test done if you don't believe me. You'll have them in your system.'

June flinched at that, but said nothing.

'Bullshit,' said Miles, but with less confidence.

'Remember the night I saw the vandal at the abandoned farmhouse?' Amy continued. 'Think back. I bet June also happened to be out that evening.'

Miles turned to his wife. 'But that's right,' he said. 'You

went out for a walk that night. You got home just a few minutes before Amy did.'

'Miles, I went out for a *walk*,' said June. 'Does that make me guilty of some convoluted crime?' She turned on Amy. 'I can't believe what I'm hearing. I've been nothing but kind to you. Were you jealous of me all along? Is that what this is about?'

Amy ignored her. 'Tell me if I've got this bit right,' she said to Miles. 'Liam asked you if he could come and live in Knockcrea, didn't he? And you were considering letting him. But when you mentioned this to June, she said it was a terrible idea. Dangerous.'

She now understood the fight she had overheard between them.

'That's right,' said Miles, staring at his wife. 'You did say that.'

'I think your willingness to let Liam move in panicked her,' said Amy. 'Made her realise she had to step her campaign up a notch. It was after that that she killed Noleen's cat.'

June's expression was pure, trembling rage. 'How *dare* you!' she spat.

Miles was blinking rapidly, like a man who'd stepped into sudden daylight.

'I should have realised,' said Amy. 'I could see how much she hated having Liam around. She was always trying to turn me against him. Making out he was this awful kid. She told me some story about how he was expelled for locking a claustrophobic girl in the school changing rooms. But I bet not a word of that was true, was it, June?'

June swallowed, but again said nothing.

'Wait,' said Miles slowly. 'I know that story. That's something that happened while *June* was at school. A girl was

locked in the changing rooms overnight and left traumatised.' He turned to his wife. 'Liam was expelled for being
cheeky to teachers. Did you tell Amy it was because he'd
done something terrible to another student?'

'No! Of course not!'

Miles pulled his arm away from her. 'How does Amy
know the story if you didn't tell her?'

June turned to face Amy. Her expression was poison.

'You *common* little bitch,' she said, her genteel voice a
twisted snarl. 'I should have never let you into our house.
I should have slammed the door in your face when I heard
that accent. Liam nearly died because of you!'

'Don't pretend you care about Liam,' said Amy.

June stood up. 'Get out!' she said, her voice shaking.

Amy stood, too, tense and wary. There was something
snakelike in June's posture, something frightening.

'June?' Miles said.

His wife whirled around.

Miles was also on his feet. 'If I get a drug test,' he asked,
'will there be sleeping pills in my system?'

For a long moment, June looked stricken.

Then she burst into tears.

'I did it for us, Miles! For our family! Liam's trouble, you
know he is. I had Tom and Poppy to think of.' She was
grovelling now, frantic. 'I didn't want to, I *had* to! He's a
drug-smoking, delinquent little ... I couldn't let my children
grow up with that influence under their own roof!'

'I'm not hearing this,' said Miles.

June's voice suddenly became low, soft, persuasive. 'You'd
be happier, Miles, without Liam around. You know it's
true ... You know you never wanted him in the first place ...'

Miles was staring at her like he'd never seen her before.

'You can admit it to me, Miles ... you don't have to feel guilty. It was Evvie's choice to keep him. The two of you weren't supposed to have a child together. *Tom* should have been your first child. You and me and Tom and Poppy – that's the way it's supposed to be!'

Tears dashed down her cheeks. She reached for him.

'Don't touch me,' he said, taking two rapid steps backwards. 'You don't know anything – *anything* – about how I feel about Liam. You're sick!'

'Amy's not right about everything!' June's voice was a high, desperate babble. 'I didn't kill the cat. It was hit by a car. I found its body and hung it up to frighten people. But I didn't kill it!'

'You think I care what happened to the fucking cat? I'm talking about my *son*.' Miles shook his head at her. 'You disgust me.'

'Oh, *please!*' said June shrilly. 'You're disgusted by me? After everything I put up with from *you*? All the affairs! Sleeping with the goddam nanny!'

'There was nothing going on between me and Georgia! It was all in your head.'

'You expect me to believe that?'

'I'm not the only one who's had affairs in this marriage!' Miles snapped back. 'What about you and Stephen the checkout boy, carrying on for months?'

June was sobbing now. 'I've had *one* affair, *one*, and you conflate it with your behaviour as if we're the same. You can't keep it in your pants for two minutes! But I always forgive you – I forgive you everything – and now you can't do the same for me.'

'You tried to destroy my relationship with my son! In the most warped, twisted—'

'To protect our family! Our children!'

'Liam is my family! He is one of my children!'

They were both screaming at the top of their lungs now. Neither of them seemed to notice as Amy slipped away. She picked up her suitcase and let herself out the front door, closing it gently behind her. As she walked to her car, she could hear the shouting rage on inside the house.

She drove away.

Epilogue

Amy and Robbie sat facing each other in plastic seats, a small table between them. The prison visiting room was chaotic with rising and falling voices, conversations bubbling all around as families greeted each other, sharing stories and grievances. But their table was silent. All Amy's attempts to make conversation so far had been shut down. Her tentative 'How've you been?' was met with a snarled 'How do you think I've been?'

Not much she could say to that.

She had driven from Limerick to Portlaoise to visit him. When her thirty-minute visiting time was up, it was Limerick she would return to. She hadn't set foot in Dublin in many months. Although Keane was in prison now, the men he'd worked for weren't, and returning to her old home would put her back on their radar.

Limerick was her home now.

When Lina had asked her if she still wanted to work for

her, Amy had been hesitant. 'You don't need to offer me the job because you feel guilty,' she'd said. But Lina had insisted that wasn't what she was doing.

'Things didn't work out with the girl I hired,' she said. 'And I always thought you were the best candidate. And I'm sorry to sound brutal, but now that your son's in prison, he's not a danger any more.'

Now Amy had a room in Lina's apartment, with freshly painted walls and a desk by the window. She pushed baby Pádraig in his buggy by the river every morning. She and Lina ate together in the evenings, and watched addictive TV like *Married at First Sight* and *Love Island*. Piece by piece, she was building a life.

Still, it was strange to think that she wouldn't have her job if her son hadn't been handed a three-year sentence.

Robbie had been behind bars for six months. It was a huge relief to Amy when he was sent to prison in Portlaoise instead of Dublin. It meant she was able to safely visit him. Every weekend, she drove up from Limerick to see him. Or to try to. This was the first time he had actually come out to meet her. She tried not to feel disheartened that he was sitting in silence, glowering at her. It was a start.

There was something she had wanted to ask him for a while. 'Robbie, you dropped my phone on purpose, didn't you? When you left Sea View. You wanted to make sure I'd have a way of calling an ambulance for Liam.'

He said nothing, but she knew from his face that she was right.

'How's he doing?' he asked after a while. 'Liam.'

Amy was quietly delighted he wanted to know. 'I was talking to Catherine the other day and she said he's doing well.'

She'd also said that Liam and Ruby were still together. Apparently they had tickets to Liam's debs the following year.

'And what about his stepma?' said Robbie.

Amy sighed. 'It seems like her husband isn't going to press charges. But he's thrown her out of the house, which is something.'

Catherine kept Amy abreast of all the news from the village. Over the past months, Knockcrea had been abuzz not only with the details of the violent incident at Sea View, but with gossip about Miles and June. The secrets of their marriage had become common knowledge. Everyone knew that June had had an affair with handsome Stephen, who worked in the supermarket in Clongrassil. Stephen even claimed he was the original owner of the Adidas hoodie that June had planted in Liam's wardrobe.

Miles had had several affairs of his own. His infidelities had left June paranoid. When Catherine tracked down Francisca and Georgia, the previous nannies, on Facebook, they both said they had left Sea View because June made them feel uncomfortable. 'She accused me of flirting with her husband,' Georgia told her. 'I had no interest in that man!' One night, after she'd been at Sea View a few weeks, Georgia found a note in her room signed with Miles's name. It said he had something urgent to tell her and asked her to meet him at the end of the road at eleven o'clock. She was uneasy, but felt obliged to go. 'He was my employer.' When she got to the meeting place, however, she found June waiting for her. 'She acted like she'd caught me out,' said Georgia. 'Like this was proof there was something going on between me and her husband! It was crazy. I left the next day.'

Since the truth had come out, Miles and June had split

up, a vicious separation in which he had kept the kids (yet another nanny had moved in), and June had returned to her mother's home in Dublin. Most people in the village were openly delighted by her fall from grace. 'There's a sense of joyous *Schadenfreude* around the place,' Catherine reported.

Amy pulled her thoughts away from Knockcrea and back to the present.

'Robbie,' she said, 'I want to be here for you. I just don't know how.'

'You want to be here for me?' he said. 'You left me.'

'I had to leave Dublin. To keep myself safe. But I thought about you every day. I was saving the money I earned. My plan was to save up enough for you to go to rehab. I never stopped worrying about you.'

Robbie's mouth worked with some emotion she couldn't read. 'Really?' he asked.

'Really.'

It was the truth. Every Thursday, when June paid her, Amy had put some cash aside, tied up with a rubber band, hoping that one day she'd be able to afford to get her son professional help.

Robbie was silent again, but his hostility had disappeared. He lowered his head. When he looked up, his eyes were shiny with tears. 'I'm sorry, Ma,' he said.

Amy reached across the table and took his hand. 'I know,' she whispered. 'So am I.'

'I wish I could go back,' he said. 'Do everything differently.'

'We can't go back,' said Amy. 'There's no point wishing. We're here now. The only way we can go is forward.'

She remembered the wish she had made on the falling star

in West Cork. *Please keep Robbie safe. Please help him get better. Please bring him back to me.* She had hope. Her son was alive, and he was sitting across from her. That was something to build on. They could start from here.

Acknowledgements

To my wonderful editors, Nita Pronovost, Hannah Wann and Molly Gregory, I can't thank you enough for the work you did on this novel. I'm very fortunate to have had such exceptional editorial guidance on this journey. Thank you for helping me to turn *Someone You Trust* into the book it was supposed to be.

To my kind and brilliant agent, Marianne – thank you for everything. I'm incredibly lucky to have you in my corner. To Alison Walsh, for her thoughtful and encouraging feedback on the earliest draft.

Struggling with second-book syndrome during a pandemic was difficult, and I got through it only with a lot of support. I have many people to thank. Lauren, for being my biggest cheerleader. Roisin, for all those long video chats during the scary Covid days. Christian, for all the long chats and for supporting me through my lockdown anxiety spirals.

To Darren, for always understanding, and for making even

the toughest times fun too. To Dylan, thanks for making me laugh, thanks for Greece (sorry I cut your hair! I really thought I could do it after watching one instructional YouTube video). To my father, for telling me I could achieve anything, while making it clear you'd be proud of me no matter what my dreams turned out to be.

To Lewis, I'm sorry I missed you on the last one! I couldn't have written my first book without all the support you gave me. You're one of the reasons I am where I am today. To Hazel, for all the chocolates left outside my door and all the small kindnesses. To Cáitín, you might be far away these days, but even at this distance, your existence makes the world a better place.

To my mother – your kindness and practical support got me through the final push. I couldn't have finished this book without you. To Ross – you were my rock in 2022. Thank you for everything. To Paddy and Conor, thank you for making my life more fun and bringing me so much joy! I'm so glad that I said 'yes' when asked to be your childminder all those years ago. It was one of the best decisions I ever made. I love you both so much. To Niamh, who read the earliest stories I ever wrote and believed in me from the very beginning.

I'd like to extend a huge, general thanks to everybody in my community who rallied around me and supported me when my debut novel was published (shout out to Trudie Gorman for buying SIX copies!). People I hadn't seen in years got in touch to tell me they'd bought my book. The Irish have a reputation for begrudgery, but what I experienced was the opposite of that. I'm very grateful.

I spent many hours working on *Someone You Trust* at the

Charleville Mall Library in North Strand, at a wooden desk in the corner. I also worked on this novel in Ballymun Library. I'm grateful to the staff at both libraries for creating such warm, welcoming spaces.